FAMILY HOME

A Sweet Contemporary Gay Romance

BLAKE ALLWOOD

BLAKE ALLWOOD PUBLISHING

Blake Allwood
Visit my website at BlakeAllwood.com

Printed in the United States of America
Box Elder, SD

First Printing: March 2023

Blake Allwood Publishing

Ebook ISBN: 978-1-956727-50-0
Paperback ISBN: 978-1-956727-51-7
Library of Congress Control Number: 2023901994

CONTENT WARNINGS

Estranged Family Member
Homophobia
Loss of Parent
Mental Illness
Trauma

Join Blake's email list to get advance notice of new books and receive his occasional newsletter:

www.blakeallwood.com

MM Romance
By Blake Allwood

Transitions Series
Aiden Inspired
Suzie Empowered (MF Romance)
Bobby Transformed

Chance Series
Love By Chance
Another Chance With Love
Taking A Chance For Love

Romantic Series
Romantic Renovations (1)
Romantic Rescue (2)
Romantic Recon (3)

Melody Series
Melody of the Heart
Melody of the Snow

Road to Rocktoberfest Anthology
Changing His Tune - 2022

Coming Home Series (2023)
A Long Way Home
Family Home
Discovering Home
Finding Home
Bound For Home
…and many more

Novellas
Tenacious
Moon's Place

Romantic Fantasy
By Adam J. Ridley

Big Bend Series
Love's Legacy (1)
Love's Heirloom (2)
Love's Bequest (3)

The Witch Brothers Series
Emerald Earth (1)
Diamond Air (2)
Ruby Fire (3)
Sapphire Water (4)

Acknowledgments

Special thanks to the following amazing people who helped me get this book finished and into your hands.

Jo Bird: Editor
Renee Mizar: Editor
Ann Attwood: Proofreader

And of course, a big thank you to my husband who puts up with my endless stories and handles the formatting and final publishing of all my books.

ONE

TODD

"**A**AAARGH! DAD, I'VE FALLEN off the roof!"

Nothing, not a sound, came from the house. *Well, crap, where'd he go?* I tried to stand up, and the second I put any weight on my right foot, it screamed with pain.

"That's just great!" I shouted toward the house.

I hobbled over to my dad's pickup. I'd left my keys next to my phone in the living room, and there was no freaking way I was going to make it all the way in there without crashing and burning, so I could only hope he'd left the keys in the ignition.

I crawled up into the truck, and finding his keys dangling, started it. *Finally, some damned luck.* Blowing out a sigh of relief, I blew the horn. Still no Dad. It was just like the asshole to leave me while I was on top of his stupid house. He must've taken Doc's truck... no surprise there, they'd been swapping vehicles since I was a kid.

I put the truck into reverse and turned around in the driveway. With my right foot hurt, I had to awkwardly drive with my left. Luckily, it wasn't far to Doc's office.

I eased the truck into drive and headed into town. Sure enough, I passed my dad on the way and flipped him off as I drove by. At least that would get his attention. There was nothing my dad hated more than his only son being disrespectful, especially in public.

I got to the doctor's office and crawled out of the pickup and up the ramp. When I hopped up to the receptionist window, I asked, "Is Doc available?"

"Do you have an appointment?"

The pain in my foot was excruciating, and I ended up taking it out on the woman behind the counter.

"Of course, I don't have an appointment, Clara Sue. I didn't know I was gonna fall off the damned roof till it happened!"

"Well, Todd, don't get your panties in a wad. We ask everyone that."

Frustrated I turned around, "I'm gonna go sit in the waiting room. When Doc is ready, come get me!"

Luckily, there wasn't anyone else there, so I was able to lift my injured leg up and prop it across the chairs beside me. I took my shoe and sock off and sure enough, the thing was turning purple and swelling. *Damn, I must've broken it.*

"Well, shit," I whispered to myself just as Ashton Nash came into the room. "Hey, Todd, what'd you do there?" he asked.

Ashton Nash. I hadn't laid eyes on the man in years. The sight of him squashed the pain and stirred up memories that spanned my childhood. We'd been best friends throughout school up until... well, until we weren't. The thought of that, of what led up to my getting the hell out of this town so long ago, caused my stomach to churn. Or maybe that was just my throbbing foot, gut-punching me back to the present.

"What's it look like, Ash? I messed up my foot. When's your dad gonna be available?"

Ash looked at me funny, amusement showing on his face. "My dad retired, Todd. You didn't know that?"

"No dammit! I didn't know!" The pain and frustration of dealing with Ash was enough to unleash my inner asshole at full throttle.

"Let me take a look at that," he said, making a move toward my bruised foot.

I instinctively pulled my foot away, "No, I prefer to have a doctor look at it. I think the damned thing's broken."

Clara Sue's chuckle from her window drew my attention, and when I looked back up at Ash, he was smiling. He pointed to his name badge. "Doctor Nash, at your service."

"How the hell did you become a doctor? You couldn't even pass tenth-grade biology," I said incredulously, unable to mask my growing frustration.

"Well, that was high school, and the reason I barely passed was because you were always hounding me to go swimmin' in the river, or whatever, instead of studying."

Through the deepening haze of pain radiating from my foot, I studied Ash. Long gone was the bright-eyed boy who'd awoken desires I'd never felt before, who'd given me my first kiss... and then ripped my heart out and stomped it into the ground.

In his place stood a man with sparkling eyes... A man who was too damned good looking for his own good... or mine for that matter.

Shaking off these thoughts I said, "Whatever... Still, I'd prefer to see your dad," I said, the unease in my tone obvious to anyone within earshot, which no doubt still included Clara Sue.

"Todd, as I've already told you, Dad retired last year. I'm the only person here who can help. Everyone else is on vacation or at the homecoming parade."

"You can't treat me, Ash," I whispered. "We were *involved*."

"Why are you whispering? Everyone in town knows we were involved. You're gonna have to see me, or go out of town. Want me to call you an ambulance?"

"Do you want a black eye?" I asked in all seriousness. "Damned if I'll ever ride in one of those things, at least not while I'm awake."

Ash chuckled. "Seriously, let me help you to the back and I'll take a look. If it's severe, and you don't want me to treat you, I can have your dad drive you into Lebanon to see a different doctor."

I gave him a dirty look, or at least I hoped it was. Unfortunately, I couldn't be sure since the pain was taking its toll and that was probably the emotion etched on my face.

I stared at my foot a moment longer... I didn't want Ash to treat me. I didn't want anything to do with him. However, since I was unable to leave under my own power, and unwilling to be ambulanced out of town, the shithead had me over a barrel.

Just then, my dad burst into the waiting room. "What the hell happened to you?" he asked, full of what I could only assume was mock concern.

I didn't respond. Instead, I stood, hopped out of Ash's grip, and moved toward the exam rooms in the back.

"He did a number on his foot," Ash told my dad.

"I thought there were rules against telling assholes personal information. What is it, HIPPO rules or something?" I gritted out through the pain.

Clara Sue giggled again, and I knew we were putting on quite a show. *Fuck, if that isn't going to be the entire town's entertainment for a week.*

"HIPAA, and when your dad can see for himself that it's blown up like a freakin' balloon, it's not a violation." Ash replied coolly.

Without another word, I hobbled into the room Ash's dad, Doc, had always put me in when I'd visited him suffering with a cold or whatever.

Both men followed me, and Dad stood over my foot as Ash examined it.

"Can you move it?" Ash asked. I tried and even though it hurt like the dickens, I could indeed move it.

"Well, that's good at least," he said. "I'll have Leslie set up an x-ray for you and then we'll know for sure."

Thank God Ash left the room, leaving just my father to deal with.

"I don't approve of rude hand gestures, Todd," he said, clearly still peeved about my flipping him the bird on my drive here.

"I don't approve of parents who leave their sons on top of a damned roof alone, so what...?" I asked accusingly, "You could go to the damned parade."

"I wasn't goin' to the parade, I was goin' to get groceries to cook you breakfast."

I looked crossly at him, but saw what appeared to be genuine concern reflected back at me.

I cleared my thoughts, surprised he was showing real concern. "Don't worry about it. I was on the lower roof that slants down. I thought I'd stepped on a nail and lost my balance. I only fell eight feet."

"I should've been there. You're right." He shook his head.

"Well, I won't disagree, but I shouldn't have been doin' it alone, either. Hell, I have an entire crew."

Dad sat down as we waited for my x-ray. I figured we didn't need to get into the fact that he'd forced me to work on his house. "This is your heritage. You need to be the one to preserve it," he'd told me when I said I could send a crew out.

Leslie Chartwell, a woman both Ash and I had gone to school with, came in a few minutes later, and with Dad's help, got me to the x-ray room and onto the table. I was now twenty-nine years old and had lain on this exact same table several times during my childhood, probably even had the same x-ray machine used on me.

My adventures with Ash often landed us both at his dad's clinic. More often than not, it was his dad bringing either him or me in for x-rays and patching up our banged-up body parts, or on a couple of occasions, broken bones.

After what felt like an eternity of waiting, Ash finally came in with the results. I huffed the moment I saw him, unable to hold back my annoyance. "What do y'all do, sit out there and do each other's nails while your patients sit in here staring at the stupid wall?"

Ash looked at my dad, then at me. "You know these things take time... Besides, if you must know, I was catching up on paperwork, since this was the time I'd set aside to do it. Technically, the office is closed right now."

Ash never got snippy with me; he was always the cool customer, so seeing him frazzled was a bit of consolation at least.

"How are you closed on a dang weekday?" I asked, purposefully needling him. "Your dad never closed on a weekday."

"I'm the only person here. My nurse practitioner is on vacation, my medical assistant has a son in the parade, and if I ever hope to get paid again, I have a shit ton of paperwork to get through. We shut the place down so I could do it."

"Oh," I said, feeling only slightly guilty. "So, is it broken?"

"Yes, but just a small fracture. We'll wrap it, and when you get home, you need to soak it in Epsom Salts. You'll need to wear the boot to keep it steady, and Todd, you will *have* to keep it steady. Don't put much weight on it, or you'll make it worse. I'm also gonna give you some crutches and something for the pain."

"Took you long enough," I said under my breath, and got a nasty look in return.

When I looked at Dad, he was trying not to smile. I gave him the same look I'd just seen on Ash's face. "Well, get on with it. Sounds like we both have a shit ton of stuff to get done."

"Leslie'll come wrap you up and get you the crutches. I'll leave a script at the front desk with Clara Sue." Then, just as quickly as he'd reappeared in my life, the man walked out... not unlike the way he'd walked out on me a decade before. Thirteen years and three months, to be exact, not that I was counting the days since Ash stopped being the love of my life. *Nope, not at all, he's an asshole, and I don't have the time or energy to worry about him.*

As I came hobbling out of the room, I went to the front desk to pay my bill and pick up whatever prescription Ash had left. Clara Sue handed me the paperwork, and I handed her my credit card.

"No charge," she said, refusing my card. I supposed I should've been grateful, but knowing whose orders she was following, it just made me mad.

"What? No way, I'm not gonna be in his debt. I'll pay for the visit and then I'll be done."

"Nope. Said he can't take your money, 'cause you two were *involved*." She winked at me while saying the last word.

I narrowed my eyes at her, and after a long time staring her down, she began to squirm. I pulled my wallet back out, counted a couple hundred dollars I'd taken out of the ATM before arriving back in town, and tossed them on the desk in front of Clara Sue.

"You tell him—" I said in a low voice, "—he can shove these where the sun don't shine." Then, with as much dignity as I could muster with my bum foot and crutches, I hobbled out of the office with my dad.

Two

Ash

I KNEW TODD WAS in town. Dad had told me—well, warned me, more like—to expect to see him. I was still not sure why my father felt like he needed to, though. What I suspected was his warning was more to protect Todd, which pissed me off. Ever since Todd broke up with me and I dated Jennifer, the town seemed to be protecting him *from* me.

It wasn't like I hadn't reminded every damned one of them that he'd broken up with me, not the other way around.

Even remembering all that still caused my heart to quake. At sixteen, I was ready to marry Todd. I never expected him—my best friend, let alone boyfriend—to throw me to the side like a piece of dung. My sister Lisa nailed me in the arm after breaking up with Jennifer after I admitted that I wasn't even attracted to women, and I'd only dated her to hurt him. Yeah, I knew it was petty, but shit, I was only sixteen. "You're smothering me, I can't do this anymore..." Even after all this time, his words rang in my ears.

Yeah, I'd been a bit much back then, and sighed as I thought about it now. "We're gonna buy your dad's house from him and fix it up, and we're gonna have a gardener who works full-time restoring the gardens," I told him, already mapping out our future. Sadness overtook me as I remembered swirling around him, confident with my teenage certainty that we'd be together forever, then kissing him on the lips.

I always wondered if it was my mentioning his dad's house that had broken us. I'd been hung up on living there—living *with* Todd—since we were little, and maybe the idea of never leaving Crawford City or his dad's house was too much for him. He hated his dad... well, hated was too strong a word, he didn't like his dad and the two fought constantly.

When we were really young, Todd wanted to impress his dad, and had done everything in his power to do so. By the time we were teenagers, his desire to impress was replaced with a desire to harass. Amos was good to me, and treated me very different from Todd, often much better. I still wondered what caused him to treat his own son so poorly.

I heard Clara Sue moving around the reception desk, and that brought me out of my trip down my miserable memory lane. I flipped open the electronic record system, but quickly got lost in thought again. Despite Dad's warning, I hadn't been prepared for Todd to show up at the clinic, especially considering we were officially closed. I'd told Clara Sue to keep the doors unlocked in case there was an emergency, but anyone else needed to have an appointment.

I was just getting into the paperwork when Todd came in, limping and looking all mad and hot as hell. My heart dropped into my stomach the instant I saw him. Medical school had been a bitch, and even though I graduated with honors, I'd had to work my ass off to get through it. As a result, my face showed worry lines and my hair had a few stray grays that shouldn't be there, at least not yet. Leave it to the son of a bitch to brink up my greatest faults, and right in front of Clara Sue. Of course, he did it while still looking just as handsome as ever.

THREE

TODD

W E LEFT DAD'S OLD pickup at the clinic, and he drove me home in silence. The moment we got back, I crawled out of the truck and gingerly made my way into the house. I found my phone where I'd left it and called my office. When my assistant, Jacklyn, answered, I filled her in on the accident. "I need you to call Warren. I need him and the crew here tomorrow morning by nine." Jacklyn told me he'd be upset, since he and the boys had plans tomorrow. "I know he's gonna be mad, but last I checked, I sign his freakin' paycheck. If he wants me to keep signing his paychecks, he and the crew *will* be at my dad's place tomorrow by nine o'clock."

I knew I probably sounded like an asshole, snapping at Jacklyn out of frustration, but my tank was near empty. I was beyond exhausted, as much from the constant pain in my foot as having seen my pain-in-the-ass former boyfriend, and I had zero shits left to give about wrecking my crew's plans for a fun day off.

I'd already looked over the work schedule, and knew no roofs were planned for the next week, which meant the crew had plans to go fishing on the company's dime. I'd only owned the construction company for a relatively short time, and my predecessor always looked the other way with those sort of things when we had downtime, but the thought of paying my men to go play when there was real work to be done always struck me the wrong way.

After the call, I contemplated soaking my foot in Epsom Salts like Ash had advised, but spotting Dad's old pickup outside distracted me. He must've hitched a ride with someone back into town to fetch it from the clinic. He was nowhere in sight, however, but luckily, I found he'd left the keys in the ignition again. I hadn't popped any of the pain pills Ash had prescribed, just some over-the-counter meds to take the edge off, so I was safe to drive. I somehow managed to get the ol' bucket of rust to meander next door to Doc's place, so I could check on him, once again using my left foot on the pedals.

I hadn't heard Doc had retired until Ash mentioned it earlier. My friend, Jen, had long been my source of Crawford City gossip once we'd moved to Nashville together after high school, and we'd remained roomies until she went to New York to launch her modeling career. Her globetrotting made it harder to talk to her about the small stuff, even though we still texted every day. My dad wasn't the best at keeping me up to date on things either, plus Ash was always an off-limits topic with me, so I was way behind on town happenings.

The minute I got to Doc's front door, it opened, and I was pulled into a bear hug by the massive man.

"Hey, Doc," I said when he released me. "I hear you've thrown responsibility to the wind and are now livin' a life of luxury."

Doc chuckled. "I hear you're falling off roofs."

"Dang, I'm not sure why I'm surprised, but the gossip mill in Crawford is a remarkable thing."

Doc laughed again. "Your dad called me, actually. Not that I couldn't tell with the boot and crutches you're sporting. He was worried and wanted to get my opinion on whether or not you need the meds Ash prescribed for you."

That shocked me... not that Dad had told Doc about my accident—they'd been best friends since forever, after all—but that he'd voiced concern for me. "Didn't know he cared," I muttered and hopped through the front door.

At one time, Doc and Ash's house had been as much my home as Dad's place. Even after Ash broke things off with me, I would spend time here with his dad or sister Lisa, helping out with odd chores whenever Ash wasn't around.

Looking back, I'd never realized just how intertwined our lives had been. I reckoned that was why it'd hurt so much when he'd broken up with me. Not that I wasn't over it, over him. He'd made sure we were done a long-ass time ago, so I'd be damned if I still cared. *Asshole.* The sound of Doc closing the front door snapped me out of my ruminating and back to the present.

"I doubt I need to take painkillers for the healing process. So far, the over-the-counter stuff is working pretty well."

"You do need to keep the foot up, though. And it wouldn't hurt for you to be soaking it either."

"Yeah, yeah. Ash gave me the same spiel. I wanted to check on you first, though. What's up with the retirement?" I asked. Doc scratched his chin, a sure sign he was pondering something, and I was immediately suspicious. "Doc, what's goin' on, you sick or something?"

"No, nothing like that, son. Come on into the living room and let me get your foot elevated."

I complied, used to following the directions of this man who was like a second father to me. Besides my dad and Doc being best buddies, they were also next-door neighbors, and both men had inherited their childhood homes when their parents passed away.

Ash and I were exactly the same age, well, As was five months older. Then there was Ash's baby sister, Lisa, who was as much my little sister as his. She'd moved to the Pacific Northwest, though, a couple of years ago, and I didn't talk to her these days as much as I should.

"So, what's the deal?" I asked Doc after I got settled in a recliner, kicking it back to prop my foot up.

"The deal is I'm middle-aged and tired of being locked down to that practice. Ash is fully capable of running it now, and I wanna spend more time fishin' and traveling."

"It's been a whole year since you retired?" I asked, feeling a little put out that no one had told me.

"Just about," Doc confirmed.

"Dad should've told me," I said, shaking my head. I'd swear that man got less and less talkative as the years went by. Doc just sat across from me and didn't respond. "What, you don't have an opinion?" I laughed.

Doc had always been my dad's defender. When I was mad, he'd console me. Jane, Ash's mom, was always shy and quiet. Wounded would be the word I'd use if I had to describe her. Even though she was friendly and seemed happy to see me, she would also quickly disappear when I came to the door.

Ash said she was the same with them really, and just didn't interact with anyone much. That always bothered him. "I know she loves me and Lisa, but there's always a wall between us that neither of us seem to be able to get over," he'd once told me.

Ash's mom died when we were in high school, but at least she'd been in his life. My dad never got married, and I'd never met my mom. She was some woman he'd met while he was visiting his family in the Caribbean and had died when I was still a baby. I never knew any more than that and never dared ask... as far back as I could remember, my mother had been an off-limits topic with him.

I shook those memories out of my head and focused back on Doc. "I think your dad has a lot on his plate," he said. "We're getting older, Todd. That comes with changes that aren't easy for anyone."

"Yeah, I know," I said, and meant it. I worried about Dad being here alone in that big old house. Of course, he was as stubborn as the day was long, and wouldn't accept help from anyone but Doc or me, when he was able to guilt me into visiting.

Looking around the living room, I spotted the old globe that I knew was full of alcohol, because Ash and I had helped ourselves on numerous occasions, and said, "Hey, Doc, why don't you offer me something to drink. I may not be willing to use the drugs, but I could probably do with a swig or two."

He eyed me skeptically for a moment. "How much over-the-counter stuff have you taken?"

"Duh, as much as the package told me I could."

Doc chuckled. "Any acetaminophen?" he asked.

"No, but that sounds like a good idea."

"Not if you wanna drink," he said. "That's a good way to develop liver damage."

"Got it, no acetaminophen. Ibuprofen, that's what I took."

Doc got up and poured a small amount of whiskey. Handing me the glass, he said, "That's the limit. Promise?"

"Yeah, yeah, I promise. I gotta have a little relief though, this sucker hurts like a bitch!"

"Son, your mouth has gotten so foul since you've been away from home. If your foot wasn't hurting, I'd consider tossing you over my knee."

"I run a construction company, Doc. What do you expect?" I laughed when he gave me his cocked-eyebrow look.

"Your dad's proud of you for that," he replied. "I know he'd never tell you, but the minute you took that job, he was over here bragging like you'd become valedictorian or something. Since you bought the business, he's been impossible to deal with." Doc shook his head as he chuckled.

"Yeah, speaking of being proud of someone, how the hell did you get Ash through medical school? Wait," I said, shaking my head. "The meds and alcohol are going to my head. I don't wanna know."

"You ever gonna forgive him?" he asked.

"That would be a hard no," I replied, and put my hand up before Doc could start the same lecture I'd been hearing for more than a decade. "I know we were young, and I know neither of us was ready for a long-term relationship, but what happened, happened, and there ain't no goin' back."

At my statement, Doc's hopeful smile slipped.

That was my cue to go. I stood up and was just about to make my exit when the devil himself appeared before me.

"Fuck me," I said under my breath, but not quiet enough that Doc didn't hear me.

"I ought'a ring your ear for that language," he said, then turned toward his son. "Come on in, Ash, we're just talking here."

"More like he was comin' to get a second opinion," Ash replied.

"That'd be my right, and *real* doctors wouldn't be intimidated by such things." I hobbled out of the room, past Ash, and headed for the front door.

Ash must've seen the empty glass near where I'd been sitting, and asked, "You been drinking? Dad, did you let him drink?"

"Now, now," Doc replied. "He had less than a shot."

"You drank alcohol with the medication I prescribed?" he asked incredulously, but with a note of concern in his voice that really got my goat.

"Fuck off, Ash," I said, and clomped toward the front door as fast as I could with crutches and the stupid boot. All the movement was causing my foot to scream in pain again.

I was out the door when Ash barreled onto the porch. "You are not gonna drive on pain medications and alcohol. I won't allow it."

His righteous indignation, coupled with the throbbing pain in my foot, was too much and I snapped. I dropped one of my crutches and drilled my finger square into the middle of his chest... a very firm chest, not that I cared. "You'll not do a damned thing to stop it either. You may have your fancy medical degree, though God help me I don't know how you managed it, but you don't own me, and you don't get to pretend like you give a damn about me after all these years."

Fuck me. Angry tears were gonna make an appearance any moment, but I'd be damned if I let Ashton Nash see me cry. I swirled around before any tears could fall, though the motion twisted my freakin' foot and sent a jolt of white-hot, searing pain through me. If Ash hadn't been a hair's breadth away, I'd have fallen to the floor.

Even as I lay in his arms, the one place I swore I'd never be again, it took several moments for me to catch my breath. When I finally did, I asked him to put me on the porch swing. "I might just get that prescription filled after all," I said as a cold sweat broke out across my skin.

"Damn it, Todd, you didn't take the pain meds?" he asked.

I shook my head and gritted my teeth, still reeling from the pain. "I took ibuprofen, and your dad gave me the little taste of whiskey. I was doing fine, at least till you got me riled up."

"Always blaming me," he said in a huff. "I'll drive you back home myself."

"The hell you will," I said. The pain might've been intense, but I hadn't lost all my senses. I'd be damned if I let this man do anything for me again. "Call my dad and tell him to come get me. This is all his fault anyway."

"No need," Doc said as he came onto the porch and turned to Ash. "I'll take him home. You go on in and get something to eat, Ash. I have supper waiting in the kitchen."

Ash looked at me with a furrowed brow. I could tell he wanted to lay into me, and fuck if I wouldn't have enjoyed a knock-down-drag-out argument with him, but I was at a distinct disadvantage both physically and mentally at the moment. Besides, I'd decided long ago that Ash wasn't worth getting worked up over, he didn't matter enough anymore.

When we pulled up to the porch in Dad's old pickup, Doc came around to my side and helped me out. Dad must've heard us coming, because he opened the front door for us as Doc helped me into the parlor and onto the sofa.

"You need to get his script filled," Doc told Dad. "He's as stubborn as you ever were." Then, my dad and he exchanged a look I couldn't quite place. They'd always shared some weird unspoken language only they knew. Growing up I mostly just ignored it, chalking it up to their being such good friends.

Sometime after Ash's mom had died, I'd even heard the two men talking about moving in together, and how that would be better for everyone. Raising teenagers was hard enough, let alone handfuls like me and Ash were, so the idea they'd want to join forces in that way hadn't surprised me. Of course, that was after Ash and I had broken up and things were complicated, so luckily for me at least, they hadn't. I couldn't imagine having to live with that teenage asshole while he chased tail in high school. Watching it from the sidelines had been bad enough.

I lay on the sofa while Dad saw Doc out. He was gone so long I fell asleep and didn't hear him come back, which was a testament to how bad I'd been hurting, because the front screen door was loud as hell.

I was guessing at least an hour had passed before my dad woke me and handed me a glass of water and a pill.

"Here, take this," he said. "Doc said to not let you give me lip. You need to rest and let that thing heal." He pointed at my foot.

I took the pill, then turned to get up off the sofa. My head spun and Dad came over to help. "Why are you so stubborn?" he asked.

I quirked an eyebrow at him, not believing he had the nerve to ask me that. "The man with a head made of a block is asking *me* this question?"

Dad chuckled. "I guess you do take after me. I sure wish you didn't," he said. "Life would've been easier if you'd have been less like me."

"Probably," I said. "Can you help me to the bedroom? I'm gonna stay down on this level in the old guest room. I can't imagine trying to get up the stairs right now."

"Sure, I'll go get your stuff and bring it down," he said.

"Why are you being so nice?"

"Was I really that nasty?" he asked. "I can't do something basic for you without you being suspicious?"

I shrugged as we hobbled toward the bedroom. "You would've told me to suck it up, or stop acting like a girl. I guess I don't know how to deal with this new you."

He helped lower me onto the bed and I tucked myself in. "I have a lot to make up for, son. I was..." He shook his head, and I could tell he was about to launch into a heart-to-heart.

"Dad, whatever you're about to unload, the pill you gave me is kicking in and I'm getting high and sleepy. I love you, I'll always love you, and I appreciate the man you raised me to be, okay? I'm successful, I own one of the largest construction companies in Nashville, so you can let yourself off the hook."

I lay back on the pillow and figured Dad would just leave me be. When I looked back at where he was sitting, though, I was shocked to see his face full of emotion.

"Dad, what the hell is goin' on?" I asked, partially annoyed at not being able to sink into a meds-induced sleep, but also concerned about why Dad was lingering at my bedside.

"I was a bad parent to you, son. Hell, even now you go to Doc for support instead of me. I have a better relationship with Lisa and Ash than I do you. I wanna make that up, if it's not too late."

I didn't know what to say. My dad had never been emotional. He didn't usually act like he gave a damn whether I lived or died. Seeing him like this instantly made me suspicious. "Dad, are you sick?"

He laughed. "Doc said you asked him the same thing."

"Well, yeah," I replied. "The two of you are being weird." When I turned to look back at the ceiling, my head spun with the medication. "Tomorrow, Dad," I said. "Let's talk about this tomorrow. Right now, I'm gonna sleep."

I was out before Dad left the room. When I woke up in the wee hours of the morning, still fully clothed, I noticed my left shoe was on the floor next to the bed. Dad must've taken it off me last night. Even that was something he'd have never done in the past. I was mostly expected to care for myself. What had gotten into the old man? I had no idea.

My foot was throbbing, so I sat up and noticed a pill bottle and a glass of water on the nightstand. Dad must've put them there last night too. "Who the hell is this man?" I asked out loud, before swallowing another pill.

Whoever had abducted my father and replaced him with this version was welcome to keep the original. Although, between his odd behavior and the way Doc had acted, I was afraid there was something wrong with one or both of them that they weren't telling me.

Something was up, and I sure as hell didn't like it. I decided I needed to give Lisa a call soon. Hopefully, she'd have some dirt on these two and could shed a little light on it. Too bad Ash was an ass from hell, or I'd just ask him.

In any case, I'd get to the bottom of it one way or another.

Four

Ash

Todd interrupting my much-needed down day, and daring to do so while looking better than a man had a right to, had me in an ill temper by the time I got to Dad's place. Walking in to find him in the living room, and to top it off, enjoying a shot of Dad's malt whiskey, sent me into a fit. Why the hell was he in my dad's house getting liquored up, and not in bed getting the rest he needed?

Todd Thompson was just as infuriating as he'd ever been, and fuck if I hadn't taken that frustration out on him.

After Todd nearly passed out on the front porch, Dad pretty-much pushed me into the house, and took him home. When Amos dropped Dad off, they both came in and headed straight for the whiskey.

By that time, I was having a full-on self-pity fest, and had already downed a couple shots myself.

"He still pissed off?" I asked in greeting.

"Less than he will be tomorrow," Amos said.

"Is he ever gonna stop hating me?" I asked, not in the mood to beat around the bush.

"Well, that depends on if he ever stops loving you or not," my father replied.

I stared at him a long moment, fighting the urge to roll my eyes. "You're getting senile in your old age," I said. "Todd Amos Thompson does not feel anything less than pure hatred for me."

Amos put his hand on my shoulder then, and squeezed. The affection startled me, though I tried to mask my surprise. The man was never affectionate with anyone, not even his son, but I accepted his comfort, and ignored the irregularity.

He didn't stay long after that, even though he and Dad tended to spend most evenings together these days, watching TV or arguing over some card game. I assumed tonight was different, because Todd was in town, not to mention, injured.

Although I had intentionally avoided discussing Todd and my unrelationship with Dad or Amos, they obviously knew our relationship was non-existent, and had been for years... hell, everyone in town knew that, including how much he now hated me.

I'd spent well over a decade trying not to think about Todd. He'd been my everything—best friend, companion, and later my lover—before the day our relationship imploded. I knew I'd never love anyone as much as I'd loved him and even though I'd briefly dated Jennifer, who for the record was the first and last woman I'd ever dated, and then there was Alex, the football jock. Both of them were more about getting even with Todd for dumping me than actually wanting to date them. It hadn't really worked, though, and only left Todd hating me all the more for it.

In college, I hadn't dated anyone. There were more than a few hookups, of course. I was still young with raging hormones, but no one lasted more than a couple of nights. How could you get close to one person when you wanted someone else?

In medical school, I tried to pretend I was over Todd and let myself date a couple of different guys longer than my two-night maximum. Both had ended in sheer disaster. The first was so bad, the guy transferred to a different school, and the second almost cost me my residency. That had been the end of my dating life.

Since moving back to Crawford City, Grindr was my wingman and Nashville my place for getting laid. I'd become religious with my two-night maximum requirement, and it'd served me well, thank you very much.

FIVE

TODD

I WOKE UP THE following morning later than I'd planned. I checked the time and saw it was way past ten. Why wasn't I hearing roof work?

I crawled out of bed and immediately put weight on my damned foot, and was rewarded with a sharp pain.

I managed to get up, and with my crutches shuffled into the parlor, where Dad was sitting and reading his paper.

"You're up," he said, smiling at me.

"Yeah, are there men here working on the roof?" I asked.

Dad shrugged. "No, are they supposed to be?"

"Yeah," I said, and turned to go back into my room for my phone, before remembering it should still be in the parlor. "Is my phone out here?" I asked, ready for my dad to hit me with a smart-alecky response.

He was always gruff, but seldom cussed.

"No, I plugged it in next to your bed."

I looked at my father suspiciously. Not wanting to get into a touchy-feely conversation again, I ignored it and went back to my room to call my office.

"Jacklyn," I said when the woman answered. "Why aren't Warren and the roofers at my dad's place?"

She sighed. "I was afraid they were going to do this. Warren threw a fit when I told him what you said. Said he wasn't comin'."

"Did any of them take a sick day or time off?" I asked.

"Nope, no one called in," she said.

"Are they on a different job I'm not aware of?" I asked, my frustration growing by the second.

"No, there are no new jobs that've come in since the day before yesterday."

"Jacklyn, I want you to pay each of those men what they're owed up to yesterday. I'm not paying them for fishin' today, you hear? And I don't give a damn how much of a fit they throw. I'll call Warren now and let him know he and his crew are all terminated."

"But, sir..." Jacklyn began before I stopped her.

"I'm fully aware of the trouble this is gonna cause, but I'll take care of it. When is the next job due to start?"

I heard clicking as Jacklyn went through the schedule. "Well, we don't have anything on the schedule, but I'm assuming Linc's job will need roofing in the next week or so."

"Have Linc call me, okay? I'll get the rundown on when I need to have replacements hired."

"Will do," Jacklyn said and hung up.

I called Warren immediately, but no surprise, his phone went to voicemail. "Warren, this is Todd. I told Jacklyn to make it clear that if you and the roofing crew weren't here to work on the roof by nine this morning, you'd all be let go. If she didn't make that clear, you need to let me know as soon as possible. Otherwise, I've instructed her to print out your final paychecks. You can pick them up at the office by the end of the day today."

I hung up, fully expecting the asshole to call me back enraged. I was sure Jacklyn made clear to him what I'd said, seeing as she was both tough and thorough. No, this was all Warren and his latest attempt to squeeze my company for more lax procedures.

I'd inherited Warren Jacobs as roofing division supervisor when I took over, and the previous owner had basically looked the other way with him, not wanting to deal with his asinine behavior. It was a bitch to find qualified roofers in the area, and because fewer and fewer locals were taking on construction jobs, we were seriously in the hole.

It was going to make replacing him, let alone his crew, difficult, but I'd be damned if I let the man control my whole company any longer. If he couldn't come to a damn jobsite when he was told, he didn't have a place working for me.

I had just dozed off again when my phone rang, and I saw it was Warren calling. I quickly thanked God I'd waited to take another pain pill and answered.

"What the fuck do you think gives you the right to fire me and the entire crew?" Warren blasted at me before I could even say anything. I could hear people—the roofing crew, no doubt—in the background.

"Warren, where are you right now?" I asked.

"That isn't any of your—"

"Before you finish that statement," I interrupted, "I should let you know I'm recording this conversation, and it most certainly *is* my business where the men I'm paying are, so if that's what you were about to say, try again." When he didn't respond, I asked again. "Where are you and the roofing crew at this moment?"

"You know damned well where we are."

"I don't, actually. Are you on a jobsite that we didn't have scheduled?"

Again, Warren didn't respond, but I could hear him breathing heavily, and imagined his face was red in anger.

"I see. I'll take that as a no. Next question, did Jacklyn tell you that you and your crew were to report to my father's house in Crawford City today by nine o'clock?"

"We ain't here to be your family's servants," he came back at me.

"So, I'm assuming the answer to that question is you were told by Jacklyn to be here by nine, but you chose not to come, because it is *my* family."

"You have no right to use company resources for your own family," he retorted.

"Is that so?" I replied. "And you took it upon yourself to take *my* employees on a fishin' trip while *my* company is paying them instead of doing what I, your *boss*, told you to do. Is that what I'm hearing?"

"This ain't your damn company," he said, the venom spewing from him nearly oozing through the phone.

"Oh, I think you might wanna check on that little detail again," I said. "Warren, my decision stands. You and your men can go pick up your final paychecks by the end of the workday. After that, I don't wanna see any of you again."

"You'll regret this, you jack—"

I disconnected before he could finish, and immediately phoned Jacklyn.

"You need to be prepared for a very angry Warren and his crew," I told her. "Have Linc gather some of the managers to be in the office with you today, just to make sure they don't do any damage. Do you want me to call them, or can you do it?"

"No," she replied, resignation in her voice. "I can handle it."

"Good, thanks, Jacklyn. Oh, and I should tell you, I fell off my dad's roof yesterday and jacked my foot up. It's just a small fracture, but it hurts like a beast. I'm on some pretty heavy pain pills, so if you need me, you should probably call my dad to come wake me up."

"Dang, boss," she said. "That sucks. Now you're having to deal with Warren and his nasty attitude?"

"I should've fired him after taking over the company, but I wanted to see if he mellowed under my leadership. So, it's my fault anyway. I'll be back in by the end of the week either way and can handle it. Oh, I almost forgot.

Call Ed and let him know about this. He's aware I was looking at letting Warren go, but he'll need to be ready in case they try to come after us with a lawsuit."

"No problem, boss, I'll let him know all the details."

"Perfect. Also, let him know I'm gonna send the recording of my conversation with Warren to him as well. That way he knows exactly how it all went down."

"Yes, sir," Jacklyn said, and hung up.

All of this wouldn't come as a real surprise to Ed, our company attorney. Warren had all but threatened the previous owner of the company with a frivolous lawsuit before I took over, and Ed and I both knew it was likely only a matter of time before Warren tried the same with me.

Oh well, I sighed, *that's what comes with being the boss*. I hadn't been running things all that long, having bought the company for nickels on the dollar, because of the financial mess it was in, but I wasn't exactly new to it either.

I'd been working for the original owner for five years, partly as the company's chief financial officer, before I offered to buy him out. The old man had suffered a heart attack a year earlier, and handed the company to his son, who proved less than capable of the job. Since the son took over, business had fallen by over fifty percent, and they'd taken on some debt they were struggling to pay back. The old man didn't want to see everything he'd built come crashing down, even if giving me the reins meant going behind his own son's back. My taking over ensured our employees kept their jobs, but it also earned me a few enemies from within.

I was only able to afford the buyout using money I'd inherited when my grandparents died, which was right after I'd been born. The money had steadily grown over the years, and although it wasn't enough to buy the company, it was a great start. The rest I'd had to borrow, and since my buddy Jake was richer than God, I decided to start with him.

I took him out to our favorite burger joint in Nashville, just down the road from where I worked, and said, "Well, I'm thinking about buying my company."

"You need a loan?" he asked as he took a bite of his burger.

"Dude, don't just offer a loan to someone," I chastised, and rather than be grateful, for thirty minutes I mostly fussed at him for being cavalier with his money.

Finally, he laughed. "Todd, dude, I want to be in business with you. You already know that. So, if you need a loan, how much do you need?"

I shrugged, then pouted a moment, cause I hated asking him or anyone for that matter for help, then I told him how much I needed. The idiot wrote me a check then and there. Well, after he finished eating the ridiculously greasy burger and fries, and cleaned up enough not to turn the check to liquid.

With Jake's approval, I deposited his grease-smudged check for a quarter of a million dollars at the bank, and that was how I became the owner of Berkshire Brothers Construction. With no debt other than what I owed Jake, we'd begun seeing a swing back into the black over the past year. Three months ago, I was able to begin paying Jake back, and I got a call from him the week after making my first payment to his accountant.

"Hey, buddy, my new client needs a house built. Can you join us at my office in an hour or so? I want him to meet you."

"Dude, I'm working. Do you really think he'll hire someone just 'cause he met me at your office?"

He just laughed. "You are clueless about how networking works. See you at one thirty," Jake said, and that was that.

It turned out his new client was country music's newest star, who wanted to build a mansion on the river in Mayville, not far from Crawford City. I put in a bid for the work, and even though mine was higher than several others, I was hired. Linc, my second in command, was leading that job, and fortunately, the construction on that, our first big project, was going up faster than we'd expected.

Nashville was growing like crazy, and other contract companies wanted to get in and out fast, not worrying about the quality of their work. My dad had been a local contractor in Crawford, and I'd learned under his strict tutelage.

"You take pride in your work, Todd, and the rest will work itself out." I chuckled remembering his words, and could even hear his mix of Southern and Caribbean accents in my head.

My throbbing foot dropkicked me out of memory lane, but I didn't want to pop another painkiller just yet. I had a feeling shit was gonna hit the fan with Warren, and I needed to have my wits about me when it did. I hobbled out of the bedroom and into the parlor where my dad was still sitting, reading his paper. I asked if he had coffee in the kitchen, but before I could make my way there, he said, "Sit down here, I'll go get it for you. You still put cream in it?"

I gaped at the stranger in front of me. "How the hell do you know how I take my coffee?" I asked.

He laughed. "I'm your father, Todd. Of course, I know how you take your coffee."

"Hey, can you grab me some ibuprofen on your way out?" I expected my question to send the dad I knew and loved, but avoided when I could, back to his usual curmudgeonly state.

"Sure thing," he said, increasing my bewilderment at his behavior.

"Hey, also ask whoever took my dad and replaced him with you to keep him, okay?"

I heard him laughing as he disappeared down the narrow hallway toward the kitchen.

When he came back in and handed me the coffee and medication, I asked again, "So what's goin' on? Why the personality change? Not that I'm complaining or anything."

Dad sat across from me and shook his head. "It's a lot to explain, but let's just say the past few years with you being gone and doing everything in your power to avoid me has helped me see what an ass I've been."

I chuckled. "You been talking to Doc, haven't you?"

Dad smiled. "He may or may not have called me a bitter old maggot a couple of times."

"Dad, I love you, you raised me on your own, well, mostly on your own. Doc sure helped, but like I said last night, you made me who I am. I'm not upset about how you brought me up. Well... okay, not anymore."

Dad sighed. "You have a right to know why, though." He shook his head. "I was so angry when I found out I was going to be a single dad, and then I lost my parents. I never intended on moving back here. Mom had taught folks around here to respect a woman of color, but that didn't mean they didn't call me every racist word they could come up with while I was growing up. If it wasn't for Doc... You know... I called him that all these years, because we were afraid if I called him by his name, people would get weird..."

Dad took a breath and shook his head. "Emanual..." That's who he is to me. Regardless, I doubt I'd have had any friends if it wasn't for him. When he married Jane the year before you were born... I felt alone...then I felt trapped."

I figured he was talking about the racism he'd faced growing up. I had my own run ins with it, but I could only imagine how much worse it'd been when he'd grown up here.

He shook his head again, his eyes not meeting mine, and let out a heavy sigh. "It's time I came clean, and admitted I was a bitter old man who blamed a baby for his own screwed-up life."

I stared at my dad, unsure how to process this usually stoic man pouring his heart out to me. What he'd just said, about blaming me for ruining his life, I'd figured out on my own long ago, and had all but forgiven him for it, although the pain of knowing my dad hated me for just being alive stung even now. I searched for the words, but too many emotions swam around inside me for me to know how to respond.

Instead, I stared at the old fireplace, hoping to buy enough time to figure out how to respond, when I heard hammering on the roof.

"Damn," I said, jumping up. "Dad, I'm sorry, I gotta handle this."

"Handle what?" he asked.

"The men I just fired are probably trying to keep their jobs," I said, pointing toward the ceiling as I hobbled toward the front door.

"Son, that ain't your men," he said as I pulled the door open and looked right into the face of Pretty Boy George.

"George?" I asked, and he smiled down at me.

George was six foot four, and used to be the linebacker on our high-school football team. He was by far one of the most handsome men to walk across God's green earth, and I'd had a crush on him since Ash had broken my heart. Unfortunately, the man was straighter than a marksman's arrow.

"Hey, Todd, I see you're up and about. That's pretty good considering you fell off the roof," he said, cracking a smile so beautiful it could rival any handsome man on the big screen.

I shook my head and stood back, inviting George into the room. "No, sorry, can't come in. We wanna get the roof on before tomorrow. Need to get it done before a storm comes up. You know it's that time of year. Anyway, just wanted to let y'all know we'd be up there."

"Yeah, that's what I hear," I replied, unable to hold back a grin of my own. "Did y'all find all the material I'd put over on the side of the garage?"

"Yep, and as you can hear, they're already installing it."

I followed George out into the yard, and ignoring the pain in my foot, looked up to the roof where a full team, at least as many as I'd have had with Warren, were spread across it, removing the old tin I hadn't gotten to yet.

"There's some damage above this part of the house," I told him. "I hadn't gotten to the back part. Also, the kitchen lean-to is a mess. It needs to be totally rebuilt. Is your crew up for all that?"

George chuckled. "We've got it covered," he assured me, and then scrambled up the ladder.

I watched him climb, admiring his very fine ass, and caught his sister looking down at me. "Kendra, is that you?" I asked.

"Yep, in the flesh," she replied.

"Well, I'll be damned. How did George convince you to do roofing?"

"He didn't. I own the company," she said with an amused smirk. "George works for me."

"Technically, he works for both of us," a woman standing next to Kendra said. "I'm Rita, George's much-better-looking other half."

I laughed. "I see that. Nice to meet you, Rita. When y'all get a break, come down and let me meet you proper," I said and hobbled back into the house. "That's cool as shit," I said to no one in particular.

"Yeah, it is, and they're the best around too," my dad responded.

"Why didn't you hire them to begin with?" I asked.

Dad averted his gaze and rubbed at the back of his neck, looking guilty. "Well, I sorta did," he admitted. "You were supposed to come down here, get mad at me like you usually do, then I was supposed to have them show up and take over the job. Son, there was no way you were gonna get this whole roof done by yourself, even if you hadn't fallen off it."

I looked at my dad through squinted eyes. "Then, why did you throw such a fit when I offered to have my men come help me?"

Dad shrugged. "'Cause it wasn't gonna be just helping you, you were gonna send your men and you weren't gonna come with them. I wanted *you* to come down."

I wanted to lay into him. Seriously, this charade had cost me, and had I not been standing on the lean-to, my injury could've been a hell of a lot worse, but the guy was trying, so I bit down on my anger, and said instead, "You could've just been honest."

He nodded. "I could've, but would you have come?"

"No, Dad." I tried to not sound accusatory, but there was no use continuing to pretend like I wasn't upset. "I'm running a multimillion-dollar company that I've got every damned cent to my name invested in. If it fails, I'm screwed."

"So, now you know why I did what I did."

I wanted to storm out of the room like I had as a teenager, but my bum foot pretty much put a stop to that. Good thing, too, because even though I felt like that same teenager who was upset with his unreasonable father right now, I wanted to maintain some dignity, considering by now all of Crawford City knew the big construction company owner had toppled off his dad's lean-to. *Thank you, Clara Sue, and all the other town gossips.*

"You're still not making sense," I said as I sat down, and brooded instead.

"I know, son. Drink your coffee, then if you're up to it, Doc and I wanna take you out to lunch."

"This where you're gonna tell me what's really going on?"

Dad chuckled, apparently seeing my retort as an acceptance of his invitation, as he walked away. "Want me to grab your laptop from your room?" he asked.

I just shook my head, perplexed. "Sure, I guess," I replied, now convinced for damned sure that something was up with Dad and Doc.

Six

Ash

Work was a literal shit show. I was booked for every appointment slot on top of treating a steady stream of walk-ins. I worked late into the night, every damned night, trying to stay ahead of the insanity, but I was failing.

That afternoon, Dr. Gibbon McCartney, a Harvard grad who I hoped would alleviate some of my workload, showed up for his interview. Despite having carved out a whole hour for it, our meeting time dissolved when a baby with explosive diarrhea appeared in the waiting room. I was sure it was salmonella, and the fact that his family lived next to a chicken farm just made me that much more suspicious.

That unfortunate little guy embodied my shitty week, and he was just one of the many patients I'd treated who hadn't made an appointment, including some regulars who came in for non-emergencies. Among them were Mrs. Wallace, who had a different ailment every week that needed to be dealt with, and Mr. Jones, who rushed to my office after every sneeze. And then there was the freshman, who I knew for a fact was struggling with high school, and was using me as an excuse for skipping school.

Amid the organized chaos of treating unplanned patients, Dr. McCartney walked into my office wearing a tie and his doctor's coat, and I almost moaned. This wasn't going to work.

"I'm sorry, Doctor McCartney, I'm buried at the moment. We'll either have to reschedule, or wait until I can get through this load," I told him.

He volunteered to stay, which probably should've given me hope, but instead, I just counted up the hours it'd take me to get through the day now that it included an after-work interview.

After prescribing antibiotics for the baby and sending the family on their way, I had to take the time to call and report the suspected salmonella infection to the health department, which, if the labs came back positive, would lead to an investigation about the farm next door to them.

I finished the call, quickly made my notes, and rushed out to get the next patient, but as I approached the receptionist window facing the waiting room, all I saw were empty chairs.

I turned toward Clara Sue with a perplexed look. She winked at me just as Dr. McCartney came out of the office with a smiling Mrs. Wallace.

After she'd exited the waiting room, I turned to Dr. McCartney, concerned, asking, "Did you see patients?"

"No," he chuckled. "When the patients you had waiting saw my doctor's coat, they began telling me all their symptoms, so I asked if Clara Sue could give us a private place to talk. I didn't offer any medical advice, but it seems these were your frequent-fliers anyway. I listened and by the time I was done, they all decided they could wait until Monday to see you."

I was flabbergasted and pleased at the same time.

I sat down with him, and learned he'd done his residency in a small-town health center, and was looking for something rural that wasn't too far from Nashville.

The man was perfect, but I still had to ask the burning question. "Why, with a Harvard degree, wouldn't you want to work in a more prestigious place?"

He sighed. "I went to Harvard, but I'm from a small town in West Tennessee."

That was all the confirmation I needed that he was the right doctor for this clinic and this community. "Well, in that case, welcome aboard. When can you start?"

"How about next week?" he asked.

At my look of surprise, he went on to explain he'd worked at a clinic after his residency, but most recently had been volunteering after a family trauma caused him to have to reduce hours, so he wouldn't have to give notice.

Glancing back over his resumé, I found he'd listed the one he'd done his residency as the same one he volunteered at. This only impressed me more. Even better was that he'd practiced in Tennessee, so there'd be no additional hoops to jump through with obtaining a state medical license.

I gave Dr. McCartney a quick tour of our little town, even showing him the Cross sisters' house as a possible purchase, before I had to rush back to the office for my afternoon patients. He ended up touring the Cross house on his own, thinking it would be the perfect place for him, then came back to the clinic to hang out while waiting for his family to come see the Cross house as well.

When the last patient left for the day, I rushed to finish up the paperwork that wouldn't wait until the next day. We helped Clara Sue close down the office, then Dr. McCartney and I walked to our town's best and only restaurant, the Crawford City Café. I was determined to show him all the good parts of Crawford City, 'cause dang, I could really use his help.

"Do you mind if I go ahead and announce that you're gonna be our new doctor?" I asked as we both filled our plates at the buffet line.

He smiled. "Sure, might as well get the gossip mill working. That way, when I come to work, I'll be able to jump right in."

"You should know that you've already met the town's most notorious gossips, and I don't just mean my receptionist. Just letting them spew their ailments like you did means you'll be so busy the day you arrive, you'll be lucky to see daylight before Christmas."

At that, he smiled happily. We continued to chat about the practice and the town as we filled our plates from the buffet.

As I suspected, given Dr. McCartney was a stranger in town, we got curious looks from everyone in the café. What shocked me was no one came over to ask questions. Finally, after the gossip around us got so intense it was like I was back in high school, I said loud enough for everyone to hear, "Doctor McCartney, when you take on your position at the clinic, you'll want to get a daily punch card here. It's saved me a pile of money."

It was as if the entire place sighed as one. The ridiculous gossip subsided, and people began coming over to introduce themselves, and welcome Dr. McCartney into our community.

When we had a moment to ourselves, I smiled and shook my head. "So, you still wanna work here?"

He laughed. "More than ever."

SEVEN

TODD

I HOBBLED INTO THE café with Doc on my injured side, so he could help me navigate the walk from the car to the table.

The moment we walked in, I knew something was up. I heard a few gasps, followed by a lot of whispered voices. When I finally spotted Ash, I knew why.

He was sitting across from a particularly handsome man. People were going up to their booth, practically forming a line that rivaled the buffet lineup, and introducing themselves to the stranger.

"Um, let's sit over here," I said, pointing to the back corner of the restaurant.

Both my dad and Doc ignored me, and to my dismay, led me to a table next to Ash and the handsome man's booth.

"Hey, Dad, meet Dr. Gibbon McCartney," Ash said.

When the guy shook his hand, Doc grinned. "I'm glad to see you. So, have you decided to take over my old position?" he asked.

The stranger, this Dr. Gibbon McCartney, smiled and nodded. "I accepted the job today. I'll start next week."

"Ah, that's good news. My son has been begging me to come out of retirement, which I've refused, of course. Maybe he'll leave me alone now."

While they exchanged pleasantries, I sat down next to my father, and began looking over the menu, doing my best to ignore them.

Doc turned to my dad then, and introduced him. "That one is Todd," he said, causing me to look at him with a cocked eyebrow. I smiled at the new doctor and decided I was going to forever call him Dr. Handsome, at least in safe confines of my own head.

He smiled at me and gave a half wave.

Doc sat down, and I immediately regretted where I'd sat. In my effort to avoid the new doctor, I'd sat at the far corner of the table, which I now realized meant I was facing Ash. *Fuck*. Well, it looked like they were about done, at least. Maybe they'd leave soon.

Luckily, it wasn't long before Dr. Handsome quickly excused himself after taking a phone call, saying something about needing to meet his family, or someone. I wasn't really paying attention... all of mine was focused on *not* paying attention to Ash, who, of course, hadn't left.

"Come on over here, son," Doc said to him, causing me to moan audibly.

Ash looked at me and shrugged. "I've not had dessert, so sure, why not," he said, and grabbing his homemade apple pie and iced tea, slid out of his booth and sat in the seat between me and his father.

"Boys, we've been meaning to talk to you, and it's serendipitous that you're both here at the same time," Doc began, and looked at my dad, who nodded his assent.

"Amos and I are officially moving in together," he said. "We're both getting older, and we don't wanna play games any longer."

Ash and I looked at them, then glanced at each other. He looked just as confused as I felt trying to figure out what they were talking about.

When we looked back at Doc, he sighed, then he turned toward Ash, and said, "After your mom died, Amos and I rekindled our relationship from when we were kids. Things had already changed so much by then, and we were both ready to accept our love for one another, but that's when things got so crazy..."

Doc choked a bit then, and shook his head. "Well..."

"What your father is trying to say—" Dad chimed in, "—is we didn't wanna make things harder on you two. So, we've held off, but we're tired of being apart. I'm gonna move in with Emanual." He then pointed to me, saying, "I'm also signing the house over to you."

My mouth opened and shut a few times. I was unsure how to react, other than being in shock. "Um..." I said, still trying to get my brain back online.

Ash collected his thoughts before I did. "Dad, Amos, I'm so happy for you both. Confused and a little overwhelmed, too, but I'm happy for you nonetheless."

Dad smiled at him, reached over, and patted his hand.

"What am I supposed to do with your house?" I asked, attempting to address one life-altering revelation at a time, since that was all my brain could handle at the moment.

Dad shrugged. "I don't really care what you do with it."

"That's not true, Amos, and you know it," Doc said, turning toward me. "*We* would like you to come home and live there. It's close to Nashville, and development between here and there is exploding, so you'll have plenty of work if you decide to set up shop here."

I did the fish mouth thing again, opening and shutting it repeatedly, before I just sighed. So, not only was Dad gay, but he was in love with Doc and had been my whole life? No wonder he'd resented my being born... maybe without me in the way they'd have had a happy life together, and now Dad wanted me to move back home to, what, fix up his house and make up for lost time?

"This is too much," I said, shaking my head and looking at my father, who was blushing so much I could see it through his dark complexion. "This is why you've been so nice to me? You were buttering me up to drop this bomb?"

Dad shook his head. "No..."

I held up my hand to stop him, because I didn't want to hear his excuses. It was all I could do to bite my tongue to keep myself from saying something I'd regret. I'd be damned if I was gonna make a scene in public, and I sure as shit wasn't gonna do so in front of Ash. Nope, the best thing to do was just get the hell out of there.

"I'm sorry, I'm gonna leave. I'm not ready to handle this right now."

I got up and was about to head for the door when I remembered the tab and opened my wallet.

"We've got it," Doc said, and I could hear the disappointment in his voice. I just ignored him and tossed down three twenties, more than enough to cover all of our meals.

I hobbled out of the restaurant, fully intending to walk the quarter mile back to Dad's place, where I intended to pack up my things before driving my ass back to Nashville where it belonged.

I got maybe a block down the road before Ash pulled his Ford F-250 up next to me, and asked if I needed a ride.

I would've told him to fuck off, except my foot was screaming, and the pain was enough to trump my equally intense anger.

I tossed my crutches in the back, and crawled into the passenger seat without saying a word.

Ash drove me the rest of the way back to the house, and pulled up in front while I piled out, not even thanking him for the ride. He and Dad—and, for that matter, Doc—could all go screw themselves. Then, I cringed at the thought that Doc and Dad had been doing that very thing to each other.

Refusing to let myself think about why that bothered me so much, I hobbled into the house and over to the bedroom, and began packing.

I was zipping the suitcase when Ash appeared in my doorway, and asked, "So, you're just gonna run away?"

"What the hell is it to you, Ash?" I asked, and had to work hard at not shedding the tears suddenly wanting to come gushing out.

"They deserve better. That's what the hell it is to me," he said.

I put the suitcase on the floor, pulled out the handle, and began rolling it toward the door, while balancing as best I could on crutches.

"How are you going to drive to Nashville with that foot? You'll get two miles before it starts screaming, and you can't take the pain pills and drive," he said.

"I'll go to Bell's," I said, referring to the old rundown motel that sat outside the city limits.

"And you'll end up with scabies or worse." Ash chuckled.

"Just get out of my way, Ash. I need some fuckin' space to process all this."

"Come on, I'll drive you to my place. You can spend the night there."

I looked at Ash like he'd grown wings. "Hell will freeze over before I stay at your place, Ash."

He held his hand up. "Don't get all weird. I'll stay with Dad. You can have your space, and I won't have to worry about you getting stuck between here and Nashville.

Besides, I think once you calm down, you're gonna feel different about the news we just got."

I shook my head, but Ash reached down, picked my suitcase up, and walked toward the front door.

I almost told him to stop, but just as I was about to, I put weight on my bum foot again, and all but fell to the floor from the pain. I glanced toward the nightstand, saw the pain pills, and picked up the bottle.

I guessed I didn't have much choice. I was either gonna stay at Ash's place or the Gonorrhea Motel, because like it or not, I wasn't gonna get home with this foot already swelling out of the boot, and I would rather sleep in my truck than stay the night in this house after both Dads' confessions this morning, then the bomb they just dropped at dinner.

"Fuck it," I said, and popped two of the stupid pills. I could put myself out of my misery, at least for now, even if it meant enduring another ride with Ash.

In the few minutes it took for us to get back to town and up to the clinic, where I assumed Ash must have an apartment or something, I was beginning to feel the effects of the meds.

Ash came around to my side of the truck and grabbed my suitcase and crutches from the back. I opened the door and went to step out, but my leg gave way under me, and I crashed to the ground.

"What the..." Ash said, and rounded the truck to help me up.

"I took pain pills," I said as a way to explain my being stupidly high all of a sudden, and he blanched.

"How many did you take?"

I held up two fingers.

"You're such a damn idiot," Ash said, and lifted me up. "Come on, you're gonna be high for a while, but at least that much won't kill you."

I let him lead me into the little house next to the clinic, thinking, in my drugged-out way, *How nice it is to live next to where you work.*

"I live next to my work too," I said, thinking of the tiny house I'd refurbished back in Nashville.

Ash just shook his head and led me to the bedroom, where I crashed onto the bed, and completely blacked out.

EIGHT

ASH

After getting his shoe and boot off and then rewrapping his injured foot, I shoved Todd to the side so I could tuck him under the covers. "Idiot," I said quietly, then flipped off the light and left the door open, so I could easily check on him without disturbing him as the night went along.

I texted Dad and told him I had Todd at my place, and that he'd taken two pain pills. I also suggested he and Amos come over here if they wanted to talk, but he declined, saying it was probably best to let things settle a bit.

Fuck. I guessed if I thought about it, everything made more sense now. Dad and Amos were *together*. Even when Mom was alive, they tended to do everything together, and at least twice a week, we'd go eat with them, or they'd eat with us.

I wondered how Mom had played into all this, if at all, and shook my head. I'd have to get to the bottom of that later.

I checked on my stupid housemate again, figuring tomorrow he'd be pissed as hell that I hadn't gone to Dad's like I'd told him I would, but that was before the idiot took two of the freakin' pills.

When I heard him snoring softly, I went back into the living room, collapsed on the sofa, and dialed my sister.

It was two hours earlier in Oregon, which meant Lisa would just be getting home from work. "Hey, Ash, what's up?"

"Hey. Well, Dad dropped a bomb on me and Todd tonight."

She was quiet for a moment, then said, "Yeah, and?"

"Did you know he and Amos were a thing?"

She chuckled. "Well, sort of, but they hadn't told me or anything."

"How do you *sort of* know?" I asked.

"Well, I may have accidentally walked in on them kissing one afternoon when Frank and I were there for a visit."

"What, and you never told me?"

"Well, I wasn't one hundred percent sure I saw what I saw, and it's not really any of my business anyway, is it?"

I let that sink in for a moment, and said, "Well, it sort of is. We're his kids."

"And if I'd walked in on him kissing some woman?"

"Then, you would've definitely told me."

She sighed. "Yeah, I probably would've, but this was a bit more loaded, with you being gay and Amos practically raising us."

"Yeah." I could tell she was busy, so I quickly added, "Well, I can let you go."

"No, I'm just about done. I'm unloading groceries, and just have to get the cold stuff put up before my ice cream melts. So, tell me what's happened."

I told her about how I was eating with my new hire when Todd walked in, being all handsome and angry, alongside Dad and Amos. Then, when my colleague left, Dad and Amos had invited us to sit with them just to drop the freakin' bomb.

"Shit, Todd was there? How'd that go?"

"I'll let you guess."

She laughed. "Like a lead balloon?"

"More like a lead balloon laced with explosives."

"Ouch, so he blew up?"

I shook my head, knowing she couldn't see me. "No, but he wanted to. It's a long story, but basically, he's messed his foot up, so he couldn't hightail it back to Nashville, and of course, you know he was wanting to run like he always does."

She laughed. "Well, he isn't one to stick around when things get uncomfortable, especially if you're involved."

"Yeah, so that makes the fact he's asleep in my guest room at the moment that much more interesting."

"What?" she asked, sounding both hysterical and amused at the same time.

"Yeah, he sort of took too much pain medication, which I prescribed, of course, and I couldn't leave him alone. So, guess who's man-sitting."

"Well, you're going to make a great stepbrother."

I almost choked on my own tongue. "Shit, I didn't think about that."

My evil sister cackled in the background. "Well, this should lead to some Jerry Springer-style family gatherings, huh?"

"You're such a jerk," I said, forgoing the insults I really wanted to throw at her.

"Well, give him my best. Do you think I should come home if all this is goin' down?"

"Of course. You should've been here tonight. I'm sure they would've preferred to tell all of us at the same time."

"Yeah, okay, brother, I'll let Frank know and I'll fly out this weekend. Oh, let Dad know you told me. I don't wanna walk into the middle of this gasoline fire without everyone knowing I'm comin'."

"I will. Okay, I'll see you."

"Not so fast, brother. If Todd is staying with you, then I'm sure you're being all weird. The whole Dad and Amos thing is surely nothing compared to that."

"We'll talk this weekend," I said, not wanting to spend too much time thinking about it.

She hesitated. "Okay, but listen, don't get caught up in this. I love Todd like family, but I know how you get about him."

"I'll be okay."

"No, you probably won't, but we can pretend you will be, for now."

I hung up and counted how many days until she'd be here. I could really use my sister and best friend at the moment. She was the only person I knew who'd understand how hard dealing with Todd would be for me. Well, except Dad maybe, but right now, he had a lot of other stuff on his metaphorical plate.

NINE

TODD

I WOKE UP WITH a headache. I didn't tend to get migraines very often but when I did, it was like having a dagger stuck into the backside of my eye.

It took me a moment to figure out where I was. The room was pristine. The curtains and the bedding were stark white. My first thought was that Ash had dropped me off at some swanky hotel or bed and breakfast, except there were no such places in Crawford City.

When I sat up on the side of the bed, the memories of the night before began to swirl through my foggy brain. Thoughts of Ash driving me to his house, leading me to this bedroom, and waking up tucked in bed... "Fuck," I whispered. *So much for avoiding the asshole.*

I crawled out of bed, wincing when I absently put weight on my foot, but too curious to see if I was indeed alone in the house. I remembered Ash saying he'd leave me at his place and stay with Doc.

It must've been pretty early, because the sun was just beginning to rise, and as I came into the living room, I was met by Ashton Nash's sleeping form lying in his recliner, still fully clothed, but his perfectly muscular build filling the chair like he was a freakin' model or something.

I went back to the bedroom, and finding my suitcase still packed, I slipped my shoe and boot on and made a beeline to escape this ridiculous situation before he woke up.

I nearly made it too. I was so close to a clean exit when I hobbled into the living room, and accidentally bumped my foot on the corner of the wall.

I screamed internally as pain seared through me, and I had to lean up against the wall to regain my balance.

When I managed to get myself under control, I glanced at the recliner and saw a sleepy yet smiling Ash watching me.

"Fuck," I said. If my foot wasn't still throbbing, I would've left, but that didn't seem to be in the cards, at least for a few more moments.

"You goin' somewhere?" he asked.

I just glared at him, waiting for the pain to subside.

"When is this gonna stop hurting so bad?" I asked.

"When you stop reinjuring it," he said in his superior, *I'm a doctor and you are a measly, stupid patient* way.

I sighed. "Okay, at this point, that would probably be with me back home in Nashville. There's way too much shit goin' on down here."

"Except, you can't drive, remember?"

"I have employees, though," I said smartly, not at all sure why I was having this debate, and not just calling Jacklyn and asking her to come get me.

"Listen, I just talked to Lisa and she's comin' this weekend. Like it or not, our dads are making decisions that affect all of us. Even if you don't move back here, your father's going to need to deal with the house and all the contents, so unless you plan to disappear again, you might as well stick around and help us work through all the details."

I listened to Ash's speech, and everything in me wanted to make some smart-ass comment and storm out. Unfortunately for me, I knew he was right.

"So, what do you propose, I shack up here with you? I'm sorry, Ash, but I'm not in the mood to see your next flavor of the month, much less be here while you're fuckin' them."

"What the hell are you talking about?" he asked. "I don't have a flavor of the month. Shit, I don't even have a flavor of the year. Do you not remember how hard my dad worked at the clinic? The population of Crawford is double what it was when we were kids, and I'm the only doctor in town, or was. I barely have time to sleep."

"Are you wanting me to feel sorry for you?" I asked, surprised he thought I'd care.

"Todd, I have no expectations of you at all, except maybe to be an ass, and block everyone who tries to help you, or wants to be a part of your life."

"Like you?" I asked, fully getting up to full steam. "'Cause, if I remember right, you were the one who ran off with the first person who looked your way."

"And you're the person who broke my heart!" Hurt laced his comment. Ash was sitting up now with his hands raking through his hair. "Listen," he finally said, "we don't have to rehash this." He looked up at me with emotions swirling in his expression. "I told you I could go stay with Dad. You can have the house. It's not like I'm gonna have much time to be here anyway. Just stay and let's work all this out. Let's help *them* work it out."

I came over and all but fell onto the sofa, abandoning my suitcase.

"You hurt me," I admitted before I lost my nerve.

"We're really gonna do this?" he asked.

"Yeah, Ash, for fuck's sake—" I said, massaging my temples. "—if I'm gonna stay here, in your house, and deal with the bomb our fathers dropped on us last night, then we're gonna do this."

He stared at me for a long moment, then took a deep breath. "You... broke... up... with... me." His voice was barely a whisper, but the power of each word reverberated inside me.

"You were pushing me too hard. We were only sixteen! I wasn't ready to marry you. Not like that was even an option back then."

Talking over me, Ash replied, "It hurt me so bad when you broke things off. It was like you'd cut off one of my appendages. No, it was like you'd cut out my heart."

"So, what...? You dated Jen and then Alex just to hurt me?"

"Probably," Ash's eyes dropped to the floor as he admitted that. "But..." he said, looking back up at me. "It was also to try to fill the void you left. Hell, we were only kids, and I'd just lost my best friend and boyfriend. I didn't know how to deal with that kind of grief, still don't."

We stared at each other for what felt like forever. I let my mind flashback to that horrible day. I'd been so nervous my voice shook as I told him I wasn't ready for all the getting married and going to college, and all the other plans Ash was piling on me. I just wanted him to calm down on the plans, not run off with someone else...

"Ash, you don't understand what that was like. It still hurts when I think about it. I didn't really break up with you. I just said I needed some space, and the next thing I know you're necking with Jen behind the bleachers. I never said we were over, that I wanted us to be over..."

Ash's face grew red then, and he shook his head. "You said we were over. I remember what you said, Todd. Do you think I wouldn't remember that?"

"I said if we didn't give each other space, we would be over. I was saying what your dad said to me the night before, that we needed to give each other some space before we ended up just like we fuckin' did."

"My dad?" Ash asked, his face registering what appeared to be shock.

"Well, of course, your dad. Who else was there for me back then? It sure as hell wasn't *my* father. I'd gone to Doc for advice after you started pulling out magazines of weddings, and were talking about which college we'd both go to. Fuck, Ash, you'd planned my entire life out, and didn't even give me a chance to share my own thoughts."

When Ash continued to stare at me, I decided to continue with my side of the story—a story I doubted he'd ever heard before. "So, I went to Doc, and he said to tell you to back off before you destroyed our relationship."

Ash's mouth was agape, his body frozen in place. "So, my dad told you to say all that?" he finally asked, disbelief in his voice.

"Told me, no, advised me, yes. And he was right, Ash, you were over the top with all the wedding and life planning. I didn't want to go to college. I never did. That was *your* dream. I didn't wanna become whatever it was you said I should become. What was it? An engineer or something? I don't even remember."

"Civil engineer. 'Cause you were so good at math," he said almost in a whisper.

"There ya go. I wanted my own dreams, not yours."

"Why didn't you tell me that? Why didn't you....?"

"'Cause your fuckin' tongue was down the throat of Jennifer Cole before I had a chance to."

Ash wiped his face with both hands and shook his head. "I was so angry, I wanted you to hurt like I was. He chuckled bitterly then and shook his head. "You know, I'm not even bisexual, but Jennifer had always shown interest, and I was so upset over losing you..."

The revelation that he wasn't even attracted to women, but had dated Jen anyway brought me up short. Ashton Nash was turning everything I thought I knew about him on its head, but I wasn't gonna let another decade go by without saying my piece.

"You goin' out with Jen is exactly why I've never been able to forgive you. I was trying to save our relationship, and you were trying to burn what was left of it to ashes, so there was nothing left to salvage."

Ash wiped his eyes, and sighed, "I... I just hadn't thought about it that way..." he said. "I always thought you'd told me to get lost, and all I knew how to do was to... react. Ash stood and paced. "I'm not even sure I can use the excuse of being a kid, 'cause I knew dating Jennifer would wreck us, but I felt like you'd already done that." He stopped and looked at me. I kept thinking you were dumping me like Mom had... I just thought you were like her. That I didn't really matter..."

"You mattered *too much*," I admitted, all the anger and frustration deflating out of me. I leaned back on his oversized sofa, letting my head fall back against the fluffy fabric.

I heard him walk to the kitchen, but didn't open my eyes. I just needed a moment to collect myself. The memories of how things had ended with us, even so many years ago, were fresh and raw for me. Hearing his version of events, and about how much pain he'd also been in for the past decade, had done nothing to make it better. My heart was still broken, we were still broken, and I still blamed him for it.

"You want coffee?" he asked.

I nodded. "Let's walk down to the bakery shop and have Linda's coffee. I haven't been there since I've been home."

"Well, Linda sort of shut the bakery down last month."

I looked at him, alarmed. "What do you mean she shut down?"

"She's seventy, Todd, she needed to retire."

"On your advice?" I asked.

He looked pained. "I can't discuss a patient's confidential conversations with you."

"Damn, so where do you go for a decent cup of coffee and pastries then?" I asked.

"The closest place is Mayville," he said, and shrugged.

"What? Mayville? That's like twenty minutes away."

He chuckled. "We could go over to old Jim's donut shop. His son, Jamie, has been helping out lately, and replaced that horrible coffee they used to serve."

I let the frustrated sigh escape before accepting the reality of losing the best pastry shop I'd ever known. "Beggars can't be choosers, I guess."

Instead of walking, we took Ash's truck and when we got to the donut shop, which had to be the oldest in the state of Tennessee, he hopped out of the cab, asking if I still liked the same kind from when I was a kid.

I shrugged. "Long John, filled with chocolate, and a bear claw."

Ash grinned and shook his head. "You're still like a freakin' sixteen-year-old."

When he shut the door, I said out loud to myself, "Except now, I'm too old to let you break me like you did before."

TEN

ASH

TODD AND I HADN'T spoken this much since the breakup. As I dashed into the donut shop and Jamie packed our order, I poured us both a cup of coffee and paid while thinking about all he'd said.

I was overbearing. I knew I was, and I knew I'd be exactly the same if we dated now. I was a planner, a plotter, really. I liked setting goals and working toward them. That's how I'd managed to get my medical degree, and how I'd managed to get through a week of seeing forty to sixty patients a day, which was an impossible feat for anyone who didn't have clear and concise goals.

When I got back to the truck, I handed Todd his coffee and drove to Lover's Lane. It was one of the few places in Crawford City away from prying eyes and ears. I figured we'd be able to eat our donuts in peace, at least at this time of the morning. It was also the scene of our first kiss... and, coincidentally, our last, but it was either there, or risk gossip mill eavesdropping.

I grabbed the donut box when I parked the truck in front of a roadside picnic table, and I was sure my choice of location wasn't lost on Todd. Luckily, he followed me to the table without giving me too much lip, not that he wouldn't give me plenty when we sat down.

I pulled my single glazed donut out, put it on a napkin, and pushed the box over to Todd.

With all the hours I spent at the clinic, I couldn't afford to even eat this one, but hell, my love of sugar and soul food was too intense for me to be a complete health nut. I tried to watch my food intake, and eat as healthy as possible to counter the lack of exercise, but sometimes a person just needed a donut.

"So, what now?" Todd asked after swallowing a mega bite of his Long John. I looked toward the grand parkway that led up to the Cross house, ignoring the *way* too tempting chocolate filling that was now sitting on the right side of his lips. Me attacking him with a kiss and licking off the chocolate would probably not be the best way to keep our lines of communication open.

When he used a napkin to clean his face, I turned back toward him. "We make a plan."

He laughed. "Should've guessed that's what you wanna do."

I shrugged off the dig, and proceeded, "We let things settle with our dads for a day or two. Lisa will be home by then, and we all three go hear them out. This time you don't walk out when you get upset."

Todd shook his head. "That's not fair."

"Fair or not, you're gay, I'm gay, they have the right to feel what they feel, and you *homosquashing* them was uncool."

"They weren't just telling us about their sexuality, Ash. They were telling us they've been in love since they were kids. How can you digest that so quickly and not... and not have your head explode?"

"Well, 'cause I'm not a kid, and I know how being anything but straight, especially in the South has been. You have to let it sink in before you react."

Todd let out a long breath, clearly taking in my words, but still looking flustered. "I do feel bad about how I reacted in the café, but, Ash, my father has been a cold shell since I was little. This week he's been..." He paused, as if searching for the right word. "He's been civil."

I let that sink in. It was making more sense now why Todd had reacted so... well, so much, but even though I felt for Todd, I loved the thought of my dad and Amos being a couple, finally bringing together that part of our family, even if it meant I had to deal with Todd from now on. I almost smiled as I thought about it... about them... then saw Todd's expression...

"Todd, I'm guessing your dad is being civil to you, cause he's not hiding from himself any longer, don't ya think?"

Eleven

Todd

*L*over's Lane. Of all the places Ash could've taken me after filleting my heart open, he brought me to a place brimming with memories of us. Not that I couldn't say the same of just about anywhere in Crawford City, seeing as we'd spent half our lives here joined at the hip, but this was where it'd all changed... where we'd become *more* than friends. Memories of feeling his soft lips gliding across mine that first time... The memories threatened to overtake my thoughts as we sat eating our donuts.

I stared off toward the parkway, using the time to focus on Ash's words, and let the revelation sink in that my dad had spent my whole life pretending to be someone he wasn't, and all for what...? Me? The idea that Dad would've sacrificed his own happiness for my welfare, as opposed to simply loathing my existence, was almost laughable. No one, especially me, would've ever accused Amos Thompson of that.

I still had so many questions I didn't even know how to ask him. Guilt gripped me. Damn, if after all this, the first time he'd tried opening up to me, I'd turned tail and run. I was beginning to think maybe Ash was right about that. Maybe I did always run... *Fuck! All this makes my head hurt.*

"Okay, I won't leave town just yet, and we'll talk to Dad and Doc after Lisa gets here. I know I have some cleaning up to do with Dad, but, Ash, I really don't wanna go back to that house. It's full of hard memories... if anything, I'd rather stay with Doc."

"Well, then you'd be staying with them both, seeing as they're moving in together," he said with a little smirk. "You do have another option, though."

"Fine, so your place *is* the best option for now, and *no*, I don't need you moving out of your own home while I'm staying there. Besides, I'm sure our dads need their space as well."

Ash smiled at me. "It'll be fine, I promise. I don't get home until late, and I leave early. So, as long as you don't get high again, forcing me to take care of you, we shouldn't see each other much anyway."

"Yeah, about that, how strong is that crap you gave me?"

"If you hadn't been so busy telling me how to treat you, you'd have heard me tell you not to take more than one every twelve hours, or, of course, you could've just read the bottle."

I sighed. "Okay, okay. That was a lesson I learned the hard way."

"Listen, Todd," Ash said, after I finished the last bite of my bear claw. "I want this to work. I want our dads to have the life they've not been able to have until now. If they love each other, and now the puzzle pieces are comin' together, I can see that they do, I want them to have a perfect life together. Can we agree to make that possible, or at least not prevent it from happening?"

I nodded. "Yeah, I want that too. Besides, your dad has been a second father to me, and I know my dad has been the same for you and Lisa. I'm good with making us a happy little family." I thought for a few minutes, our conversation making me feel lighter than I had in years. "Since you're a rich doctor now, I have a nice long Christmas list for you too. Something along the lines of a new car, or maybe a new bulldozer for the company."

"Um, dude, I work in a small town where a third of the patients I see can't afford to pay me, so Mr. Richie Rich construction-company owner should be the one buying his poor stepbrother a new car or medical equipment that wasn't made sixty years ago."

As we got back into Ash's truck, we were laughing and teasing each other again like old times. That hadn't happened in over a decade, and it felt good. Like the planets were realigning or something.

"Want me to drop you somewhere?" Ash asked.

"Um, yeah, I need to brush my teeth, since I didn't get to do that this morning, and then I should go over to Dad's. The construction crew he hired is reroofing the old place, and I wanna see how it's comin' along. I might just have a few jobs for them if they're doin' good work."

"You aren't gonna try to climb up there on that foot of yours, are you?" he asked, looking concerned.

I shrugged. "No, definitely not, but I'd like to watch their progress and then have my foreman, Linc, come out and do an inspection when they're done."

Ash winked at me, and we drove back to his house. Simply seeing him wink sent my heart racing. Fuck, the man still had way too much control over me, if just a wink could undo me.

While Ash showered, I used the kitchen sink to brush my teeth and clean up some. I probably should get a shower as well, but I could do that at Dad's place. That way, I wouldn't make Ash late for work.

As he drove me the five minutes to Dad's driveway, I could smell the soap on Ash, and it was by far the most erotic smell in the world. With his intoxicating scent invading my senses, and my mind racing with ways to put his freshly showered body to use, I wasn't so sure if this stepbrother thing was going to work out after all.

I crawled out of the truck, and waved as Ash disappeared around the circle drive and then back toward town.

"Looks like you two are making good," Kendra said as I walked up toward the big porch.

"Looks can be deceiving, but for our fathers' sake, we're trying."

Kendra's face broke into a knowing smile. *Shit*, did the whole town know? Of course, it did, we'd been at gossip central—otherwise known as the Crawford City Café—last night when Dad and Doc told us.

"Kendra, how much more do you have on the roof before you're done?"

"Well, storms are expected this evening. So, we plan to have it done or almost done by tonight. We got all the old stuff pulled off yesterday in time to replace rotten boards and put up the plywood. I've got a few extra hands on duty today, so we should be done by quittin' time."

I nodded. "Good, do you mind if I watch ya'll?"

She looked at me funny. "If'n you're a mind to sit and watch, I guess I don't mind if you do."

I chuckled. "I appreciate it. I'm gonna get my laptop and sit under the shade tree and do just that."

She nodded, then disappeared up the ladder.

I went inside and gave Linc a call. When his voicemail picked up, I left a message asking if he had time to come this way to inspect the work of a potential new roofing sub-contractor to replace the redneck idiot I'd fired yesterday.

I decided to skip taking a shower, since it was hot enough to boil eggs, and I knew I'd need one when the day was over anyway. Instead, I set about creating up a makeshift office under the monster oak tree that I'd spent many a day climbing as a kid.

Jacklyn called off and on throughout the day, mostly about setting up potential new customers, which I told her to put off until I knew if Kendra's roofing crew would be able to cover our needs, or even be interested in working with us.

Dad came by with Doc about noon, and each man pulled up a chair on either side of me to watch the progress. At one point, Doc went to the house, and grabbed a padded footstool, an ancient thing that had belonged to my grandmother, and propped my foot on it before sitting back down.

I just shook my head and thanked him before I got a return call from Linc, saying he'd have time to do the inspection today, and should arrive here in about two hours.

Only after I'd hung up did I notice my dad was staring at me.

"What?" I asked.

"You trying to scalp my contractors?" he asked.

"You're retired, and yeah, if they're as good as I think they are, I'm in need of a reliable roofing crew now that I fired mine."

Dad gave Doc a look that conveyed some secretive message only they could decipher, more of their wordless communicating that I'd learned long ago to ignore. I went right on ignoring them, and focused on working through my bid for a new project, making sure I'd put in enough contingency before we committed to the three-million-dollar build on just the other side of Lebanon.

Then, it was Dad's turn to disappear into the house. When he came back out, he was carrying an ancient silver platter with a glass pitcher of lemonade and three matching glasses.

I cocked an eyebrow, willing myself to ignore the fact that the platter had been polished and shined for the first time since... well, I'd never seen it polished and shined before.

I took the lemonade he offered and drank, surprised when it was the perfect blend of tangy and sweet.

I glanced at Doc, and caught him smiling before he ducked his head behind his glass, and took a drink.

"It's the freakin' Twilight Zone here," I said, causing my father to shake his head. "Dad, stop being weird for a minute, and give me an opinion about this bid. I'm gonna need some fancy work done on this section where the architect has some harebrained idea goin' on with the two roof lines. I'm guessing I'm gonna have to put reinforcements under this area." I pointed toward the architectural drawings. "But, I'm not sure if it'll require steel, or if I can do it with a reinforced beam."

Dad took my laptop and stared at the blueprint for several moments. "My first thought is that's not an appropriate angle, and it's gonna give your new homeowner a lot of grief, but the architect seems to have remedied that here with this overhang. I'm surprised, though, that the codes, especially in Lebanon, will tolerate it."

I noticed the address in the corner of the blueprint. My dad didn't miss a thing, which was why I was glad to get his opinion.

"So, should I send it back to the architect for a redraw?"

He studied it a moment longer. "Yes, I saw something similar to this on a build I did back in the eighties. Two things you'll have to prepare for. First, the runoff will have to be redirected away from this part of the roof like the architect has shown here, but they didn't give you enough clearance. Ask them to raise that by a couple feet, here and here." He pointed at the screen, then pondered a moment longer, before continuing, "The second thing is inside clearance. I'm guessing you've got this weird roof pitch, because of how they designed the interior. If that space is going to be finished, and they sacrificed roof pitch, then the interior isn't going to be adequate for a huge beam. Why don't you have your architect put the weight on supports under the increased space on either side? That way, you can hide the beams here instead of having to support this area."

I looked at the area and smiled. That really did fix the problem, and when I jumped to the interior design, I was able to show my dad the huge window that was meant to go there, a window I'd thought we'd lose due to the beam.

"Thanks, Dad," I said, and quickly wrote an email to the architect asking her if she could redesign the roof with my dad's suggestions and redistribute the weight away from that section of the build. When I was done, I smiled at my father, who was busy sending more meaningful glances to Doc. "Okay, you two, cut it out. If you've got something to say, spit it out, otherwise, go somewhere else."

Doc chuckled. "Well, your dad isn't happy about his retirement, and wants to be involved…"

"Involved with what?" I asked, feeling a gurgling form in the pit of my stomach.

"I miss the work, son. I mean, I don't wanna be the one swinging the hammer any longer, and my blood pressure would be a lot better if I wasn't managing multiple crews, but I miss being a part of the daily work."

"And, what, you wanna come to work for me?" I asked. He looked hesitant, almost worried. "Dad." I considered his words carefully before I responded, which I'd admit hadn't occurred much when talking with my dad. "I'm not sure. I can't have you screaming at me in front of my crews. You and I never worked well together. There's a lot at stake here."

Dad nodded and I could tell he was disappointed. I looked at Doc for support, and he'd pasted a neutral expression on his face, which didn't make me feel any better.

Luckily, Linc pulled into the driveway behind us, and I was happy to let him be the excuse to end the conversation. It wasn't before I looked at my father, though, and realized he really was disappointed and maybe a little hurt by what I'd said. *Well, shit. So much for my extending an olive branch to the man.*

"Hey, how about you write up a proposal for me. What you'd be doin', how you would help out, and, most importantly, how you won't be undermining my authority. We can go over it later, okay?"

I could tell I'd bruised his ego, and this was about when I'd expected our conversation would go down in flames. I waited for the *screw you* to spew from my dad's mouth, but Doc made eye contact with Dad instead, and before I knew it, he nodded and actually smiled. "Son, that sounds like a great plan. I'll get that to you tonight or tomorrow, okay?"

"Sure," I said, and gave Doc my best, *Has hell just frozen over?* look.

Doc grinned at me, and he and Dad took the tray and glasses back into the house, while Linc walked toward me.

"Hey, Linc, thanks for comin' out."

"You're the boss," he said, which caused me to laugh.

"Like that's made a difference before."

Linc smirked. "Well, it sure shocked the shit out of Warren yesterday."

I cringed. "He givin' you shit?"

"Nah, he tried to recruit me away from the company to join him, but, Todd, I'd rather have every tooth pulled out of my head. That man couldn't manage a pig eatin' slop."

"He's pulling some away, though?" I asked, feeling concerned.

"Yeah, but mostly they're the ones we need gone." Linc was one of my most trusted employees, who I'd met when I first came to work for the company. At just shy of seven feet tall, he was, at that time, the size of a pole, but had filled out considerably between working out and working hard in construction in the years since, and his ebony skin seemed to glow with health and vitality.

I'd considered dating him a few years back, but my survival instincts told me not to get involved with a coworker, even if he was also gay and had flirted with me for a while.

As time went on, we seemed to come to the unspoken agreement that we preferred to be friends, and when I took over the company, he was the first person I promoted, and was now my second in command.

Linc smiled. "You won't be surprised at who's givin' notice."

I quirked an eyebrow in question.

"Jones the electrician, for one."

"That's a blessing. I thought you were about to fire him anyway."

"I should've, but he promised to do better."

"Did he?"

Linc laughed. "No." Then, he continued down the list. "We lost a couple subs, but they were horrible anyway. The fact is, we only lost the worst of the worst, but that leaves us in need, across the board."

I thought about Dad's offer to help, then looked skyward at Kendra and Rita, who were telling their men to begin cleaning up the mess around the house. "My dad wants to come aboard," I admitted.

Linc had met my dad early on, when I talked him into comin' down to moonlight for Dad when his crew got sick with the flu, and they were up against a major deadline.

Linc cringed. "Is that a good idea?"

I shrugged. "No idea. I told him he had to come up with a plan not to undermine my authority, but if you're asking if we could use his expertise, and more, his old crews, like the one on the roof of his house at the moment, yeah, I think we really could."

Linc clapped his sizeable hand onto my back, and said, "I wish you luck, man. I really do."

"Shut up," I said teasingly. "Just get up there and see if that roof is as good as I think it is."

Linc left me smiling. The moment he got on the roof, he shook hands with the two women and made nice before he inspected their work. I'd known Linc for a long time and trusted his judgement. I could tell from here he was impressed.

Kendra and Rita were helping clean up debris alongside Pretty Boy George, who, even sweaty and exhausted, lived up to that secret name I'd long ago given him.

Linc sat next to me in one of the chairs Dad and Doc had vacated. "That's impeccable work," he said. "You'd be a fool not to hire them on the spot."

I nodded. "I figured my dad wouldn't have hired them if they weren't top-notch, but I've also known Kendra and George all my life. Their father was Dad's competition for years, and the man had a reputation for being as much of a hard-ass as mine was."

"Well, you want me to hang out while you hire them?"

I chuckled. "You worried about getting back to working on the country singer's house, huh?"

"More than. That man's wife is scary as shit. I think if we don't get the place done soon, she'll kill me and bury me in the foundations."

Having met the woman, I couldn't help but see his point. "Okay, but, yeah... if you don't mind waiting, I'll go get them."

I stood up, only to realize my damned injured foot must've fallen asleep after sitting with it propped up on that old footstool so long.

"Well, hold on. I'm not goin' anywhere for a minute."

By the time my foot stopped tingling and I was able to move toward the house, Rita was climbing into her truck to leave.

"Hey, Rita," I yelled across the yard. "Do you have a minute to talk before you go?"

She gave me a quizzical look, not unlike Kendra had when I asked if I could watch them work, but met me halfway across the lawn.

"Can you get Kendra too? I wanna talk to both of you, if you've got time."

Her expression was wary, but she nodded. I managed to get up the stairs and into Dad's parlor, where I plopped down in the same Victorian side chair next to the fireplace that I'd seen Dad sit in a thousand times when he was doing business with potential partners.

When Kendra and Rita came in and sat on the sofa, Linc sat in the other side chair. I almost laughed with how ridiculous he looked sitting in the dainty little chair.

"Sorry," I said. "My stupid foot is getting the better of me, or I'd have talked to y'all outside."

That seemed to relax the women a bit before I got down to business. "So, I just let my roofing guy go yesterday, and need to either hire a new crew or hire subs I can rely on. Linc here is impressed with y'all's work up there, and even the cleanup your crew is doing now is good, so would you like to bid on a job for me?"

Rita looked at Kendra and they both smiled. "We're pretty new, and we've already got quite a bit of work, but sure, we can shoot you a bid."

I nodded. "It's a big one. The house is almost ten thousand square feet. Luckily, the roof on this one isn't crazy, it's just a basic design."

Rita smiled, before responding, "I worked for a local construction company, before Kendra and I decided to go out on our own. I'm not afraid of the more complex rooflines, but if yours is straightforward, that'll make us cheaper."

"Good, when are you available to meet Linc at the jobsite to look at what needs doin'?"

They exchanged information with Linc, including the address of the project, and headed out the door.

Linc hung out a bit longer, and we discussed some of the people we'd have to replace with the changes, thanks to Warren.

While we were hashing through it all, Dad came in and sat across from us. "Sounds like you boys might need some more help."

I nodded. "Yeah, the idiot I fired yesterday is ripping my crews apart, and even though we're glad to see the back of most of them, it's them leavin' all at once that's creating problems."

Dad smiled. "I might be able to help. I have a list of folks like Kendra and Rita who are either starting out, or want more reliable work. If you can give that to them, I think you'd be pleased with their work."

I made eye contact with my dad, and knew what was going on. He knew his worth, always had. In fact, he'd taught me to know my own value when I was growing up.

"Okay," I said, ignoring the fact that I was walking into my dad's trap just by agreeing to it. "Why don't you and Linc discuss it. I'm gonna go pop some more ibuprofen, and talk to Doc about how I'm gonna deal with you being my newest employee."

I ignored Linc's chuckle as I hobbled out of the parlor and into the kitchen, where Doc was sitting on the old fifties dining chair, reading the local paper.

"So, now that I've been tricked into a working relationship with Dad, what sage advice do you have for me? Preferably advice that keeps one of us from killing the other."

Doc put the paper down and winked at me. "I think you'll be surprised with the new leaf your father has turned over. He's not as... as angry as he used to be."

"I've noticed some changes, but you sure those aren't superficial?"

Doc leaned forward when I sat in the chair across from him, and placed a hand over mine. "Listen, son, the angry man was the superficial one. The man you're getting to know now, he's the one I've known and loved all these years. I know it's hard, but if you can give him a chance to show you his true character, I think you'll be... I think you'll be surprised."

I sighed. "Well, for my sake and the sake of my company, I hope you're right." I stood up and moved to stand by his side, putting my hand on his shoulder. "Your sake as well. I couldn't imagine you shacked up with the old son of a bitch he used to be."

Doc howled with laughter. "So, you comin' to terms then?" he asked.

"Oh, yeah, of course, you're my dad as much as him. I'll admit, I never thought the two of you were... well, I was a kid... but yeah, if you are, and you're happy, I'm happy too."

Doc stood up then, and pulled me into a hug. "We are."

When I pulled back, the old man was swiping at a tear. "Do I finally get to call you Dad now?" I asked, teasing him.

"I told you long ago you could call me Dad."

I nodded. He had. When I was so angry at my dad that I stayed at his house for a week, I'd asked if I could call him Dad, and he'd said sure, just like that, except that was right after I started messing around with Ash, and it felt a little wrong to be calling Ash's father Dad at that point, but that was a different time, and while my relationship with Ash might have changed since then, my relationship with Doc never had. He'd always been a father to me, so even though I might never do it, but the idea of calling Doc Dad just felt right.

Twelve

Ash

MY WORK WEEK FROM hell continued through the weekend. I'd initially planned to close, given Rachel, my nurse practitioner, was on vacation, but damn, we had so many unscheduled patients come in on Thursday that I begrudgingly agreed to open on Saturday as well.

"Keep the schedule light," I'd told Clara Sue, seeing as I was doing three people's work, but I knew my request was futile.

I barely had time to see Todd, although seeing him curled up on my sofa watching TV when I got home late and his pointing to food my dad had fixed and brought over, felt wonderful. Despite how good it made me feel, though, I was so exhausted that I couldn't do much more than smile, eat, and crash.

By the time Sunday came along, I was too tired to do anything but lie in bed. Unfortunately, this was also the day Lisa was flying in from Oregon, so Dad and Amos agreed to pick her up from the Nashville airport. I was glad, because I only had today to rest before my crazy schedule resumed on Monday. At least Rachel would be back at work and could take on some of the workload, although her appointment calendar was already booked out three weeks in advance, as was mine. She could handle some of the walk-ins, until Dr. McCartney got settled in, and could start seeing patients.

Todd rode with Dad and Amos to pick Lisa up and get a few things he needed from his office. I heard him talking to his assistant, about leaving things for him to grab yesterday, when we'd made plans to manage all today's activities.

I knew I was an idiot, but I couldn't help but feel excited that I'd have another few days with Todd in my home. Maybe with Rachel being back, I'd get home in time to actually see him for more than a few minutes before I fell asleep.

I managed to get myself up and showered before they all made it back to Dad's place, and was about to head over there when I got an emergency call. When I checked the message, it was about little Tyler, a kinder-gartener, who had a pretty serious infection that I'd already tried to treat twice this week. If he was spiking again, that meant the antibiotics weren't working.

I called his mom back immediately. "Hi, Kim, yeah, bring Tyler to the office. I'll have a look, but you need to go ahead and pack a bag. If he's got a high fever, he'll probably need to go to the hospital in Nashville."

As I suspected, Tyler was way too sick for me to treat at the clinic. I immediately sent the family off, before calling the hospital and informing the receptionist I was sending a six-year-old to the ER, and noted his spiking fever, suspected sepsis, and resistance to both antibiotics I'd prescribed.

By the time I finished documenting my notes, I'd gotten a text from Dad telling me they'd arrived at the house. Luckily, the pediatrician soon rang me back from the hospital in Nashville, letting me know the family had just arrived at the ER.

We chatted briefly about Tyler's clinic visits last week, and when I told him which antibiotics I'd used in treating Tyler, he sighed into the phone. "It's unusual they didn't work. Okay, thanks, we'll get him worked up."

When he hung up, the relief of knowing little Tyler was in good hands, Rachel would be back to work tomorrow, and that we'd also be welcoming Dr. McCartney into our clinic, hit me all at once, and almost made me want to sit down and weep.

I closed the clinic back up, and left a note for Leslie, my medical assistant, to have Dr. McCartney fill out his necessary paperwork asap when he arrived Monday morning. I wasn't going to waste one minute before officially making him an employee, so he could get started seeing patients.

Thirteen

Todd

Dad and Linc were like two peas in a pod from the moment I walked out of Dad's parlor, leaving the two to chat. So, it was no surprise that every opening we had was soon filled by tradespeople from Crawford and other nearby towns. Also not surprising, was how they were all formerly associated with my father's business in one way or another. Dad hadn't officially told me he was retired, in fact, until Doc had mentioned Dad's retirement the other day, I'd thought he was still in the business.

I did know he'd slowed down, which explained why he'd needed the roof done, but not knowing he'd quit the business altogether, just showed how out of tune I'd become with my family. Honestly, I thought that might be why I'd accepted my dad's request to help so easily. I felt the emptiness where my family should've been, and I was ready to fill it again.

I'd yet to see that written list of things I'd requested, but the truth was, even though it'd only been a couple of days, I was enjoying having my dad around. Unlike when I was a kid, he was chipper, funny even, and always had a solid, reliable answer to anything I asked him. The kind of valuable advice only years of experience could produce.

Finally, on Saturday afternoon, I relented. "You'll come on as supervising foreman, same as Linc, but you still have to answer to me."

A smile bigger than I'd ever seen from my dad slowly spread across his face. He and I both knew, when push came to shove, he wasn't going to answer to me. The fact he could smile and not rub that fact in my face was a glimpse of the miracle transformation Doc said was the real him.

My only concern was, if Dad's old personality—the one I'd grown up with—came back out, would I once again be struggling to find skilled workers?

For better or worse, I didn't have time to dwell on that thought at the moment. I had six more potential jobs coming in from the famous country singer's referrals, now that his house was almost done. That meant I had over ten potential building projects all between here and Nashville, and I needed a reliable team in place before even considering accepting them. In fact, at this point, I didn't know if I even felt comfortable bidding for the work, until I had my crews in better shape.

I was staring at the bids, when at seven, Ash still hadn't gotten home from work. The man was going to work himself into an early grave. As I had the past two nights, I bundled up food from Doc's before he or Dad dropped me back at Ash's for the night.

It seemed weird that I was staying here, with Ash, after all these years of hating him, but it felt oddly right too, and I was glad for it. While things had been up in the air with Doc and Dad, not to mention letting my father come to work for me, I needed neutral ground. Now *that* was a strange thought, thinking anything to do with Ash was neutral.

I was worried about him, though. It wasn't healthy for him to be working this many hours. He was headed toward burnout, and fast.

While Ash was still at work, Lisa had called asking if I knew where he was, because she needed to talk to him about changes to her upcoming flight tomorrow. Apparently, he was supposed to be picking her up at the Nashville airport, and I was surprised he hadn't shared those details with me.

After taking down her new flight information, we ended the call, and I immediately phoned Doc. Driving any great distance was still a pain, literally, with my healing foot, so it'd be up to our two dads to bring Lisa home, but that didn't mean I couldn't bum a ride with them.

Ash walked into the house, looking totally spent and ready to drop, when Doc answered my call. While we discussed Lisa's travel arrangements, I pointed Ash toward the food still in the microwave, so he'd get something decent in his system before passing out.

"If you don't mind, I'd like to join you and pick up some stuff from my office while we're in Nashville. Jacklyn has already put it out for Linc to bring to me next week, but I'd rather not pull him off the job if I don't have to."

"That's no problem, son. We'll be by to pick you up around seven forty-five, which'll give us enough time to fetch Lisa and then we'll go get your things."

"Thanks, Doc," I said, and hung up as the microwave beeped. "I guess you heard. Lisa's flying in earlier than expected tomorrow," I said to Ash.

"I guess you figured out Lisa's itinerary."

I shrugged. "Any reason you didn't tell me?"

"Forgot, I've had so much on my plate this week."

Silence fell between us, not uncomfortably so, but that was mostly because I wanted to tell him he was working himself to the bone, and knew it wasn't my place.

"So, we'll head out early to get her. You can sleep in." He nodded, and just like the previous nights, all but fell onto his meal. "Do you have to work this hard all the time?" I finally dared to ask.

"It's busy, but no, the nurse practitioner is out, which means I only have late nights like this occasionally. However, we've needed another doctor since before Dad retired. Even when Dad was still with us, it was busy, but now it's almost impossible." He chuckled, which seemed to take energy he didn't have to spare.

"Why did you wait so long to hire someone?"

"Supply and demand. There's a shortage of family care docs, and an even bigger shortage of doctors willing to come to the middle of nowhere to work."

"Seems like they'd have plenty of patients though."

I nodded. "I was about to try to hire another nurse practitioner when I got word from my headhunters that they had someone who wanted a rural job. That's how I found out about Doctor McCartney, the guy you met the other night at the café. We just got lucky. Thank God, too, 'cause, with us being fully staffed again, I might get to have a normal life for the first time in years."

"Good," I said, and left Ash to finish his supper, while I showered and got ready for bed.

By the time I came back out of the bathroom, Ash's empty dish of food was in the sink, and he was nowhere to be seen. He'd probably barely made it into his bed before crashing.

I shook my head as I rinsed the dish and put it into the full dishwasher, so I decided to run it while we slept. I could clean it out tomorrow night before I went to bed. That was the least I could do for Ash for letting me spend time here without putting pressure on me to talk.

Ash was sleeping like a log when I gathered up my laptop, and crept out of his house early the next morning to collect his sister from the airport. It'd been at least a year since I'd seen Lisa, although we chatted at least by text once a month.

After hugging our dads, Lisa literally leaped into my arms, causing Doc and Dad to laugh. "Todd, it's been too dang long since I've seen you," she said when I let her go. "Come on, I overpacked and will need you to carry some of this luggage."

She wasn't lying. While she managed her carry-on bag, a purse, and what appeared to be a laptop bag, the rest of us each wrangled a large size suitcase to Doc's extended cab pickup.

"You moving back home?" I asked, after hauling the last piece of luggage off the conveyor belt.

"Shut up, I'm a woman. I need my things to make me feel pretty."

"You need to learn self-restraint," I said, and earned myself a slap on the arm, which was lucky for me. Usually, she'd have belted me with all her strength. Lisa Nash had left more than a few bruises on my arms when I'd pissed her off over the years, same as she'd done to Ash. She really was like a little sister to me, minor squabbles and all.

We crawled into Doc's pickup after throwing all of Lisa's luggage into the back, and recapping the rubber cover over the truck bed.

Lisa chatted on and on about her life in Oregon, her husband, Frank, who was serving his first year as the state's attorney general, and how happy she was that I'd returned to Crawford and wasn't hiding in Nashville, pouting like a baby, any longer.

I'd have just ignored her, except I was sitting beside her in the back seat, and ignoring Lisa was difficult at the best of times. It was dang near impossible when she had you in her line of sight.

At least she wasn't practicing psychology on me... yet.

"So, you moving back to Crawford City then?" she asked out of the blue.

You could've heard a pin drop as her loaded question hung in the air. Had I been sitting up front, I'd have turned the radio on to distract everyone while keeping my trap shut. *No such luck.*

"No. I've not committed to that. Why? Have people been telling you I'm moving back?" I asked, and looked between the two guilty parties in the front seat, who conveniently kept staring straight ahead.

She shrugged. "It would make it easier, you know."

"Easier for what?" I asked.

"Easier to spoil your niece and nephew."

The confusion must've shown on my face at trying to figure out what she was talking about, because a wide grin spread across hers. Noticing a hand splayed across her middle, left no doubt as to her meaning: Lisa was pregnant. "You're expecting?" I heard our dads chuckling at my question, which told me they already had this nugget of family information. I wondered if Ash already knew too. "Um, you're having twins? Like, you're having two babies?"

She laughed, like she used to when she thought I'd said something ridiculous, and launched herself into my arms again... well, as much as she could while still wearing a seatbelt. "Yes, Uncle Todd, I'm having twins."

I felt myself get emotional. *Uncle Todd.* That was so cool.

"When?"

"I'm four months along, and my due date is around February fourteenth."

"You're having Valentine's babies?"

"Well, sometime around then, yeah."

"Cool," I said, misty-eyed for a moment as the woman I considered my baby sister would soon have babies of her own, and was going to raise them up to consider me their uncle.

After a brief stop at my Nashville office to gather the paperwork Jacklyn had set aside for me, then at a restaurant outside Lebanon for a late breakfast, we continued on to Doc's place. I stayed with Doc and Dad, while Lisa took the truck to get her brother. I ducked into the living room and used the time trying to hash out bids again. Only the sound of truck doors slamming shut and Ash's voice carrying into the living room, were enough to force me out of work mode.

FOURTEEN

ASH

I WALKED OUT OF the clinic feeling happier than I had in a long time, only to find my baby sister pulling up in front of my house. She hopped out of Dad's pickup and right into my arms.

"You are a sight for sore eyes," I told her as I pulled back and looked at her small frame clad in designer clothing. "When's the last time you ate?"

She shook her head. "Really, that's how you greet me?"

"No, I told you that you were a sight for sore eyes, not that I'd be able to see you if you got any thinner. Oh, well, Dad'll remedy that soon enough."

"Shut up, you pest," she said, and pulled me back into a hug. She followed me into the house, helped herself to a soda out of my refrigerator, and plopped down on one of the counter stools in my kitchen.

"So, what's with Todd staying here with you?"

Although I knew an inquisition was likely coming, I tried to keep my expression neutral. "What about it?"

"Don't play coy with me. You said we'd talk about it this weekend, so talk. If Todd Thompson, who has hated you with a vengeance for years, is staying with you and hasn't murdered you in the night, there's plenty to tell."

I shook my head. "Well, you know most of it already. Dad and Amos came out to us, told us they were moving in together, and Todd freaked out. He started staying with me that night, and since I've been too busy to be home, at least while being awake for more than five minutes, we've been two ships passing in the night."

"And how do you feel about that?"

"Now you're pulling the therapist thing on me?"

"I am a therapist, but no, this is all for my own pleasure."

"I could have your license revoked."

"You could not. I'm not *your* therapist, you nincompoop. I'm your baby sister, and this is juicy gossip."

I laughed as I sat down with a sandwich that had somehow appeared in my refrigerator since the last time I'd looked.

"You hungry? Want part of this?"

She shook her head. "No, Dad and Amos took us out to eat at that huge restaurant off the interstate. Oh, my god, the chicken fried steak and homemade biscuits were so delicious. I swear the food in Oregon doesn't even begin to compare."

"Why don't you come home, so you can eat more like that all the time?"

"I'm guessing my politician husband wouldn't be too happy that his wife left for Tennessee, and I seriously doubt he'd be able to commute to work from here."

I chuckled. "I miss you, though. You should at least come home more often."

She nodded. "Well, and now that I'm about to become a mom, I will."

It was my turn to nod in agreement, and I continued chewing my sandwich until her words finally registered. My eyes grew large, and I jumped up and pulled my sister into another hug, swirling her around the kitchen. "You mean I'm gonna be an uncle?"

"You are, and I intend to raise babies who have distinct Southern accents, so we will definitely be here more often. In fact, I've already warned Frank that the kids and I will likely spend the summers here, and probably the holidays as well."

"I'm sure he's gonna be fine with that."

"He will, he adores me, and the twins will only make that worse."

"Dear God, did you just say twins?"

She giggled. "Yep, from what it looks like on the ultrasound, I'm having a boy and a girl."

"Frank must be impossible to live with."

"You have no idea. I swear that man follows me around just to wipe the sweat from my brow. A woman needs some space, especially when her hormones are all whacked out. That's why I'm glad Dad and Amos finally came out, so I had a good excuse to get away."

I hugged my sister again, and said, "You know Dad will be just as bad, and now you've got Amos on top of it. You were always his favorite."

"Amos's favorite?" she asked, and I nodded.

She sighed. "I love him. He's always been more like a parent, even more than Mom was, really."

The mood grew a little somber at the mention of our mom. I wondered how she would've reacted to becoming a grandma, and if and when she and Dad would've ever divorced. "Yeah, at some point, I'd like to know more about that. Was their sexuality the reason she was so... so withdrawn?"

Lisa shook her head. "No, I know some of that. Mom told me before she died."

I stared at her. This latest revelation almost more than I could digest, especially after just getting hit with the news that my sister was about to become a mother herself.

"Do you ever intend to share that with me?" I asked.

"She didn't want me to, didn't want you to know her history, but I'd already decided you needed to hear it. Eat your sandwich, and I'll tell you. It might help with all this stuff too."

I sighed, but bit into the sandwich anyway. I really was starving.

"You already know Mom had been abused as a kid. She'd been in and out of foster care. What you didn't know was that she'd been sexually assaulted as a child. Unfortunately, several times. Mom suffered from various mental illnesses, but the most debilitating was multiple personalities."

Lisa walked toward the living room and leaned up against the back of the sofa. "She never knew when they'd show up, so she hid herself away. Dad tried to get her help, but... well, I think that's sort of why I went into psychology. I wanted to understand more."

I shook my head, a bit stunned by this revelation. "Why did Dad marry her?"

"That's the part of the story I don't have, and the part I'm hoping he'll explain to us, now that the truth about him and Amos is coming to light."

"Do you really wanna know?" I asked, my mouth full of sandwich.

"Yeah, I do. I mean, she was our mom and I loved her, but she wasn't... lovable. Even when we were little, she was distant." She smiled, though I could see old pain behind it. "Even back then, Amos seemed more like a parent to us than she was."

"She was like an ever-lurking shadow," I admitted, remembering times as a little boy when I'd tried to get close to her. When I was young, I'd tried by knocking at her door just to be ignored. I'd even once snuck in and lain on her bed until she came back. She smiled, kissed me, and sent me on my way. The woman was such an enigma.

Lisa nodded and we both let the subject lie. It wasn't the first time we'd talked about our mother being so distant and unavailable, physically and emotionally, but like those other times, the subject always ended in helpless sadness, and more questions.

We sat in silence, both lost in our own memories of Mom, and the endless times she'd disappear into her room, and not reemerge for days. Lisa, I thought, struggled more than me. She had clearly wanted a relationship with Mom... needed it, probably.

I had always felt an emptiness where Mom was concerned, too, but having Dad and Amos as a steady presence had made it easier on me. It was like Mom had been more of a ghost in my life than a real person.

"Anyway—" Lisa said, disrupting my thoughts. "—now that you've inhaled that sandwich, Dad wanted me to bring you over there, so we could all sit and talk."

"So, no rest for the weary?"

She studied me a moment, then smiled sweetly. "No, brother, no rest for the weary... and speaking of that, why you do look like warmed-up poop?"

FIFTEEN

TODD

BEING AT DOC'S REMINDED me of the many days I'd hung out here growing up. I felt equally at home here as I did at Dad's place, *more* at home, really. I'd preferred it with Doc, Ash, and Lisa, and even their mom, although she didn't often make an appearance.

When Ash and Lisa arrived, they came into the living room and sat across from me. That, too, reminded me of our shared childhood. The difference was, I was usually playing some silly handheld game, or reading a book, rather than huddled over a laptop.

"Whatcha doin'?" Lisa asked.

"Trying to get caught up on work. When I fell off Dad's roof, it sorta put me behind."

"Yeah, Amos called and told me about that after it happened," she said. "It really scared me... no more falling off roofs."

I put my hands up. "That's kind of an occupational hazard, considering what I do for a livin'."

"I've never fallen off a roof," Dad said as he came in and sat next to Lisa on the sofa. "And Lisa did just about have a stroke when I told her." He acknowledged what I figured was true. Lisa was not one to react in subtle ways.

"Well, me neither till now," I said.

"At least it was the lean-to," Doc said when he came in with a tray of glasses filled with ice. I didn't notice until after Doc put the tray down that Dad had carried in a pitcher of iced tea. *Domestic*, I thought. *Had they always been like this, and I just never noticed?*

I put my laptop away, and reached for one of the glasses of tea when Doc sat next to Dad, slipping his arm around him. The two glanced at each other lovingly and parts of my heart began to quake a bit. They really did love each other. This was the first time they'd shown it around me, though.

"Since you're all here, let's get the heavy stuff out of the way, so we can just enjoy each other's company. What do y'all say?" Doc asked, smiling.

Dad and Ash looked at me, as if they were expecting me to jump up and leave again, like I did last time. Couldn't say I blamed them, seeing as I'd behaved like an inconsiderate ass, but still... *I didn't always overreact*, I thought... and caught myself pouting. Shaking it off before anyone noticed, I said, "Doc, go for it," and gave Ash a look, since we'd basically already had this discussion, and he knew I was good now.

Doc smiled and patted Dad's leg. "Amos and I are a couple, and after all this time, we've decided to *be* a couple and no longer keep it hidden. Hell, with things changing like they have, we'd even like to get married and make it official. So, that's the first part. Amos and I are engaged. We have the venue booked already for Fall Creek Falls State Park. As you know, we've always loved it there. We'd like all three of you to be part of our ceremony."

We all sat quietly listening to Doc. When he finished speaking, Lisa got up and kissed him on the cheek, before leaning over to kiss Dad as well. "It's the best news I've heard in a long time. Who's decorating the venue at the falls?"

"Well, we were hoping, you and your brother would help us with all that," Dad said to her.

When I looked at Ash, he was blushing. Not for all the money in the world would I make some smart-assed comment about him being a wedding expert, although I sure as hell was thinking it.

Dad looked shyly at me, which was a first. "We were hoping each of our sons would give us away."

I wasn't sure whether it was how vulnerable my normally impenetrable Dad was when he asked, or if it was because of the emotion of the moment, but the tears came unbidden.

I nodded. "Yeah. I'd be honored to give you away to Doc," I replied.

Both Dad and I wiped tears, and neither of us spoke, until Lisa said, "My god, you're like clones. Go hug each other for God's sake."

We both stood up and embraced each other. "I'm so happy for you," I said, and opened my arms to pull Doc into the hug. "I just wish y'all had done this sooner."

Doc was wiping tears, too, as he embraced us. Lisa and Ash joined our little huddle, and at that moment, we five, not counting the two grandbabies Lisa was carrying, officially became a family. We'd been family my entire life, but from this point forward, the world would know it too.

"Now, about them grandbabies," Dad said when we all sat back down. Lisa laughed as she cuddled up against him.

"Yeah, I can't wait until you two spoil them rotten."

Sixteen

Ash

Lisa kept herself busy helping Amos officially move into Doc's house. Now that they were engaged, and word was out, there was no reason to keep up the pretense that they weren't together.

Todd continued to stay in my guest room, which to everyone's surprise including mine, I was enjoying. Not that it made much difference, though, seeing as I was so far behind at the clinic I was rarely home during waking hours, even with Dr. McCartney and Rachel easing my workload.

Luckily, Rachel agreed to take Saturday by herself and was on-call Sunday, so I could have some downtime.

Dr. McCartney—or Dr. Gib, as he wanted to be called—was still spending most of his time running interference, since we had to wait until all the insurance companies transferred him from his previous place of employment to here. Even so, he was already a tremendous help just by listening to our frequent-fliers, given it cut our workload by a third.

Saturday morning, I crawled out of bed happy I didn't have to be at work. I danced into the living room celebrating my temporary freedom, momentarily forgetting I had a houseguest.

I was startled when I caught sight of Todd settled in my recliner, working on his computer.

"Hey, you're up early," I said when he looked up. He was smirking a little, so I guessed my busting a move hadn't gone completely unnoticed.

"Yeah, haven't been able to sleep. Too much goin' on in my head. What about you? I didn't expect to see you till noon."

I chuckled. "Well, I did fall asleep at seven last night, so I'm saying I slept late, considering."

Todd looked over his laptop at me, and smiled. "Oh, I made coffee." He gestured toward the kitchen. "Why are you still using that old contraption anyway?"

I laughed. "I usually just drink coffee at the office. Clara Sue always makes it there."

As I headed to the kitchen, Todd hollered, "Hey, why don't you warm me up while you're at it."

"If you're lucky," I said without thinking, then blushed when I turned around and saw his cocked eyebrow. "I'll just go get your coffee," I said.

I put the pot on the coffee table, on top of some magazines that'd been there forever. I should've taken them to the waiting room long ago, but I never seemed to remember. For now, they made good coasters.

I sat on the sofa and propped my feet up onto a clear space, drank my coffee and enjoyed not having to rush to see a patient.

"When did the dads want us over?" I asked, causing Todd to do the eyebrow thing at me again.

"'The dads'?" he asked.

"Well, it seemed the best way to describe them now that they're livin' together."

He chuckled low and deep, reminding me what that deep vibration felt like when he was kissing me years ago. His voice had mellowed even deeper since then, but it sent a shiver down my spine same as ever. *Shit, time to stop thinking about that.*

"They said anytime around noon," Todd said, and I was thankful he couldn't read my heated thoughts. "They're grilling hamburgers and dogs, so nothing fancy."

"Speaking of fancy, have you noticed they're now using silver and crystal, and all sorts of stuff they never used before?"

He nodded. "I have. Dad served lemonade to me on a silver platter that probably hadn't been cleaned since before I was born, and it was spit-shined like you'd see in one of those British movies where butlers would serve wealthy people everything on silver platters."

I laughed. "They're both really comin' into their own. It's fun to see."

"It's weird as shit, but good… I guess," Todd remarked, causing me to look over at him. He was smiling as he stared down at his computer.

"How's it goin' working with your dad?"

"Weird, and he's transformed into some nice guy who I even like being around. I swear it's like aliens abducted him and replaced him with a droid. At any moment, I expect some sorta bloody beast to burst out of him, and chase me down the road."

"You know, don't take this the wrong way, but that's the man I always knew. He was… different with me and Lisa. He was… kinder."

"I know, it always perplexed me, and I'd probably be really bitter about it, except that's how Doc was with me. We should've just switched parents. Our childhoods would've been better."

I smiled, since we'd discussed this many times in our youth. My dad was always more attentive to Todd, and Amos was always more attentive toward me. It felt weird even back then.

"Why do you think that was the way of it?" I asked, pondering.

"I'm guessing 'cause we represented a part of the other. Dad couldn't show his love for Doc, at least not openly, but he could show you, and the same with Doc and me. In a way, I think we got the attention they would've normally shown the other."

"Regardless," Todd said on a sigh, "I'm glad your dad was there for me. Mine definitely had an issue with me, and if it wasn't for Doc, I'd have been a basket case."

I just nodded. We'd entered a weird gray area of our new neutral ground. In the past, I'd have comforted him, maybe even held him. Now, I didn't quite know where things stood between us.

I finished my coffee, and was about to get in the shower when I heard Todd's phone ring. I grabbed it out of his bedroom, so he wouldn't have to hobble there to get it, and noticed his father's name displayed on the screen. To keep it from going to voicemail, I answered, "Hey, Amos, it's Ash. I'm bringing Todd the phone."

I heard him chuckle. "It's strange to hear you answer Todd's phone."

I didn't respond. Again, that was a loaded subject for me, which could also be said of nearly anything involving Todd, and one I'd rather just ignore. I handed the phone to Todd, and headed back to the bathroom for my shower.

"Hey, Ash," Todd yelled from the living room. "Dad wants to know if you can take me to his house early, he's wanting to talk about something."

"Yeah, no problem. I'm getting in the shower now."

I heard him tell his dad he wanted to grab a shower, and if I didn't drain the hot water, we'd be over in an hour or so.

"I don't drain the hot water," I said, loud enough for him to hear, but not giving him time enough to respond before I shut the bathroom door, smiling to myself. It really felt nice to be back to how things had been before, when teasing was our main mode of communication... at least, when we weren't kissing. I missed our playful banter, even if it only lasted for this moment, and even if it caused my heart to yearn for all the other things we used to share.

SEVENTEEN

TODD

ASH DROPPED ME OFF at my dad's house, and drove to Doc's, leaving me to deal with whatever Dad wanted to discuss. Frankly, I didn't see what the big deal was, given it was probably about the business. It wasn't like Doc seemed to mind us talking shop, since almost every day since Dad took on the foreman job, he and I discussed the company, or something related to it.

I hobbled in on my crutches, although putting weight on my foot didn't hurt as much as it had in the beginning. If I wasn't careful though, it would start throbbing. Ash still forced me to keep it in the damned boot all the time, and his rigid requirements were reinforced by his father.

I found Dad sitting at the little desk in the parlor, which he never did. When he looked up and saw me, he smiled. "Hey, son, come have a seat."

"Okay," I said, confused, but a bit intrigued as I took a seat.

"Do you know the history of this house, at least, since it's been in our family?" he asked.

I shook my head. "Sorta. Your parents lived here with their parents, that's about all I know."

Dad took a deep breath. "Yeah, that's my fault too. Your great-grandparents bought this place. I was just a little kid, so I don't remember much, but my dad told me things about it, stuff you should've been told long ago."

He reached into the desk drawer, pulled out a photo, and handed it to me.

"That's my grandparents and parents shortly after they moved in here. They were from the Bahamas."

I looked at our house in the old photo, and cringed. "It looks like it's about to fall down."

Dad laughed. "It was. Even *I* remember that part. My dad had worked in construction, and since they basically got the house for nothing, they invested what they had in restoring the place."

He sighed, and I could tell by how his expression changed that his memories were turning from fond to less pleasant ones... painful even. "Well, son, I didn't ever plan on staying. We had relatives in the Bahamas, so the minute I turned eighteen and found out Emanual was gonna marry Jane, I didn't hesitate. I packed and left. I had just enough money to get to Nassau."

Dad took the picture back and placed it in front of himself.

I turned toward him then, giving him my full attention. My dad had never told me much about his family, or my mother, just that she was from Cuba and had died right after I was born, but his somber tone told me that I was about to get a crash course in family history.

He used a key to unlock another drawer in the desk, the contents of which I'd never been privy to, then pulled out a picture of a white woman I'd never seen before, and handed it to me. "She's pretty," I said, suddenly becoming emotional. Although I didn't recognize the woman, I did recognize some of her features as my own. I was looking at a photograph of my mother.

"She was, and she was also wild as a buck," he said on a chuckle. "Her mom, your grandmother, had emigrated to the Bahamas from Cuba after Castro took over. They'd been wealthy there, huge landowners. Castro's people took it all and killed her father and grandfather. They barely escaped themselves."

Reluctantly, I handed the picture back. Dad stared at it for a long time. "She was my best friend while I was there."

"I'm confused, Dad. Are you gay, or bisexual, or...?"

He shrugged. "She was a great friend. I loved her, but not like Emanual. He was and is the love of my life."

"So, why have you never told me about her?"

"That, son, is a mixed bag of reasons. The most pertinent one was because she'd been wanted by several countries for... well, I don't actually know what all for. All I know is she was in deep trouble, and by the time you were born, she was planning to leave. She'd said she couldn't tell me where, but she never made it there anyway."

He took a deep breath that caught as he let it out.

"I found her, son... I'm the one who found her." The tears spilled over as he described the scene where he came upon her lifeless body, bleeding out after having been shot multiple times. "I think whoever killed her wanted me to find her, and that they'd eventually want to kill me too. At least, that's what her friends led me to believe. I was only nineteen, and you were only a few weeks old at the time. My aunt was too old to help, and I could barely afford to take care of myself. I didn't know what to do." Dad looked at me sadly, the pain of the memory etched on his face, before continuing, "I called home, and Mom wired money for me to get you a passport and fly us back here."

My mind was whirling with the knowledge that my mother hadn't simply died, she'd been murdered, and Dad had basically fled the Bahamas with me to keep us safe. He slipped my mother's picture back into the drawer and locked it, then put the key on top of the desk.

"Emanual's parents had moved up north when he and Jane got married. I hated him for marrying her, but he was a man of honor. He knew his parents wanted grandkids, and 'a faggot can't get pregnant'... that's what they'd told him." The hateful words reverberated around the room and he shook his head. "I was so bitter. Anger was the only emotion I understood for a long time. I was angry at Emanual, his parents, whoever killed your mother, and hell, I was even angry at her for dying and leavin' me to raise you alone. I wasn't alone though, not really. Emanual basically took over caring for you even then. I managed to get myself together enough to stop hating him, and thank God I accepted his help, because you were a pill to raise." He chuckled then, and wiped at his tears this time smiling. "Every stubborn trait that ever existed in me or your rebellious mom seemed to course through you. Emanual was the only person on Earth who could calm you when you went into a temper tantrum." He chuckled again, causing me to look over at him after such a serious conversation. "I guess, Emanual has that effect on both of us."

Dad's revelations didn't exactly erase the difficult childhood he'd put me through, softened as it may have been by Doc, Ash and Lisa, but it did cast my dad in a new light that he'd only begun revealing to me. Doc was right, Dad was a changed man from the one I knew as a kid, and I almost didn't know how to reconcile the two. He got up then, and went to the old secretary that sat behind the sofa-settee thing. He pulled down three photo albums and handed them to me.

"Emanual took them all. Every picture of your childhood came from him, not me..." Dad was still wiping at the silent tears that had continued to flow as he spoke. He went back to the desk again, pulled out an envelope, and handed it to me. "I've already signed it all over to you. The house and all the contents, most of which is original. My grandmother reupholstered most of the furniture in here. In fact, the backs on both chairs as well as the settee were handstitched by her."

Like I was seeing them for the first time, I really looked at the scenes stitched on the backs of the chairs, and was surprised. "Why are they all scenes of rich white people?" I asked, causing my dad to laugh.

"That's what she knew to do, I guess. It was a really different time."

"You've given me the house? Don't you just wanna sell it?"

He shook his head. "No, I won't sell it. The moment you were born, this house became yours. I didn't accept that until recently, but no, I couldn't... wouldn't sell it. It's your house."

"Dad...?"

"I know, son, it's a lot, but I'm ready to be free. I know I made your life hard, much harder than it should've been. Thank God for Emanual, 'cause he loved you like his own from the moment I put you in his arms. I don't care what you do with this house. Really, you can sell it, tear it down, burn it... I've let go, and now that I'm with my one true love, I want you to have what is rightfully yours."

Dad reached into his pocket, pulled out a ring of keys, and put them in my hand, then he picked the keys up that were on top of the antique desk, and put those in my hand as well. He pulled me into a hug then, and when he pulled back, he was smiling. "I love you, son, and as God is my witness—" he said, mocking *Gone With The Wind*, a favorite pastime of his. "—I will never miss dealing with this monstrosity again."

He literally jumped up in the air and clicked his heels together on his way out before getting into his truck. I couldn't help but chuckle at the sight of my dad appearing so carefree for the first time... um ever. He waved at me and drove toward Doc's house... their house.

Dad had lightened his burden with our talk, but I felt weighed down by my racing thoughts, a pile of keys, and an envelope containing the deed that I just didn't have in me to open yet. This had been too fucking much to process all at once, and I hadn't been prepared for it.

Feeling antsy, I wandered through the old home looking at it with fresh eyes. I was no longer seeing it as my dad's place, the place I wanted to escape from, but rather as something I owned, something with a legacy.

I walked down the long corridor, past the kitchen to the room I'd stayed in the night I'd broken my foot. It wasn't originally a bedroom, you could tell by the makeshift walls, but it'd long ago been converted to a bedroom, probably by my great-grandparents. I saw the four-poster bed from a different perspective. Now that I really looked at it, I could feel the age coming off the thing. *It must be original to the house.*

I hobbled up the stairs, which was a real bitch on crutches, and wandered through my old room. There was an outdated bathroom on this floor that occupied what was clearly the back part of the original hallway. There were also four bedrooms on this floor, all roughly the same size, except my old room, which was toward the front of the house and a bit smaller.

I lay back on my old bed, thinking about all that'd happened. I'd lain there for many years trying to process problems usually associated with Ashton Nash.

Just thinking his name seemed to conjure him and within moments he yelled up the stairs. "You up there, Todd?"

I chuckled. His hollering to track me down wasn't an uncommon sound in this house either.

"Yeah, I'm in my old room."

I heard him running up the stairs, and moments later he was sitting next to me on my bed. At one time, such a sight had been common as well.

"So..." he began.

I couldn't help but smirk at his awkwardness. "Did Doc tell you, or did Dad?"

"After I dropped you off here this morning, my dad told me what your dad had planned. When Amos came in and swept my father off his feet a little while ago, and planted a huge kiss on him before announcing to us all that he was free, I decided I had better come check on you."

I patted his leg, and said, "Thanks."

He looked at me and smiled. "Want me to show you what I think you should do with the place?"

"Really? You came here just to hash that old business up again?"

"Hey, I didn't say I was gonna be the mistress of the house like I used to. Just that I have some ideas that would bring this old lady into the twenty-first century."

I chuckled. "Go ahead," I said, conceding that he was going to, whether I wanted to hear it or not.

He giggled like I hadn't heard since we were kids, and began talking about how this room would stay the same, but I should build the staircase up to the attic, and convert that space into the master suite. He'd talked incessantly about that same scheme after my dad had sent me and Ash up there once to fetch something he'd needed for work, and Ash had immediately fallen in love with the space.

As I followed him downstairs now, thankful he couldn't see my graceless hops down the steps, I had to force myself not to go glossy-eyed over the hundred and one things he wanted to do, including a new idea of turning it into an open concept layout. As a teenager, he'd wanted to turn it into a museum and charge admission.

The back half of the house was to remain the intimate family space, though. He hadn't changed that vision. Instead, he'd added some concepts like a big fireplace, and huge doors that opened onto porches. He was convinced the original home had a big porch wrapped around the outdoor kitchen, where the cooks would work when the kitchen got too hot.

The problem was, as he talked, especially about this part of the house, I could envision it. I could imagine the comfortable country room with a cathedral ceiling. This part of the house was only one level, so adding a fancy ceiling made sense.

As Ash's enthusiasm washed over me, I became uncomfortably aware that I could much-too-easily see myself sharing this space with him. If I was being honest with myself, I'd always seen myself living here with him one day. That was cause enough for my stomach muscles to twist into knots, like they always did when I thought about loving Ashton Nash. *Loving Ash.* I'd *always* loved Ash, and had always wanted to be here, with him. The thought left me feeling euphoric. The difference this time, however, I was finally ready to admit it, even if only to myself.

Eighteen

Ash

"**I** DID IT AGAIN. Fuck, if I didn't just do it again."

Lisa sat across from me, drinking her hot cocoa and burying her face in the mug, so as not to laugh at me. Although it was clear she was.

"What is it about Todd's house that makes me so crazy? You've always loved that old place. Even when you were little, you'd go over and start rearranging the furniture."

"Yeah, but we've just started talking again, and I go over and start redesigning the house, like we're gonna become lovers and live there forever."

"Did you tell him that?" she asked with what sounded like a mixture of curiosity and hope.

I gave her my most appalled look, and shook my head. "Of course, I didn't tell him that. Do you see streak lines across the lawn? If I even pretended like I was still interested in him, he'd be gone so fast, it'd take years to find him."

Lisa put her mug on a coaster and came over, slipping into the tiny space next to me in Dad's big recliner.

"I'm gonna give you a little insight. He isn't as against you showing interest as you may think. The fact is, that man still loves you, almost as much as you still love him."

I pushed her off me and got up to stretch.

"You're insane. He hates me." Despite that, my heart still skipped a beat at the thought.

"And there is a very fine line between love and hate, brother. A very fine line."

I shook my head. There was no need to get into it with her, she thought everything could be solved with love and improved communication—whatever that meant.

She followed me into the kitchen and sat down next to me. Dad and Amos were happily putting supper together. The two worked around each other in a well-choreographed dance. I wasn't sure why it had taken so long for me to see they were lovers... *are lovers.*

Occasionally, one of them would put an affectionate hand on the other's shoulder, or rub a hand across the other's arm as they passed. I was sure if we hadn't been here, there would've been sweet kisses to go with it.

"How long have you two been like this?" I asked, curious as to why I'd missed it for so long.

Dad smiled at me, understanding what I was asking. "Off and on for years."

"But not together, like we are now," Amos added. "When Lisa went to college, Emanual gave me an ulti-matum—commit or he was done." He sighed. "I'd been so angry with the world. Of course, I wrongly placed that anger onto your dad, and pretended like it was somehow his fault we'd ended up in these circumstances. So, after things changed when you all moved out, his ultimatum forced me to figure out what I wanted. I was tired of being mad at him, and tired of being alone."

"It took you ten years to tell us about you, though?" I asked.

They both stopped preparing the meal and looked at us. "You have to understand how different things were when we were kids. Gay people were reviled. We were both working in businesses that would've been destroyed if we'd come out even ten years ago."

I nodded. "But, you could've told us." Lisa hit me, forcing me to look at her and ask, "What?"

"How do you think you'd have handled learning Dad and Amos were a thing ten years ago? Hell, you'd have reacted worse than Todd did," she said.

"'Worse than Todd did' what?" Todd asked, coming into the room behind us.

Lisa blushed, which she deserved. "Ash just asked our dads why they didn't come out years ago."

"And you were saying it would've been worse than when they told me this time?" Lisa shrugged, embar-rassed. "I did take it bad, but for reasons other than them being together." He gave his father a pointed look, and Amos nodded and looked down.

"Lisa's right," Dad quickly said, putting the loaded Todd and Amos conversation aside. "We were afraid of what your reactions would be."

"Were you always lovers?" I asked, then waited. I both dreaded their answer, and needed to know at the same time.

"No, we were lovers when we were young, in high school, although that was very secretive," Amos replied.

Dad nodded. "Back then, we didn't really think there was any hope that we'd actually get to be a couple, so we both dated women."

Amos looked at Dad sadly. "When your mom got pregnant with you, Ash, the reality that Emanual and I weren't ever gonna be together sank in. That's when I left town."

Dad's response mimicked Amos's. "Things were strange when Amos came back with Todd in tow. Shortly after he got home, both his parents died, and he couldn't take care of Todd on his own, so naturally, I began to pitch in. I knew your mother had figured out I was in love with Amos, but she didn't say anything, at least not then. Your mom and I had stopped being intimate long before that." He sighed sadly and shook his head. "Your mom's psychological issues were difficult for her to overcome. We were still young adults. Occasionally when she felt safe, she'd come to me. I let her be in charge of our love life."

I cringed. "Well, that was more information than I needed."

Lisa elbowed me again, this time harder. "Were you intimate with each other while married to Mom?" she asked.

At her question, I glanced in Todd's direction, expecting him to look uncomfortable, since he was learning way more about Dad than he probably ever wanted to know, but to my surprise he appeared just as curious as we were.

"Mostly no. Amos had his hands full with Todd, and I had my hands full with medical school and raising you two. When Jane got sick, she sat both Amos and me down and told us it was time to stop acting like we weren't who we were. I was so alone and lonely while she was passing. She was our friend. We'd not been lovers for many years before she got sick, but we'd been friends. So, during her last few months, Amos comforted me... even though he still sort of hated me too."

Amos nodded. "That's true. I loved and hated him for marrying your mom, but she really was an amazing and special person."

"I barely knew her," I said, and slumped a bit in the chair, the weight of the realization feeling especially heavy in that moment.

"She did the best she could. In fact, she did better than most in her situation. Lisa already told me she told you about her psychological problems. She'd grown up with mental illness as well as the abuse, and she didn't want you two to be affected by it, so she withdrew."

"I would've liked to have known," I said regretfully, and could feel all the years of sadness and loss flow through me.

Dad nodded. "Now you do."

We all sat around processing the information we'd just shared with each other. The room was silent, until Amos moved over to the stove, and Dad joined him as they began to stir the boiling pots.

"You need any help?" Lisa asked.

Dad shook his head and forced a smile. "No, it'll be done in about half an hour. Todd, if you walked here on that foot of yours, you probably need to elevate it, otherwise, it's going to give you fits tonight."

Todd nodded and headed back to the living room.

Lisa and I stayed where we were. There remained a big question I hadn't known how to bring up, but it seemed like the right time to ask, though Lisa beat me to it.

"Did you love her, Dad?" she asked.

He nodded. "Yes. I did love her. Not like I love Amos, but like you love a dear friend."

I mulled over his answer a moment, before asking, "If you had it to do over, would you marry her again?"

Dad shook his head. "Listen, son, you're asking an impossible question. I wouldn't redo the past if it meant I wouldn't get to be your parent, or if it meant we didn't have Todd, but I loved Amos so much, and for years we had to pretend not to feel how we did. If I didn't know what it felt like to be your dad, would we have married one another? Probably. Now, here's the amazing thing. You live in a time where that will never be something you have to choose. You can love the people you love and not be ostracized because of it. You don't have to hide, or choose one life over the other."

Amos came up behind Dad and slipped under his arm, hugging him. Amos was only a couple inches shorter than Dad, but he seemed to fit so perfectly into his side, like they'd always been meant to slot together like that.

"Son," Amos said. "There's no answer to those questions, because we were forced to make decisions you'll never be forced to make. The answer that might help you, though, is we love you... all of you. And, yes, we loved your mom and your mom loved us. We all did the best with the circumstances we were given. Now, because the world has changed for the better, your father and I are together, and can spend the rest of our lives together. We can only hope that you and Lisa and Todd can maybe learn a few things from our experiences."

We all understood that he meant Todd and me, and I wished Todd hadn't already left the room, so he'd have heard the words, but that didn't mean things would change or be different. In the end, we'd screwed up so badly that finding the way back to each other, to where Dad and Amos were now, seemed impossible.

Nineteen

Todd

I'D HEARD EVERYTHING DAD and Doc had said, and maybe, because I wasn't in front of them as they explained, the message landed harder. Doc had basically told me I needed to stop letting the past dictate my feelings, but now I understood why that'd been so important to him. Dad had basically kept them apart because of his anger. Funny, I'd done the same thing with Ash.

I had already begun to forgive Ash, and was enjoying our snippets of life together while staying with him. Even though I barely saw him, it felt good, and it felt right when I did.

That night at supper, I was so engrossed in my thoughts, I barely paid attention to the conversation. So much had happened since I'd come back to Crawford City to fix Dad's roof. We'd begun making amends, and only now was I understanding him as the angry kid stuck in a place he didn't want to be in. Not to mention living next to a former lover he'd thought had jilted him. Yeah, I could relate to Dad on so many levels.

Ash was saying something about his clinic that had the rest of the table laughing. I smiled, not because of what he said, but because seeing the humor and happiness on his face always made me happy too.

I'd barely eaten, so I was surprised when Lisa went to take my plate. "Wait, sorry, my mind was elsewhere. I'll take my plate in when I'm done."

"Nothing different there," she said, and I gave her a withering look.

"It's true," Doc said as he helped clear the table. "You were always stuck in your head about one issue or another."

Ash didn't return my glance. I used to share those thoughts with him.

They brought a huge bowl of homemade banana pudding over and placed it in the middle of the table. Dad got the china bowls out and passed them around, chuckling when he said, "Banana pudding just tastes better in fancy china."

I shook my head, but resisted the urge to ask again where my father had disappeared to.

Lisa brought in the coffee and poured a cup for herself. I shook my head when she offered me some, saying, "You've been in Starbucksville so long you can drink caffeine this late at night?"

"I live in Portland, not Seattle, but yeah, they do love their coffee up there."

"I can make decaf if you like," Doc said, but I waved him off.

"No, I prefer milk with my pudding. Thanks, though."

Doc smiled. "It makes me all kinds of happy to have us all together around the same table again. I've missed this."

We all nodded. I guessed I'd missed it too. It wasn't something we'd done, since Ash and I broke up all those years ago. I'd refused to be in the same room with him, until now.

We all went to the living room after we'd cleaned up the dishes and stacked the old dishwasher. Doc had said I needed to elevate the foot again if I wanted to resist the swelling, so I sprawled out on the sofa.

Somehow, there was an unspoken rule that the two recliners—the one that had always been in this room and the one brought over from Dad's—were theirs. The two recliners were close enough that when they sat in them, they could join hands.

Lisa sat in the lady's chair, as we'd all called the dainty seat her mom had inherited from her parents.

When Ash came in, I pulled my foot back, so he'd have room on the other end of the sofa. He sat down and immediately pulled my foot onto his lap. "You should keep it elevated. Dad was correct."

It shouldn't have bothered me, but the act was so intimate, so reminiscent of how we'd been... before. I had to fight the urge to pull it away. Luckily, the conversation took my mind off it as Doc and Dad reminisced about our childhoods.

We continued rehashing old memories for a long time. Finally, I noticed Ash was crashing. Knowing how intense his work life had been the past week, I made the excuse that I was getting tired.

As we drove back to his place, I smiled at him. "You know, I forgive you for being a stupid kid."

He swerved the truck a bit and glanced toward me, as if I'd just said the world was coming to an end. "How'd I get so lucky?" he asked sarcastically.

"'Cause, everyone is stupid when they're a kid. I also want more nights like tonight, when we can all be together as a family. I didn't realize till now how much I needed that."

He sighed. "I'm not sure what to say. I've wanted to fix what happened between us for a long time, but..."

"But, I wouldn't let you?" I asked, and he blushed.

"More like I didn't know how, but yeah... you didn't really want me to either."

We rode in silence to his home, and when we got there, I excused myself and went to brush my teeth and get ready for bed.

Ash was sitting in his recliner when I came back out to the living room. When he saw me, he stood up, came over, and pulled me into a hug.

"I've missed you so much," he said over my shoulder. He pulled away without looking at me, then went into the bathroom to get ready for bed himself.

Ash and I danced around each other the following week. I could tell he wasn't sure how to navigate the new cease-fire between us, and I wasn't sure how to either, so with his busy schedule and me having to navigate all the changes in my life, it was just easier to go with the flow.

I met with Tom Baskin, the old rickety architect who'd lived in Crawford most of his life, to go over the renovations to my inheritance. I'd come to the conclusion that I'd be much better off making Crawford City my home base, mostly because I could sell my Nashville property, and use that money to completely pay back my buddy Jake for the money he'd loaned me to buy my company, not to mention I'd have enough left over to refurbish the house. I also quite unexpectedly wanted to be back in Crawford... back home.

"I wanna rip the lean-to off completely," I told Tom. "Then, I wanna add offices." The lean-to had been added sometime after the Civil War, and held a bunch of crap that didn't do anything, except breed snakes and who knew what else.

I drew a simple picture of how I'd like the addition to look. "I also want the parlor to open up into offices, so they can be used by the house's occupants, but it can also be a place for us to meet potential clients."

I took him through the house, and asked him to combine the parlor and the extra living room. He told me it was a library, and in the olden days, it would've been where the men would retire to smoke and get away from the women.

"Regardless, I want it to be one large room, maximizing the formal gathering space. I also want the fireplace to work. I'm guessing it's in rough shape, and since it runs through the center of the house, I'd prefer to fix it properly before we move in. I want it to be natural gas, though, since I have a natural gas well here on the property. Same thing with the fireplace above this one. That's going to be a guest room, and I want the gas fireplace to work there as well."

Ash's dreams for the home were second nature to me. I continually smiled as I showed Tom how I wanted the kitchen to be built into the addition with the cathedral ceilings, and how I wanted to combine the old kitchen and dining room to become a large dining option. "My family seems to be growing, and I want us to all have a place to gather comfortably."

When I showed him the back area, he smiled. "Your idea of turning this space into a large family room is perfect. I won't know how possible it is until I get into the walls..."

I shook my head. "No, trust me, it's a mess. It'll cost three times as much to try to retrofit this into what I want. Instead, it's gonna be a teardown, but we can preserve the old wood beams and use as much of the reclaimed materials as possible. We're just gonna preserve the original structure, the rest will be new construction."

He nodded his approval. He'd done his share of old home renovations, and he knew as well as I did the headaches that went with that kind of addition.

We walked up the stairs and I showed him the simple renovation there, mostly insulating walls and replacing windows, so the air would stop blowing through during the winter. We were going to preserve all the windows on the first floor, but we definitely needed energy-efficient windows in the sleeping areas.

I showed him a video I'd made earlier of the attic. "It's a magnificent space. I want cathedral ceilings here too, but leave it open. The only thing you'll be adding is the en suite, and walk-in closets," I told him.

When he left, he told me he could have the basics drawn up for me by the end of the following week. *That's pretty good*, I thought. This was a massive project, and a big section of it would be new construction. Making that fit with the historic home would be difficult at best, although the home's current condition did give a clue what it'd eventually look like.

I then met with Grady and Lewellen, a local thirty-something couple my dad had recommended to draw up plans for the gardens. Dad and Doc were going in with me on the landscape work between our two properties, since they were so close together.

I wasn't sure yet how I was going to break all this to Ash, since I knew how attached he was to the property, so I talked the dads—yes, I'd started calling them that too—into letting it be our secret, until I got the blueprints back.

Ultimately, I'd mostly gone with Ash's ideas with a few basic changes, like the new construction, which couldn't be helped. Still, for the most part, I'd heard so often what he wanted the place to look like, it was all but burned into my mind. It'd be hard to see it any other way than he did at this point anyway.

Jake called me the following night. "Hey, buddy, where'd you disappear to?" he asked.

"Yeah, sorry, things have been interesting."

"How so?" he asked.

Jake was in every way a space cadet, but our friendship was real, and I felt guilty about not communicating more about how things were progressing for me.

"Well, I fell off a roof."

"What? Did you break anything?"

"Just a little fracture in my foot. I ended up getting stranded here in Crawford City."

"Wow," was all he said.

"Jake, I'm thinking about moving here permanently."

"Really? I thought you hated that place."

"Yeah, so did I, but I might have misjudged it. Besides, there's a lot of business in these parts as people move away from Nashville and into quieter, more rural areas."

"Yeah, I've got a couple more people wanting to talk to you about building out that way."

"They'll have to wait, I'm afraid. I'm having to reject a couple of potential clients because there's no way I can fit into their timeframes as it is."

"You need to expand..."

"Yeah, this isn't like your fancy PR firm. I can't just add new workers without someone I trust to supervise them."

"Oh well, at least you have plenty of business."

"Thanks to you. Hey, why don't you come down to Crawford and spend some time here? I just inherited my dad's house, and I'm gonna do a full-blown reno on it. You might enjoy seeing the before and after."

"Sure, I can take before and after pictures and put it on your website too."

I chuckled. When I'd borrowed money from Jake to buy Berkshire Brothers Construction, he'd become obsessed with my company's public image. "You need to show what you're selling," he'd told me repeatedly.

"You can knock yourself out," I said, and we made plans for him to come for the weekend.

"Oh, if you still have people interested in my property in Nashville, let me know. I'm going to sell up there and move my operations here. It'll be a heck of a lot cheaper to store stuff, and get me out of the middle of the city too."

"Really? My friend, Christian, will be over the moon. You know he's been spoiling for that property for years."

My construction company owned over five acres in total, including the tiny house I'd renovated when I'd bought the business. There was a great deal of potential for development in that area, even if it did mean tearing down a whole bunch of buildings that currently housed storage and offices.

"Hey, make sure you talk him into offering what I owe you. I wanna be out of debt."

He hesitated for a minute. "You're wanting to get rid of me?"

"No, buddy, I just don't wanna have debt. Right now, we're doing good, and you know construction has good times and bad times. While things are good, I wanna make sure I'm square with you before it changes."

He sighed, but agreed. If I knew Jake, and I really did know Jake, he'd get me top dollar, and the buyer would still smile all the way to the bank.

I thought again about the tiny house that had been just a shack when I'd gutted it and turned it into my home. I hated to give it up, because, frankly, there'd probably be times when I'd want to go back to Nashville, and the little house allowed me access to Centennial Park, the university campus, and a variety of other areas, all within walking distance. I quickly texted Jake.

Make sure Christian knows I'm going to keep my house and a little swathe of land it sits on.

If I were lucky, I'd get Jake paid off and still have enough money to do the renovation here, as well as purchase anything else I'd need for the company to relocate.

After texting Jake, I decided I should go spill the beans to my father and Doc. They'd be the most likely to be able to help me find what I needed to replace the storage space I was selling.

I met Dad and Doc in the kitchen, where they were putting lunch together. I sat at the counter, and when they both looked at me, I launched into my news.

"So, and I don't wanna see you gloat, Dad, I've decided to sell up in Nashville, but now I need to find storage space here."

Dad smiled, and before I knew it, grabbed me into a hug. Although it was still disconcerting that he was so affectionate, after years of getting the cold shoulder, I was beginning to get used to it.

"Come, and I'll show you where I think you should go," he said, and all but dragged me out of the house and into his truck. "When I began shutting down Thompson's Construction, it forced the local lumber yard out of business. They were just barely hanging on as it was, and old Mr. Oliver was ready to retire anyway. I felt bad, so bought the place from him."

He pulled into the parking lot of the old lumber yard that I'd spent so many years coming to for Dad's business.

"You own this?" I asked.

He shrugged. "Yeah, I was considering opening the business back up, since it's so far to get to another hardware store, but then I was enjoying spending time with Emanual..."

I chuckled. "In other words, you bit off more than you could chew."

For a second, he gave me one of his squinted-eyes looks I was accustomed to seeing. That expression usually led to me being firmly put in my place, but this time it quickly morphed into a smile. "Not more than I *could* chew, more than I *wanted* to chew."

"Dad, this really couldn't be more perfect. It's got all the storage we need, plus it appears to still be in good shape. Do you think we could get the hardware store part back up and running? I'd like to have an ongoing supply of odds and ends without having to run back and forth to a different town."

"Well, if you're gonna be your own best customer, I'm guessing you could keep the place running."

"I'm not sure I wanna run a hardware store, though." He smiled at me and winked. "No, you aren't gonna tell me you have someone in mind?"

He just laughed. "You know, Mr. Oliver has a great-nephew who helped him during the summers. He recently got a divorce, and he was thinking about moving back to Crawford City with his kids. He approached me a few months back about reopening the store."

"I'm not sure how to take all this, it's almost like you planned it all."

That earned me another wink, then he laughed, before admitting, "No, I wish I could take credit for it all, but to be honest, it's just luck."

"So, how much do you want for all this?" I asked, gesturing around the property.

He hesitated, before answering, "Well, son, I don't really wanna sell, but I've got a proposition for you."

Shit, here it comes, I thought to myself.

"Like I already said, I miss the business. I miss working with the men, and seeing the properties change and improve. Emanual and I both wanna be able to travel and spend time at home, just us when we want, and now that Lisa's gonna have babies, we'll wanna go to Oregon and spend time there, but I still want my hands in the middle of things. So, I want you to consider a partnership. I also want you to change the name of your company from Berkshire Brothers to Thompson's. Maybe you could even change it to Berkshire and Thompson's, if you wanna keep the name, but, son, we've got a good reputation here, one that goes back to your great-granddaddy."

He looked so hopeful and vulnerable. I just wasn't used to seeing my dad like this. He was one to demand things, not ask or hope I'd see it his way.

After we finished meandering through the old store building, I sat down on a folding chair I'd found, while Dad leaned up against the counter. "I've already been thinking about the name. You're right, Thompson's has a great reputation here in Crawford City and the surrounding area, but Berkshire has that same level of respect in Nashville. If I combine the names, it'll go a long way to giving the business that much more credibility."

Dad nodded, and I could see the hope on his face. "Dad, I wanna say yes about the partnership." I got up and stared out the window. "The truth is, I've got my hands full, and I don't have enough people I can rely on to help me keep my projects on task. In fact, with all the business that's being thrown at me, I need you more than ever."

I turned toward him then, wanting to see his expression, as I said this next part, "Dad, I'm having a hard time believing you won't slip back into being *Dictator Dad*. I can't be in business with him. Hell, I could barely stand bein' around him. I know what you went through, and I get it, I really do, but throughout my entire life, I thought you hated me, and before you say anything, I think you sorta did."

He plopped onto the chair I'd vacated a moment before, looking a bit resigned. "I know, I told Emanual it was too early for all this. I need to prove myself to you. I never jumped into relationships with people until they did, and I've trained you the same way. I know I don't have a right to ask you to trust me, I've been a hell of a shit to deal with, but I *have* changed. It's something deep inside me, and it's got everything to do with being with Emanual, not pretending we aren't who we are anymore, and embracing our lives together. I never did hate you, but I resented you in a wholly misplaced way, however, I've always loved you. If you want the truth of it, I loved you so much it scared me. You were so much like me. Stubborn, willful... then when you and Ash broke up, you were angry. That anger was like looking into a mirror. I was so afraid you'd eventually leave me that I pushed you away. If it wasn't for Emanual, I'd have lost everything, because I was too damned angry and blockheaded to see it."

He got up and walked over to where I was standing. "I won't force you to sign anything, son. I'll give you a lease on this place, and I'll make it reasonable, so you can afford to make it work, but I do wanna be a part of it.

I don't *have* to own part of your business, but I *do* wanna be part of it. Will that work?"

I nodded, which was about all I could do in that moment, what with a frog lodged in my throat. I'd never heard such honesty coming out of my dad, and I didn't quite know what to do with it, other than agree. Just the fact that he'd be willing to give in, and not force his own agenda, spoke volumes.

When I got home, I called my attorney, Ed, and asked him to draw up papers to create a partnership between my dad and me. I still wanted to retain the majority ownership in case he did turn back into his old self, but he was bringing to the table so much more than I'd ever hoped for, and deserved to get something in return. Besides, he *was* my dad, and Doc was too. If Dad's expertise and other assets lifted us to where I figured we were going to end up, I wanted them both to benefit from it.

ASH

With Dr. Gib and Rachel both taking patients, my workload finally began to level out. Unfortunately, as I began getting home earlier and earlier, Todd showed up later and later. I'd hoped that we'd see progress toward resurrecting our relationship, especially now that he'd said he'd forgiven me. Unfortunately, life kept getting in the way.

"I think the universe is working against me," I admitted to Lisa, during an extended lunch break I'd taken to spend with her.

"No, you're just both grown men with responsibilities and careers. It's what we've all got to deal with. If you want him, you're gonna have to go through the process. Invite him out on a date. Schedule time to spend with him." She looked at me when I cringed, then chuckled,

"Sweetheart, you aren't a couple of kids any longer. It's gonna require some effort on your part."

"I don't know. What if I ask him out and he freaks?"

"Then you back off and give him space."

"Maybe," I said, even the thought of asking him out causing nerves to bounce around inside. Luckily, Lisa quickly changed the subject to the twins.

"So, before I go home, I want you to help me surprise Dad and Amos. I wanna convert my old bedroom into a room for the twins, so when I come home, and I intend to come home often, there'll be a place for us to stay. That way they'll know I'm not gonna keep their grandbabies away from them."

I smiled. "That's a great idea. So, you're totally thinking of Amos as one of the grandparents?"

"Of course, I would've even if they weren't a couple. He's been another parent to me my entire life."

The grin on my face grew bigger. "Yeah, he has. I guess it's different for me, though, 'cause I love Todd so much. He's my dad, but also the dad of my... well, whatever Todd is to me."

She smiled at me knowingly, and only then did I realize I'd said I loved Todd, and not in the past tense. "Right now, he's your friend. Start there."

I nodded. "Yeah, that's right, we're great friends, actually."

Something about that acknowledgment shifted the angst inside me, made it seem less stressful. I still had a friend in Todd, and I knew we'd become even better friends with time. The love stuff just made that stronger.

"Okay, when do we start putting that nursery together?"

Lisa squealed. "I'm so happy you're helping. I haven't asked Todd yet, but I want his help as well. This is gonna be so epic! Oh, I forgot, Frank is gonna fly in for the big reveal. He wants y'all to see he's supportive of the family's involvement too."

"You mean, he understands the consequences of getting between you and us."

"He does, and that's why I love him."

I leaned across the table and kissed my baby sister on the forehead. "You've done good, sis. Really good!"

"I have, haven't I?" she asked, before wiping at a tear. "Damn hormones," she said.

"Please, you've been a sap your entire life." I laughed out loud when she reverted to her childhood self, and stuck her tongue out at me.

"I'll take Friday off if you wanna head into the city to shop. You'll have to see whether Todd's free or not, and let me know."

"You can get away from the clinic?"

"Sure, I'm supposed to have a day a week just for paperwork. That hasn't happened since Dad retired, but Fridays were supposed to be my day, so I don't have any appointments."

"Cool, I'll go ask Todd now."

It'd be fun to be out and about again after all this time. I really was looking forward to it.

I was back to work when she texted me, but I managed to see the message between appointments. Todd was free, but only until five. He had plans Friday night. I wondered briefly if that was code for him having a date, but brushed the thought aside. I had no claim on Todd, not yet anyway. The more I kept reminding myself of that, the better.

The week, like all other weeks before, sped by. By Friday, I was more than excited to get away from the clinic and Crawford City. It'd been months since I'd had a day to just go to Nashville and hang out.

Luckily, Todd's fracture had improved enough that he could handle all the shopping, which was good, because Lisa was nothing if not a shopper.

By the time we were done with store number three, though, I was more than a little done with all the shopping. "Lunchtime," I announced after we walked out of the mall. "Let's do tacos!"

Todd took us to his favorite taco truck, which was parked close to his neighborhood, and the three of us had a picnic in a nearby park. Lisa picked on us both equally, and more than ever, it really did feel like we were a little family.

Lisa managed to pull us into two more stores, before Todd put his hand up, and said, "No more. I have to be back by five to meet a friend, and I can see if someone doesn't put the skids on, this could go on all day."

Lisa pouted, but I knew behind it all was good humor.

As we drove back to Crawford City, we discussed the different nursery furniture we'd looked at, and when we all agreed with Lisa's choice, she called the store and arranged to have it delivered to Todd's place.

Todd's place. How strange it felt to call his childhood home that. It'd always been Amos's place. Now Todd was the owner, and he'd decided to stay. I'd caught that much from snippets of the conversation. The revelation thrilled and concerned me at the same time.

What should I do? Tell him I miss him, make a move, or just accept our friendship for what it is?

Before we got home, I'd decided to let the friendship settle before I tried anything else. Lisa was right, I needed to build our friendship back up first, no matter how much I already wanted more.

Road construction put us about thirty minutes behind, and Todd ended up calling the friend he'd intended on meeting at five o'clock to say he'd be late, and that he should just go on into the house.

So, Todd's friend would be staying with him? That could only mean he wasn't going to be staying with me any longer. The thought left me feeling unsettled, and began to move through me like wildfire. *Todd was moving back to his house?* I'd admit I also felt a little upset by it. Why hadn't he at least let me know? Unless there was a reason he hadn't told me.

When we reached Crawford, Lisa drove directly to Todd's house and let him out. Within moments, an incredibly handsome man rushed out and scooped Todd into a giant bear hug. Todd barely remembered to wave at us as he was pulled inside. My heart beat fast and my brain started overthinking things. *Todd had said the man was a friend. Just like we are friends. Except, Todd never hugged me like that, at least, not since...*

Lisa had borrowed Dad's truck for the trip, and after what I'd just seen, I needed air.

"I think I'm going to walk home," I said, and she shook her head.

"You have no idea if that's what it looked like."

"I have no rights to him either way," I said, trying to downplay the intensity of so many emotions—jealousy, anger, frustration, desperation—swirling inside me all at once.

"Doesn't mean it doesn't hurt."

Damn my little sister's perceptiveness. I sighed. "Yeah, okay, tell Dad and Amos I'm going back home. I'll be back tomorrow to help you put the nursery together. They said delivery would be here before noon, right?"

She nodded, but didn't try to hide her sadness.

Twenty-One

Todd

DAMN, IT FELT GOOD to see Jake. Even before I'd come here to put Dad's roof on, it'd been weeks since we'd hung out together. He'd had a couple new stars that'd hired him to do their PR stuff, and one had dragged him all the way out to Nevada on tour. I'd missed the nutty man.

He wanted a complete tour of the home, filming each section while providing commentary, and asking me how we were planning to change it up. I'd swear I felt like the host of some reality renovation show for a moment.

After the tour was over, I took Jake to meet Dad and Doc, and, of course, he charmed the pants off them. The man could charm the devil himself, given half a chance.

I got a call from Tom, the architect, right before we were about to leave their house. Tom told me he had the preliminary sketches done on the property. "Why don't you come over and pick them up, and then you can add what you like before we make the final decision."

Cool. I had already planned to surprise Ash with the designs, and I was getting excited as I considered what his reaction would be when I showed them to him tonight. Jake had already told me he'd have to head home tonight to meet a client, who'd at the last minute scheduled a meeting with him for tomorrow morning, so Ash and I would have the house to ourselves. There was intimacy to that, especially knowing how much Ash cared about the old homestead.

"You hungry?" I asked, and Jake, the bottomless pit he was, nodded. "Okay, we'll stop by and pick up the blueprints and then we can run over to the Crawford City Café for supper, before you have to rush home."

"Perfect," he said happily, which wasn't surprising, since Jake was almost always happy.

I drove him by the old lumber yard, and explained what my dad wanted to do there and that I was going into business with him. Jake almost had to pick his chin off the ground at my news.

"Um, I thought your dad was... less than supportive."

"I did too, but since he and Doc have decided to get hitched, everything seems to have changed."

"You don't think you're jumping the gun here?"

I shrugged. "I think if there's a chance he is different, I'd be a fool not to use his resources. That includes this property. Not to mention, it feels good having a dad I can just hang out with for a change."

He smiled and gave me a had pat on the shoulder. "I'm happy for you."

"Me too," I said happily.

We got the blueprints from Tom and headed to the restaurant. Jake was starving, of course, so we ate first. Friday night was catfish night at the café, and I'd swear Jake ate his weight in fish and hushpuppies, before we put our plates aside, and opened up the prints.

Jake was just saying how beautiful the addition would be when my skin prickled at sensing a familiar presence behind me. I turned around and saw Ash staring over my shoulder at the plans.

"Dang, this was supposed to be a surprise," I told him.

He blushed and swallowed hard, before he asked if it was the plans for the house.

I nodded, happy to show him I'd incorporated a lot of what he'd said we should do.

He looked at Jake, then back at me. "I'm really happy for you."

Then, he left without another word. He simply walked out, not even picking up a to-go meal.

"What was that about?" Jake asked.

"I'm not sure. I thought he'd be happy to see the plans."

Jack laughed. "I'm guessing he wasn't happy seeing you show the plans *to me*."

"Don't be ridiculous. We're just friends."

"Does he know that?"

I stared at Jake for a moment, then down at the plans. "Hold on, let me go talk to him."

Jake just nodded as I rushed out of the restaurant.

"Hey, Ash, hold up!" I yelled, but he ignored me as he jumped into the cab of his truck and left.

"Shit," I said, but froze when I saw Mrs. Natasha standing a few feet away.

"Um, sorry, Mrs. Natasha," I said to my fourth-grade teacher.

"You've never had good control of that tongue of yours," she said, and winked at me as she headed into the café. I followed her then paid for our meals, and by the time I got back to the table, Jake had already rolled the plans up and was ready to leave.

"You gonna be okay?" he asked.

"Yeah, it's just a misunderstanding. These plans represent something he's wanted for a long time. I'll show them to him tonight. I'm sure he'll be okay."

I drove Jake back to my house, knowing he'd have to leave soon.

"I want you to come stay for a few days, help us figure out what we're missing on the property. You're better than me at figuring that stuff out."

"You sure Mr. Sexy will be okay with that?"

"He and I are just friends... almost stepbrothers, actually. It's just that renovating the house was his thing."

"Ooh, kinky," Jake said, causing me to give him a look.

"It's not like that." It wasn't. *Was it?*

"Not like what, you and your stepbrother having the hots for each other?"

"Listen, he and I had the hots for each other a long time ago, long before we realized our dads were a... well, a thing."

Jake just laughed. "This is sounding more and more like a porn flick, you know that, right?"

"Shut up!" I said, and pushed his shoulder. We got out and sat on the porch steps. "I hope I'm not making a mistake with all this, but it feels right."

"Todd," Jake said, putting his hand on my shoulder, and squeezing. "You know your business better than anyone I've ever met."

His words surprised me. "What do you mean by that?"

He shrugged. "Dude, I've tried pulling you into my life on both a personal and business level, and you've kept me firmly at arm's length. The time I tried to get you to go in with me to refurb that old building in downtown Nashville, you told me the whole thing would fail, and it did just that. The truth is, I think I knew it too. You also knew we would fail if things turned romantic, and because you kept us only being friends, you've become one of the best friends I've ever known."

"I borrowed money from you. That's not keeping you at arm's length."

"That was a no-brainer, and you were desperate. We both knew you'd make this a success, and you have. Hell, you're going to take it over the moon with your innate business sense, and skill for predicting successful projects."

I shrugged, unused to the praise. "I think you're putting too much faith in me, and my love life is purely fucked-up."

"Doesn't have to be, though, does it?" I looked at him, not sure I was ready to hear what he was about to lay down. "Well, I'm guessing that guy, your kinky step-brother-to-be, is Mr. Hunky Heartbreaker from high school."

"How did you know that was him?" I asked.

"Please, the teenage angst was pouring out of you. You both looked like you were going to melt where you stood."

"You saw him for what, two seconds? You didn't have enough time to figure any of that out."

He pulled me into a hug. "But, I'm right, aren't I?"

I sighed deeply. "You know you are."

"Why don't you stop being an idiot and go after what you want?"

"It's not that easy."

"'Cause, *you're making it hard.* Something else you're an expert at."

I gave him my withering look, but he knew me too well, and I ended up just laughing, "I hate that you know me so well."

"No, you don't, you love me, and you know it. Now give me smooches."

I pushed him away as he tried to kiss me. This was so common between us. I loved Jake like a brother, and there was the truth. Jake *felt* like a brother. Ashton Nash? He very much did *not* feel like a brother, and Jake was right. It was time to stop acting like an idiot, and let Ash know how much I wanted him, a thought that scared me half to death.

Twenty-Two

Ash

I CAN'T DO IT. I just can't watch Todd in love with someone else. Now, I understood a little too well how much my dating Jennifer and Alex in high school had hurt him.

I decided to do what any red-blooded man would do in my shoes, get drunk and try to forget what it looked like to see him with another man—a really, *really* handsome man.

Rather than making the situation even sadder by drinking alone, though, I opted to go drinking in a bar like a civilized person. I slipped into the Red Saloon, our local bar, and ordered three shots of tequila just to get the party started.

"Hey, Doctor Nash, what brings you here?" I heard a tentative voice behind me, and I cringed.

"*Fuck,* this won't work," I said under my breath. "Just blowing off a little steam." I turned around and saw my nurse practitioner Rachel's daughter, Kristin. I forgot she worked here.

"I've heard things have been hectic down at the clinic."

"They have, and I don't get out and socialize nearly enough. I also miss tequila," I said, thinking maybe I'd somehow given a plausible reason for why I was here.

"Well, you drink up."

When I turned around, the bartender winked, and put three more shots in front of me.

I'd managed to convince myself to just down one and maybe sip the others when, fuck me, none other than Alex Lessen walked in, looking like a million bucks.

Yeah, this just gets better.

I sucked down the other two shots and sat back to enjoy the buzz. Six shots of tequila when I hadn't had a drink in months... that was all it took.

I watched as Alex stuck his tongue down a woman's throat, then turned and kissed some man too. Alex was the worst player in Crawford City. I'd been one of his toys, but just once, and accepting that turned my stomach.

When he caught my eye, he winked. I turned around and paid my bill. Nope, I was not going to play that little game.

I stumbled a bit as I started walking out of the bar, and when Kristin came over to check on me, I giggled. "I'm great now. That's exactly what I needed. I'm gonna walk home and hopefully walk some of the buzz off."

Like fuck I am, I thought as I left the bar, and walked my buzzing ass up to Kandy's drive-thru liquor store. I bought a bottle of brandy, not caring what brand. "It all works the same," I said to the young woman I didn't recognize behind the window.

At that point, I hauled my ass back to my house as fast as my legs could carry me to get drunk in private. The whole *drinking in private turns you into a freaking alcoholic* was a bunch of bologna anyway. Well, *no*, my scientific mind quickly added, *it wasn't*, but fuck it. "One night of drinking while *fucking* Todd is *fucking* some *fucking* man of the month from some *fucking* sexy man-calendar is just fine."

I didn't realize I'd been talking out loud, until one of my patients pulled over and asked if I needed a ride home.

I blushed, which was probably impossible to see, since I was already flushed from the alcohol, before politely declining. "I'm nearly home, but I thank you."

She shook her head before driving on. *Great!* Public drunkenness, that was all I needed on top of everything else.

I managed to get home before I made a bigger fool of myself, and turned the TV on, flipping the channels until I came to some cartoon I didn't recognize. I poured myself another shot into a glass I'd snagged on my way through the kitchen, and downed it while watching some weird-looking, spiky-haired old man run around screaming about something onscreen.

I'd gotten through half the bottle, and was in the middle of a full-on pity party, when I heard a key turn in the lock and the front door open.

Fuck, I didn't expect him home tonight. Did he bring that handsome man here to fuck in my house? *Oh, hell no.* I'd put a stop to that.

I stood up just as Todd entered the living room.

"Nope, get out. You are not going to fuck some hot man in my house." I thought that was what I said, or meant to at least, but the words didn't seem to be coming out right.

"*What?* What man?"

I looked around the room. "Where'd he go?"

Todd took a deep breath and walked over to sit on the sofa. "There's no one with me, Ash. Why are you drunk?"

"'Cause you're fucking some other man. I know you fuck other people, and I can't stop you from fucking other people, but you don't get to fuck them in my own house," I said, and the tears began to flow.

"Ash, baby, I'm not fucking other people, and I sure wouldn't fuck them here. I wouldn't be with anyone where you could see it. That wouldn't be okay."

"No, it's not okay, and I shouldn't have done it to you. I'm such a stupid, shitty person. Why did I hurt you so bad?" I sat next to Todd on the sofa, then leaned over and kissed him, saying, "I'm so sorry, baby. I'm so sorry I hurt you."

I felt more than heard Todd let out a deep breath, before a strong arm snaked across my shoulders.

"Shh, it's okay, sweetheart, come on in here and I'll get you squared away."

"I just feel so damned bad. I feel bad all the time, Todd. I didn't wanna lose you, and I miss you all the time. Even now I miss you all the time."

Todd's arm only tightened around me at my drunken admission, or maybe he was just helping me stay upright. Even if it was only a half-hug, and even though I felt like shit in more ways than one, feeling his body pressed up against mine had never felt so right.

TWENTY-THREE

TODD

OF ALL THE THINGS I'd expected, seeing the perfectly put-together and respectable Ashton Nash drunk in his living room was not one of them.

After pawing me and rambling on about me fucking some hot guy in his house, which I assumed meant Jake, I managed to get him to his bedroom. He fell asleep the moment his head hit the pillow, even though he was still grabbing me, and apologizing for hurting me.

I let myself feel the emotions around all of Ash's drunken confessions. I wasn't quite sure how to feel about the jealousy though. That'd always been my re-action in our relationship. Regardless, drunk Ash, had left me mostly amused, and maybe just a little buzzed by his comments, even if he would forget them all by tomorrow. Thank God it was Friday, so I could fully enjoy the hangover and mortification that was coming. Was I that shallow? Yes, *yes*, I was.

I found the half-empty bottle of cheap booze, screwed the cap on and tossed it. "You aren't going to need that any longer," I said to the vacated living room.

I texted Lisa and told her to be at her brother's place by nine, because he was going to be sporting a serious hangover, which I was sure she wouldn't want to miss.

Seconds later, I got a phone call. "Why is my brother smashed?" she asked.

"I'm not one hundred percent sure. I got something about me dating hot men, and screwing them in his house, which before you yell at me, I wasn't screwing anyone, much less in his house."

"Oh," she said. "This is about the hottie you had waiting for you when we got back to town."

"Maybe, but regardless, I think it's best if you're here instead of me tomorrow when he wakes up."

I waited for her to contradict me, but instead, she said, "Yeah, I think you're probably right."

After ending the call, I went to check on Ash, and seeing he was fine, and not so drunk he was in danger of dying or anything, I went to the guest room and packed up my belongings. Even though I was totally gonna enjoy the show tomorrow, this situation had just gotten a hell of a lot less comfortable, and I needed to give the man his space. Fuck, *I* needed the space.

When I got back to my childhood home, I tossed my stuff into my old room before texting Jen.

Hey, so guess what's just happened?

What? she texted back immediately.

You know I'm back in Crawford?

Yeah...?

So, I didn't tell you everything. I've been staying with Ash.

Three dots came and went several times, before she called. "What the hell do you mean you've been staying with Ash?"

I sighed, "Well... things here got strange. My dad and Doc are dating, and they moved in together."

"*Shut the front door!*" Jen said, and cackled in the background.

"Shut up! That's why I didn't tell you. You want the whole world to be gay."

"Oh, baby, you freaked out, didn't you?" she asked.

"Yeah, and I couldn't stay with my dad, so I stayed with Ash instead."

"Wow, talk about jumping out of the frying pan and into the fire."

I sighed again and we sat silently on the phone for a moment.

"Anyway," I finally said again. "I, um, well, we... well, it's been nice. We've been working through our stuff, you know? I was even enjoying staying with him."

"And?" she asked, knowing I'd contacted her for a reason.

"Well, and... I went to his house tonight, and he was smashed. He probably thought I was having sex with Jake."

"Why would he think you're having sex with Jake? How does he know Jake?" she asked, sounding perplexed.

"Well, we went with Lisa to pick up baby furniture to create a nursery in Dad and Doc's house. That sounds so weird to say... anyway, when we got back, Jake was waiting for me here on the porch."

"Oh, you didn't explain to them that you and Jake are friends?" she asked.

"No, it didn't feel important. I mean, it didn't at the time."

She laughed. "You two are a fucking mess. You'd think after all this time, you'd get it together."

"Uh-huh. If I remember right, you were just the same last time we talked about Ashton Nash."

"Well, that's more for your benefit, though. Honey, I'm not in love with Ash... I never was. Pissed, yeah, but never in love."

I sighed and plopped down on my dad's old sofa. "I still am, aren't I?"

"Yeah, baby, you always have been. I'm glad you and he are talking, though. That's good."

I nodded, not even caring that she couldn't see me. "Jen, will you come home? I need you right now."

"To Crawford City?" she asked, clearly stunned.

"Yeah, I'm sorta moving back."

"Shit. I was afraid this was coming. I do need to visit my dad. I promised I would like three months ago, but damn, you know I hate Crawford City."

"But you love me..."

"Fuck, Todd," she said, frustrated. "Don't manipulate me. I get enough of that from my father."

"You can stay with me. I didn't tell you, my dad gave me his house."

She was quiet. "You mean the house Ash drew up the blueprints for when he was like ten?"

"That'd be the one."

"Damn, this did get deep. Okay, I'm coming... damn," she said again. "I can't believe you're dragging me back to Crawford City."

I felt better when I got off the phone. Jen was my go-to for all things Ash. I probably should've already talked to her about all this, just to keep my head from exploding, but I thought I had it under control. Now, I realized just how wrong I was. *Hell, I'm moving back to Crawford City*. Until that moment, I didn't think that'd settled into my head, not until I told Jen, but *that* had made it real.

I made the up the four-poster bed in the downstairs bedroom, thinking of my great-grandparents, who'd once called this room their own. When I crawled into the bed, it felt... different. It was as if I could feel their presence here, and I welcomed the feeling.

The next morning, I woke up completely relaxed. It was still too early to go to the dads' house, so I busied myself looking through the old desk in the parlor. The only picture I had of my mom was the one Dad had shown me. I stared at it for probably half an hour, memorizing her features.

I had her nose. It was pointed, and although I'd never thought so on me, on her it looked aristocratic. Her hair was long, light brown and parted in the middle, and it hung down along her shoulders. I could tell she'd spent a lot of time in the sun, because the brown hair had natural highlights.

"Who are you?" I asked the photo. I decided I'd hire a family history researcher, to see if they could help me figure it out. What dad had told me about her family emigrating, and the circumstances of her death, and how he'd feared for his own life afterward made me wonder if she had been involved in espionage, or some other top-secret government work.

I admit that thinking her some kind of government agent was probably fanciful on my part, but the arrogant and ornery look of her made me think there was much more to her story than anyone knew.

I rummaged through the other things I found in the desk. I found some love letters from my grandparents that looked like they'd been written while they were still dating. I put those aside to read later. There were also several pictures of my grandparents and great-grandparents. Most of them were taken in the Bahamas, but there were several from here as well.

"Were you happy here?" I asked their pictures, not unlike how I'd talked to my mom's photo. I compared the photos of them when they first got here, standing in front of the broken-down old home, to ones where my dad was little. I wondered how a black Caribbean family could be happy in a backwoods Tennessee town in the early eighties, but I couldn't argue with the evidence scattered across the desk in front of me. Their smiling faces told me they'd been happy here.

I put the pictures away and went over to the sofa, where Dad had left the three photo albums from when I was a kid. I laughed when I opened the first page, and there were Ash and me sitting in the middle of this very room, playing with baby toys. Even then, Ash was all but lying on top of me.

I flipped through the pages, and it was rare to find a photo of me without Ash or Lisa in the picture too. We were together. We'd *always* been together.

By the time I got to the end of the third album, I'd nearly looked through the entirety of our childhood together. The final handful of photos had been taken around the time when Ash and I broke up, and the last photo almost ripped me in two. Ash was looking at me from across the room. Clearly, neither of us knew we were being photographed. I was busy reading on Doc's big sofa, and Ash was sitting across from me. The look on his face conveyed nothing less than the purest love.

I couldn't help but stare at it, willing myself to remember that captured moment I'd been oblivious to at the time, and wiped away tears. I pulled the photo out of the album, snapped pictures of it with my phone, and sent the best one to the local drugstore, ordering an eight-by-ten print. I got confirmation that the photo would be ready by the end of the day. I put the precious original back in the album and closed them all before reshelving them in the old secretary.

It was almost eight, but before I texted the dads that I was back at the house. I decided to wander through and see what I'd need to do to prepare for all the renovations that I hoped to start sooner rather than later.

Most stuff in the house I didn't want to keep. I'd never been into dainty Victorian furniture. For me, the big, overstuffed furniture at Doc's place better suited my tastes. The Crawford City Historical Society had built a museum a few years back, and although it was small, I thought at least the antique parlor furniture would look good there.

I found some straight pins and notecards and began marking the furniture I'd like to donate to the museum. By the time I was done, my foot was beginning to hurt, but I was feeling good about ensuring the historical artifacts in the house would be appreciated and preserved elsewhere.

I was almost dozing off on the sofa when a knock on the door woke me. I pulled myself up and walked to the door, opening it and cocking an eyebrow when I saw Dad and Doc standing in front of me.

"Um, when did you start knocking at your own house?" I asked Dad.

"When it stopped being mine," he said matter of factly. "Now, invite us in. We brought donuts and coffee."

I chuckled. "Someone needs to open the bakery shop back up before we all end up fatter than pigs," I said.

Doc shrugged. "Fatty carbs are fatty carbs... don't really matter what form they're in."

I smiled. "You'd know, I guess."

Dad came in, and when he saw the pinned notecards, he looked at me questioningly. "I'm going through the stuff I'd like to donate to the historical society," I informed him.

A sadness passed over his face, before he nodded. "I think that's probably a great idea. Can I recommend that you require that they keep the upholstery as it is now? I'd hate for them to get rid of your great-grandmother's needlework."

"I can do whatever you'd like. In fact, I'd like it if you'd go with me to speak to them."

Doc smiled and patted Dad's back. "I'll go put these in the kitchen," he said as he walked away.

"Would you prefer I keep this stuff, or do you wanna keep it at your place?"

"No, no... I really don't want it, and the truth is, I never liked it. More like hated it, to be honest," he admitted, laughing.

"I never hated it, but I don't really like it that much either. Hey, I got the preliminary blueprints back from Tom. Do you two wanna look them over with me?"

I couldn't believe how excited I was about all this. I never dreamed I'd like the idea of moving back to Crawford, much less taking over Dad's house... *my* house.

Dad smiled. The sadness was still there, but I guessed it was because even though he hadn't really liked, or maybe even hated this place for a long time, it was still a part of who he'd always been.

As Doc, Dad, and I looked over the plans, they both oohed and aahed at the appropriate times. I could tell something was eating at Dad, though. "You gonna tell me what it is you don't like, or are you gonna pretend like it's nothing?" I asked.

Both Dad and Doc chuckled. "Can I be honest?" he asked, again shocking the crap out of me. The man I'd always known would've never asked, just yelled out his opinion, and forced me to accept his way or the highway.

"I prefer you to be honest. I've always admired that about you, maybe not the stubbornness that went with it, but honesty, yeah."

"If you build the offices here and attach them to the parlor, you're gonna completely compromise the historical aspects of the house." I nodded. I'd already decided I was okay with that. "If I could suggest that instead of building it on the left side of the house, build it to look like it's a carriage house that sits next to the home. It'll look authentic for the time period, give you the space you're looking for, and provide you much better sightlines as well."

I looked over the plans, then got up and walked outside to take a good look at the house in real time.

Dad's suggestion was perfect. I mean, like, *duh*, perfect. I could easily use this side of the house as the big open parlor room, move the kitchen and dining to that side, and even add a long porch behind the house that ran alongside the new addition in the back. That'd mean the space would always be private. It also meant the family side of the house would face the dads' place.

I walked back inside, shaking my head. "Dad, you're a genius. Maybe you should go back to school and become an architect. Hell, Tom is like a hundred years old, and you'd do excellent taking his place."

"Never going back to school, son, but I appreciate the compliment."

I nodded. I felt the exact same way. I'd rather pull my fingernails out one by one than sit in another classroom.

I made notes about the changes. The entire home was going to end up gutted. I'd thought I'd be able to stay in the house during the renovations, but with the entire downstairs being stripped, it'd be better for everyone if I moved out.

"Now all I have to do is let Ash see it. The man has his own ideas where this house is concerned."

Both dads nodded. This house needed Ashton Nash, and if all went to plan, when I finally confessed that I still had feelings for him, I hoped maybe one day this would be his home too. I sure as hell wasn't going to announce that to my fathers, though.

We spent the rest of the morning talking about odds and ends in the house, and what should be done with them. Mostly my dad didn't care. I couldn't donate everything to the historical society, its museum just wasn't big enough for all that. Unless...

"Hey, Doc, what's going on with the old mercantile building downtown?"

"There's been talk about tearing it down. The old thing is sturdy, but don't really have much use."

"Hmm. I have an idea. It's a crazy idea, but... the first floor could be a great place for several shops if it were divided adequately, which downtown desperately needs, and with all the new folks moving into town, I think we could use some more commercial space."

Dad and Doc both nodded, encouraging me to continue. "If we were to convert some of the space into an interactive museum, and move the historical society out of the basement of the Town Hall, I think more people would enjoy visiting it. Not only that, the space could be rented out for social events too. In fact..." I was beginning to get excited. "You know that used to be an old boarding house back in the day? We could renovate parts of it to be a small bed and breakfast. The historical society could take on part of the upstairs and the first level could be commercial. Y'all, I think that could be a great place for all this old stuff."

Doc smiled. "I've been threatening to open a bed and breakfast in my house, even tried to get Amos here to turn this into one, but he said he didn't want the worry. If you did that, I could help you get it off the ground."

I looked at Dad, and to my surprise, he was smiling. "So, you like the idea?" I asked.

"I like seeing you becoming a part of this town. It's a good place, Crawford City, it just needs a little TLC, and it could be a great place."

"I agree, and you know what the best part is?" I asked.

He shrugged. "No, what's the best part?"

"I know a guy who owns a construction company."

Twenty-Four

Ash

W HEN I WOKE UP to the mother of all hangovers, I made myself stumble into the kitchen, resisting the urge to puke. I wasn't surprised there was coffee made, since when Todd got up before me, he usually fixed a pot.

Remembering Todd made me moan. *Fuck*, I just remembered in vivid detail how I accused him of fucking some guy last night. I also remembered he came back here alone, and I'd ended up... *God help me*, I'd ended up kissing him while I begged his forgiveness.

I poured the coffee, slammed the most Tylenol I could without damaging my liver, and dragged myself into the living room, fully expecting to see Todd smirking, or, more likely, fuming at me.

What I found instead was my baby sister sitting in my recliner, reading one of my magazines.

"Lisa?" I asked in a whisper, trying to preserve my head.

"Yeah?" she said as loud as she could without screaming.

I took a moment to let the loudness of her reply settle in my head again.

"Quietly this time, can you tell me why you're here?"

"'Cause, Todd texted me last night telling me you were on a bender, and would need company this morning."

"I see," I whispered, hoping that would encourage her to start doing the same thing. After putting the coffee down on my coffee table, I lay down on the sofa, and covered my eyes with my arm.

"So, wanna tell me what's goin' on?" she asked.

"No."

She chuckled. "You know I'm not leavin' until you do. Might as well spit it out."

"What I need is a shower and copious amounts of painkillers. I do not, however, need my nosey baby sister digging around in my business."

"Yet, here I am. Okay, you get the shower and copious amounts of painkillers, then you come back in here and spill."

I sighed, knowing I wasn't getting out of this, at least not that easily. Even before my sister became a licensed therapist, she was good at pulling information out of people when she needed or wanted, and now she was impossible.

I managed to down the rest of my coffee, drank two whole glasses of water, and climbed into the intense heat of my shower, hoping that would at least bank the hangover long enough for me to get rid of Lisa.

When I came out, she was at my stove cooking eggs and bacon. As usual, the entire kitchen was a mess. No one could dirty as many dishes as Lisa when cooking the simplest of meals.

I went to the sofa again and lay back, letting all my remedies kick in, while I waited for her to finish and force me to talk.

I drifted off while waiting, and woke to the clang of a plate on my coffee table. I'd swear there was nothing elegant about Lisa Nash Bradford when she was on a mission.

I lifted up, took the plate, and began to stuff my face.

Lisa watched me until I swallowed, and said, "Okay, now spill."

"What do you want me to say, Lisa?" I said after loading my mouth with more food. I knew how much she hated people who talked with their mouth full, so I could at least get a little passive-aggressive revenge. I swallowed, and continued, "You already know what this is about. I'm in love with a man who I'll never have again. I can't even fuckin' date anymore, 'cause I compare every man I meet to him. I thought we were doin' better, and I'm confronted with him dating someone else, and showing him the blueprints to the house I always dreamed of being a part of. Yes, I know it's pathetic, yes, I know I should be beyond this point, and no, I'm not. You can't therapize me out of this, I've got to come to terms with it on my own. Last night was my attempt at doing that."

"God, you're so full of shit." Lisa shook her head, and lifted the foot of the recliner, letting it pop her back into a reclining position.

"What? Is that how you treat your clients?" I asked, before stuffing another forkful of eggs into my mouth.

"No, and you aren't a client, although I'd like to kick some of them in the ass like I'm about to kick yours. Listen, you and Todd are both idiotic men. You dance around each other, instead of having a straight conversation about your feelings. You saw him with a guy last night. That don't mean shit. You can't know why he was meeting with him. Maybe he is dating him, maybe he's a friend or a business associate. Just 'cause you fucked up doesn't mean he is acting like you did, and no, before you get your panties in a wad, I'm not blaming you. You were a kid acting like a kid, but you still hurt him, and now you're feeling all sorts of guilty. I get it... the whole fuckin' town gets it."

She drew in a deep breath, shook her head again, and closed the recliner before she stood up. "It's time for you both to have a heart-to-heart and be honest with each other about how you feel. That's why I texted him and told him to get his stupid ass over here. He should be here any moment."

"What? He's comin' to talk?" I looked back at the guest bedroom. "Is he not here already?"

"No, he moved his shit back to the big house. Which is probably better, at least until the two of you get all this teenage angst worked out." With that, Lisa grabbed her purse, a bag almost bigger than her, and walked out the front door.

I collapsed back onto the sofa. I didn't really want to talk to Todd, especially when I had a hangover. I'd loved spending time with him again, and admitting how I felt... well, that seemed like the wrong thing to do. I didn't want to chase him away again.

I took my empty plate into the kitchen, and thought about cleaning up Lisa's mess but decided against it. Instead, I went to the bathroom and brushed the horrible day-after taste out of my mouth. God, I could almost taste my bad breath.

When I came out, Todd was sitting in the same recliner Lisa had vacated only a few minutes before.

I sighed and collapsed back onto my sofa.

"Well, you might as well tell me what's goin' on. If not, your pushy-ass sister is gonna come force us."

"You're the one who told her to get involved," I said, feeling irritated at him and the world in general.

He smiled. "Yeah, but she would've been involved eventually anyway. At least, this way we could get it over with before she did her hokey psychology practice on us."

I shook my head, thankful the meds had worked, and it was no longer pounding as it had been a while ago.

I sat up and put my head in my hands. "Todd, I don't wanna lose the ground we've made these past few weeks." I looked over at him, and sighed, "I apologize for last night, but can't we just leave it as it is? You're dating someone, and well, it don't matter now anyway."

Todd shook his head. "I'm not dating anyone. I've not dated anyone seriously since we broke up. Have you?"

I didn't dare look at him. The emotions were too overwhelming. "No... it never worked out for me."

"Because?" he asked.

"'Cause, I love you." I'd always been overly emotional, but add to that a hangover, even a banked one, and I was too vulnerable. There was no way I could hold back over a decade worth of regret and pain when I didn't have all my faculties about me.

I was about to get up and go hide in my bedroom when I felt the cushion next to me dip with his weight, and two glorious arms come around me, pulling me to him.

He held me as I cried like a total idiot, then after a moment, he lifted my chin, and looking into my eyes, said, "I love you too. I always have, Ash, and I think I always will."

I had never wanted to be held by anyone as much as I wanted to be held by him. I melted into him and clung to him as if my life depended on it. Maybe it did. I didn't think I'd lived, not fully, not completely, since we'd broken up all those years ago.

I pulled back, just enough to see his face. "You're my one. I don't think I'll ever love anyone as much as I do you. I've missed you so much, Todd... so much it hurts to even think about it."

He smiled down at me. "I understand. That's exactly how I've felt too."

I leaned back into him and had a nice cry. Somehow, we ended up lying down on the sofa, his larger frame embracing mine. In all the years since we'd broken up, I'd never felt so safe and secure as I felt right then. It was like a huge missing piece of me had been found. It was almost like while being in his arms, I was whole for the first time since I was a child.

TWENTY-FIVE

TODD

WE LAY TOGETHER FOR so long, Ash fell asleep against me. He smelled so good. Like soap and the fancy shampoo he used every day. God, it felt so good to have him in my arms again. I loved this man with every ounce of my being. He filled me in ways I couldn't even begin to explain.

He'd said I was *his one*... yeah, that was right. He was my one too. I wasn't sure why or how other people could go from one man to another, but not me. I was his and had always been just his.

After a while, I too fell asleep. I was honestly not sure how long we slept like that, but I was sure we could've slept the entire day, if there hadn't been a knock at the door.

I roused Ash and turned him onto his back as I got up to answer the door.

Lisa, Dad, and Doc were standing there looking concerned. "What's going on?" I asked.

"We wanted to check on you, since neither of you would answer your phone."

I smiled. "We were sort of busy."

"Oh... *OH*," Doc said, with a knowing look of surprise on his face, and I couldn't help but laugh.

"Well, not in the way you're thinking. Y'all come on in."

They did, and Ash sat up, smiling like the cat that'd eaten a canary.

"Since y'all are here, I'm gonna go grab the plans I got yesterday for the house. I want y'all to see them, so we can discuss them together."

Ash was blushing, which was so fucking cute. I really was over the moon for this man. Yeah, we still had a lot of shit to work through, years of it, but thank God he was at least back in my life, and back in my arms while we were doing all that talking.

I put the plans on the table, turned the dining room light on, and asked everyone to come and take a look.

When Ash came over, I slipped my arm around him. "It's almost exactly like what you'd asked for. Dad recommended some modifications, but I think you'll like those too."

As he looked over the plans, tears slipped down his face. "You were listening," he said with a wet chuckle.

"Of course, I listened. It's been your dream, but now it's mine too."

When he looked up at me, I kissed him. "I was showing Jake yesterday to get his opinion about the interior, 'cause he's a whiz at that kind of thing, but ultimately, it's your ideas that matter."

"Jake? The guy who was at your house?" Ash asked.

I nodded. "One of my best friends, but still just a friend."

He kissed me again, both of us ignoring the rest of the family.

Dad cleared his throat. "Okay, well, seeing as the two of you are fine, we'll let you get back to making up. But, we're fixing supper tonight, and we expect to see you both at our house by six. That should give you enough time to... well, work things out."

We both laughed as Doc and Dad skirted out of the front door. Lisa, however, lingered behind, and kissed us both on the cheek, before saying, "Damn, I'm really good at my job!"

Both of us kicked her out of the house laughing. It was just like her to take credit for us getting back together. Not that I cared. All I cared about was after all this wasted time, I finally had this man back in my arms where he belonged.

TWENTY-SIX

ASH

I COULDN'T STOP CRYING. Did that make me a sap? A basket case? Whatever it made me, I was happier than I'd been in a long time. Todd went over the details of the house plans with me, but I was too emotional to respond. All I could do was smile and try not to blubber too much.

Note to self, don't go on a bender and then try to have a reunion with the man you love the next day. It just makes you look nuts.

After everyone left, we didn't talk much, or do much of anything really, other than cuddle, watch some TV, and just enjoy being in each other's embrace.

Finally, after five thirty, we got ourselves together enough to go to our parents' house. I'd completely forgotten about setting the baby room up with Lisa, but when we came in, I could hear her and the dads putting stuff in the room.

"Shit, we forgot Lisa's nursery surprise."

Todd chuckled. "Trust me, this is probably better anyway. This way the dads have their hands in the middle of it. I'm sure they're happier for it."

I nodded in agreement. We went up and leaned on opposite sides of the doorway as we watched three completely occupied people arrange the baby furniture in Lisa's old room. Lisa was always into pastels, so the room's color was already perfect for a baby girl and boy. She put the bassinettes together side by side, and put an old rocker I hadn't seen in years next to them. I was guessing Dad had it stored up in the attic bedroom.

Todd cleared his throat, and all three of them turned to us smiling. "Um, so I see the cat's out of the bag," he said.

Lisa jumped up and down and rushed into Todd's arms. "Isn't it amazing? The rocker is what Dad used to rock us in, and the mobile used to be yours. She looked alarmed for a moment, and said, "Your dad got it out of the attic of your house. I hope you don't mind."

Todd smiled down at her. "Of course, I don't mind. I love that you all thought of me in putting this together."

A meaningful yet sweet look passed between his dad and him. It did mean a lot that we were all included in this room. This was the next generation, and Todd and Amos were as much a part of it as Dad and I were. It warmed me all over that we were all actively a part of this. We were a family.

They messed around the room, while Dad told Todd and me where to store Lisa's old bedroom furniture. Clearly, Dad and Amos had been so occupied with decorating, that no one had thought about food. I went downstairs when no one was paying attention, and ordered a couple of large pizzas, remembering that Lisa loved Canadian bacon, and Todd loved pepperoni. Two pizzas prevented a war, one we'd experienced time and time again while we were growing up.

When the pizza arrived, I rushed to put it on the table, and not finding paper plates, pulled out the same dishes Dad and Amos had served us food on before. "Y'all come on down for supper," I called, and they all came down the stairs smiling.

"I thought I smelled pizza," Dad remarked, looking pleased.

"I figured you got sidetracked, so I just ordered pizza to be delivered."

"Had to have been a while ago. Pappies is delicious, but slower than cold molasses."

I chuckled. "Yep, I ordered it shortly after we got here. Anyway, Lisa, your Canadian bacon is over there, Todd, your pepperoni is over there. No need for bloodshed tonight."

As we sat around the table, eating and laughing about all that'd gone on, I slipped my hand in Todd's. We were back to how things were supposed to be, back to where we'd been before my world had fallen apart.

Unfortunately, in the back of my head, I kept thinking, *I wonder how long this'll last.*

Twenty-Seven

Todd

O N Sunday, Ash and I stayed at his place cuddled up watching TV, while Lisa, Doc, and Dad ran to Nashville to pick up Lisa's husband, Frank. Jen was flying in also, and they'd agreed to wait and bring her to Crawford as well. I'd already warned Ash she was coming, and he just laughed. "You know she's gonna have a heart attack when she sees we're back together."

"Nah, she was already pushing me that way. She's gonna give you a ton of shit, though. I can't wait."

Ash smiled but looked a bit concerned. Jen was tall, thin, and dainty looking, but if you got her mad she could do some real damage. I was sure Ash had been on the receiving end of that damage. I knew I'd sure experienced it more than once. I understood his reticence.

"So, you willing to come stay with me at the house for a while? I'm gonna have to put her up, and there's no room here."

Ash looked at me for a long moment. "No, as much as I'd like to, I think we need to move this along slowly. Baby, I love you so much... I've missed you in every way possible, and I never wanna lose you again. So, go be with Jennifer, just y'all include me in your plans, don't leave me sitting out in the cold," he said, and began singing.

I didn't recognize the song, but I did recognize the voice I'd heard so often back when we were young, and he'd started singing with a band.

"The sun is shining,

The air is soft.

My heart is yours and I'm not lost.

You left me here, but not alone.

The feel of you, will not be gone.

I sing your name, and sigh your voice.

I'll be yours forever, if you'll just have me.

Don't leave me out in the cold.

Don't forget me when you're gone.

I'll be yours forever, if you'll just have me."

He was smiling when he pulled me into an embrace and began dancing with me as he hummed the rest of the song.

"You wrote that about me, didn't you?" I asked.

He shrugged. "Doesn't matter," he said, smiling up at me. "I got you now... and it's not cold."

I didn't say anything else for a moment, guessing the next few verses weren't as nice. He was never one to stop singing one of his songs.

"Are we changing the ending of that song?" I asked.

He looked at me sadly. "I'm not sure. I hope so."

"You ever gonna sing the ending for me?" I asked.

He pulled away and sat on the back of the sofa. "I never gave it one, to be honest. I tried a few times after we broke up, but it was... well, it never felt like we were over... then I went to college and medical school, so my music career was pretty-much toast," he said, chuckling.

"But, you remembered enough to sing it now."

He nodded. "I remember the songs I wrote all those years ago, especially my mad songs. I could sing a few of those for you," he said teasingly.

"No, that's okay. It's probably best that you not. If I remember correctly, you got a bit angry Carrie Under-wood. *Dug your key into the side of my four-wheel drive* before you disbanded your band."

He smiled. "I'm no American Idol, but I did express myself with music back then."

"Baby, you were always very expressive in everything you did. It's one of the things I loved about you the most."

He leaned back into me then, and I held onto him. We'd been like this since yesterday, each holding the other, as if at any moment things would fall apart again.

I think it's just how it was supposed to be. Before we could even begin to work through our stuff, we just needed to be with each other again. Despite that, I was beginning to feel a bit antsy, so I asked, "Wanna let me show you something?"

"Sure," he said, and pulled back smiling.

"Can I show you my company stuff? I'm kinda excited about it."

"Of course, shit, I've been so caught up in our reunion, I haven't even thought about all that. We have time before everyone gets back. Show me."

I couldn't contain my excitement. I had no idea why it was different with Ash than it had been with everyone else, but it was. I wanted him to see my plans, and maybe, even more surprisingly, approve of them.

We went to the hardware store, and he chuckled. "Do you remember the times your dad sent us down here to pick up stuff? Hell, we didn't even have a license. I don't know how we didn't get pulled over."

"'Cause, Sheriff Lemon was friends with Dad. Besides, it's not like we hadn't been driving all over creation since we were like, what, ten?"

He chuckled. "More like eight," he said. "So, you gonna reopen?"

"Dad thinks we should. I think he'll run that part of it, though, thank God. I don't know how I'll find time to run a dang hardware store on top of my existing business."

"Oh, that reminds me," Ash said, catching my attention. "Dad said you were thinking about buying the old mercantile building and redoing it. Is that true?"

"Yeah, but don't be spreading it around. I called down to the mayor's office, and since the city owns it, he began making quite a stink. You know that old man never did like us."

"Don't feel bad, he don't like anyone."

"I figured he likes me a little less than you, don't you think?" I asked, and Ash cringed.

"Yeah, he's always been a bigot," Ash said on a sigh. "Well, if you're interested, you can go around the old fool. I know the city council would love to have you redo the building, especially since last I heard they were debating tearing it down. I happen to know if they had the funds, they already would've."

"I heard that too," I said, smiling. "Maybe, since Doc is friends with most of the council members, I'll ask him to sniff around and let me know. It'd be perfect for mixed-use."

"You're gonna have your hands full with just your projects. When are you gonna find time for everything else?" Ash asked.

"Well, the mercantile isn't a for-sure thing. My house is a perfect opportunity to try out my new partnership with Dad. I figured if things go south, it'll be there. Linc, my second in command, is handling my other project. So, I've got some leeway."

Ash slipped into my embrace. "I'm so happy for you, and more than happy that you're comin' home. I've missed you."

I kissed his head. "Yeah, I think that's why it's so important I show you all this. Reckon we should go on over to the house. My foot's a lot better, but it's beginning to hurt again. I don't wanna be too worn out when Jen gets here. Besides, I can't wait to see how she messes with you."

Ash looked at me sideways and shook his head. "You're pure evil."

"Nope, just enjoying the karma show."

Ash began tickling me. Dang, I forgot he knew how ticklish I was, and he never was. "No fair, no fair!" I yelled, until we were both laughing. When he stopped, I bent back and kissed him again. "I love you."

Ash blushed, a sight I'd missed more than I knew I could. Seeing his handsome face blush while he was in my arms, I could honestly say that look did things to me as a man that the boy never experienced before. It reminded me of all the things we hadn't rekindled yet.

When I kissed him again, I deepened it. When Ash pulled away again, his breath caught. "Um, maybe this is a bit too fast. Let's slow it back down."

"What's wrong?" I asked.

Ash looked at me concerned. "I'll move this too fast, Todd, you know me. I lost you once because I couldn't keep things simple. I'm not gonna make that mistake this time, okay? Slow and steady, that's how I've got to do this one."

I stared at him, and I could see the layers of pain. I wasn't sure why so much of it had left me. I was ready to be all in, but if he wasn't, well, that was okay with me.

"Slow and steady wins the race," I said, quoting something I couldn't remember from where, but he nodded, and gave me a tentative smile.

My stuff was still at the house. I knew if I spent the night at Ash's place again, I wasn't going to be able to keep my hands off him, and I sure as hell wasn't going to stay out of his bed.

When we got back to Dad and Doc's, the whole party had arrived. We walked into laughter, music, and food cooking in the kitchen.

Jen jumped into my arms, and as was her usual way, she kissed me smack on the lips. When she pulled away, she looked to my right and into the eyes of Ash.

"Well, as I live and breathe, if it isn't my *horrible* ex, Ashton Nash."

"Hi, Jennifer," he said, blushing deeply.

I enjoyed watching him squirm under her intense stare, before she said, "So, if your sister's gossip is to be believed, my dearest and closest friend here has given your sorry ass another chance."

The entire room had turned to watch the interaction. Of course, I knew my friend better than almost anyone in the world, and I recognized when she was giving someone the business.

He nodded, and said, "He's givin' me another chance."

She squinted her eyes, took a deep breath, and said, "And it's *about fucking time!*"

When she grabbed Ash in a bear hug, his eyes were as big as saucers.

"Oh, how I wish I had my phone out. *Damn,* that was a priceless expression," Lisa said, laughing her ass off.

I couldn't help but chuckle too, and Ash gave me the evil eye.

"So, you forgive me?" he asked Jen then.

"Oh, hell no. No other man has ever dumped me, Ashton Nash, and no other man ever will. That is something I will never forgive you for. Do you hear me?"

Ashton smiled, a little nervous still. "If it helps, it's 'cause you're a girl, not because you aren't the prettiest girl in the world."

"It does help, and I knew that before you went out with me. So, as long as you never do it again, and don't hurt my babycakes here, we are square."

Ash smiled at me, and before I knew it, he was snuggled up under my arm. "He's the only one I want," he said, causing me to blush, and Jen to smile happily.

The next day, I went with Jen to have breakfast with her dad. I'd always thought Jennifer's dad was the funniest man in Crawford. He loved to cut up, and was just as quick to make himself the butt of his jokes as he was to pick on others.

"So, I hear through the grapevine that you're planning on settling back down in our fine Crawford City," he said with a twinkle in his eye.

"Yes, sir," I said, smiling. "I'll be selling my property in Nashville, and moving business operations here in the next few months."

"Oh, that's good news, son, very good news."

I could tell he was mulling something over, and not wanting to encourage him to get too personal, I turned to Jen and asked her about her last photoshoot in Paris.

We were chatting like that, until Mr. Cole said, "Jen, girl, when're you gonna settle down like young Todd here?"

She shook her head. "Here we go. Dad, we've already had this discussion. I like my life. I love traveling. I don't want kids, I need a man like I need a hole in the head, *and* I'm *never* moving back to Crawford City."

Mr. Cole's face distorted as he hmphed.

"So, what about those Volunteers? They're having quite the season," I said, trying to change the subject to the state's adored football team. Just then, Clara Sue walked into the restaurant.

Clara Sue and Jen were intense frenemies. They'd both been cheerleaders, they'd both competed at the local beauty pageants, and Clara Sue was intensely jealous that Jen had been as successful as she had been in her modeling career. The fact that Jen jumped up as quick as she did to talk to her was testament to how much she hated our current conversation.

As soon as she was out of hearing range, Mr. Cole's friendly disposition returned. "I wish I could get that girl to at least move back to Nashville. I'm getting older, and want to have my family around me."

"Would you mind if I gave you a little advice?" I asked, fully expecting him to say no.

"Sure," he said, surprising me.

"My dad's been after me for years to move back here, and the truth is, it was all a scheme that got me back here to begin with, but I know the more he pushed, the further away I went. If you want your daughter to come home, you have to give her a reason to wanna be here."

I hesitated, knowing I was stepping into uncharted territory, but he seemed interested in what I was saying, so I continued on, "It's just that, if every time she comes home, you're givin' her the business about moving back, she's just gonna stay away."

The man across from me deflated. "I guess I already knew that. When I was y'all's age, I was a new dad with grand ideas. My mom and dad wanted me to move here and take over the drugstore. I couldn't imagine moving back to a podunk town in the middle of nowhere."

"What changed your mind?" I asked.

"Jennifer. Her mama left me, and I was stuck with a baby to raise on my own. I moved back to have help, then I learned how much I loved hanging out with my dad, when he wasn't trying to be my dad, and controlling my every move." He stared off in thought for a moment.

I waited, watching Jen do her typical Southern "bless your heart" stuff to Clara Sue, when he lifted his coffee mug to his mouth.

"It seems to me, if you just give her space and make her stay here fun, it's likely she'll wanna come back more often."

"Look at you being so grown up and smart," he said, causing me to chuckle. "No wonder young Doctor Nash is so taken with you."

The smile dropped from my lips, a knee-jerk response that hadn't gone away, even though he and I were getting past all the... well, all the past.

"I'm guessing the gossip is pretty ripe."

He laughed out loud. "Son, when he got all drunk, clearly upset about you and that fancy fella you had on your arm, you know the town's gonna talk."

I cringed. "That fancy fella is just my friend. I didn't know Ash got drunk in public."

Mr. Cole grinned ear to ear. "Yep, walked right back to his place with a bottle of something under his arm, stumbling and everything."

I shook my head. "You'll have to repeat that so Jen can hear. She'll love that story."

"But, you, not so much, I see."

"Well, after all this time, we're making up. He's gonna be my family either way. Did you hear Dad and Doc are engaged?"

"Oh, yeah, there's been talk of that for years. I'm glad those two finally got their heads out of their rear ends and got on with it."

I chuckled. "The whole town knew, but I didn't."

He looked shocked. "Well, you haven't been around much, but I thought those two woulda told you."

"Nope, not till a few weeks ago. It was a surprise to Ash too."

"Well, parents don't always want their kids in the middle of their love lives," he said, and looked off toward Miss Jamison, owner of Crawford City Café.

"Do I detect a little love interest in you, Mr. Cole?" I asked tongue in cheek. He blustered a bit, but I could see the hidden smile. "Well, I'll be," I said. "Miss Jamison? How long have you two been... whatever... you're dating?"

He sighed. "Young man, you need to keep these wild-brained ideas to yourself, especially when talking to my loud, obnoxious, opinionated daughter!"

"Keep what to himself?" Jennifer asked as she walked up behind her father and sat back down.

Mr. Cole sighed. "Now you've done it," he said, giving me a stern look.

I had to bow my head and keep from chuckling.

"Well, y'all, it's been fun, but I'm gonna head back to my place. I'm meeting with my foreman today about what it's gonna cost me to refurb my new home. Jen, come on over when you're ready."

Both Jen and her dad gave me the exact same look of frustration, and I almost burst out laughing. I couldn't get back to the house alone, but I'd be damned if I was gonna sit through the heat of the conversation that was about to happen here.

I hobbled down the block to Ash's clinic, and slipped in through the side door where Ash and I used to talk old Mrs. Henderson, Doc's assistant, into sneaking us sodas and treats while Doc was too busy to notice.

I sat next to Leslie, who was manning the reception desk while Clara Sue was out. "Is he busy?" I asked.

"Lord, yes, but no more than usual. He'll be out in a minute."

"How's the new doc handling things?" I asked.

"He's doing pretty good," I heard a male voice behind me say.

I jumped. "Um, sorry..."

"No need, we didn't get to meet properly the other day. I'm Gib."

"Hi, Gib, or is it Doctor McCartney?"

"Oh, you can call me Gib, or Doctor Gib, if you're gonna be one of my patients."

I cringed when Leslie said, "Well, you probably will be." She put her hand beside her mouth, and making fun of the day I fractured my foot, whispered, "He and Doctor Nash were... *involved*."

"Shut up, Leslie. I was in a lot of pain, and, well, Ash and I..." I looked at the new doc, and shrugged. "Ash and I have a past."

"Oh, I've only been here for a little over a week, and I'm fully caught up on all the gossip about you and Doctor Nash."

I groaned. "I shoulda known."

He nodded. "Yep, you probably shoulda."

I liked Dr. Gib a lot more than I did when I thought Ash was dating him.

"Where ya from?" I asked, having noticed he had a slight accent, although I could tell his education had covered most of it up.

"I'm from West Tennessee, a small county just south of Jackson."

"Oh, you're from Tennessee. I thought you went to Harvard."

He smiled companionably. "Well, us country bumpkins can go to Harvard too."

I chuckled. "Well, those of us crazy enough to wanna."

"Touché," he said. "Touché."

Ash came out a few minutes later with one of the Linden kids. He smiled when he saw me. "To what do we owe the pleasure of a visit from you?" he asked.

"Just avoiding a knockdown drag-out between Jen and her dad."

He nodded at me. "Do you need a ride back to the house?"

I shook my head. "No, Linc is supposed to be here to pick me up in a minute. I wanted to show him the old hardware store and lumber yard. I've already texted him to meet me here."

Ash just smiled, but I could read all the meaning there. I was comfortable enough to come here when I needed to. Seeing that it made him happy warmed my insides as well.

Twenty-Eight

Ash

THE TIME SPENT WITH Todd was magical. I tried not to overthink it, knowing if I did, I'd just make a mess of it again.

Todd and Jennifer spent copious amounts of time together, and that gave me time to hang out with Lisa and Frank. I hadn't initially liked my brother-in-law. He was the opposite of everyone I knew. He was open and gregarious, a bit awkward, and at the same time a little pompous. However, when I got over myself and watched how well he and my sister got along, I let it go, and now, I enjoyed the man as much as I did anyone.

Dad and Amos made over Frank's new position, asking questions about what it was like to work with Oregon's power-woman governor.

I just enjoyed watching them, especially how easily both couples interacted with their loved ones. Simple brushes of a hand over the other's back, or holding hands. I'd thought that'd never be me. I didn't believe Todd would ever give me another chance, and I'd come to the conclusion that without him, I'd never be in love again.

Now, as I watched these two couples, I thought he and I would probably be the same. We'd probably have the same mannerisms, the same little displays of affection. The thought warmed me deep in my core in a way nothing had before.

Lisa and Frank helped Dad and Amos finish the nursery while I worked. We got together every night for supper. Jennifer and Todd were usually there as well, and it felt right on so many levels.

I knew I was an overly emotional idiot, but part of me remained apart from it all, unable to believe it'd last long. I kept thinking either I'd do something to fuck it all up, or Todd would get tired of me, and I'd lose him again. I tried not to feel that way and just live in the moment, but it was such a powerful thought that I couldn't quite shake it.

I probably should've used my sister's expertise and asked her about it, but she and Frank were having so much fun with the dads that I couldn't quite bring myself to ruin their conversation. So, after an amazing and wonderful visit, I hugged her and Frank, before watching them leave down the long hallway toward their plane.

As usual, I felt sad when my sister left after a visit. I couldn't be happier for her and Frank, especially now they had new family members on the way, but I missed her. It was just a shame she hadn't settled back here.

TODD

LINC PICKED ME UP a little after noon, and declared he was hungry, which meant I ended up back at the Crawford City Café for the second time today. When I walked in, I got a look from Miss Jamison, and I just shrugged and pointed at Linc. "Gotta feed the help."

She smiled, and for the first time, I noticed some of the hard lines that'd always been on her face had softened. Love could do that to a person. I knew that from experience.

After Linc had eaten enough to feed a small army, we paid and headed to my dad's property. Linc was talking about the process of moving the supplies from Nashville to here, when we pulled onto the property and came to a stop in front of the store's big plate-glass window. *"Get the fuck out of Crawford, Faggot!"* The words were painted in blood-red across the storefront. *"Leviticus 18:22"* was written underneath.

"What the fuck?" I said as I climbed out of the truck, shock making my legs weak.

I looked at Linc, who had paled at the sight. "Dude, you should call the sheriff!" he proclaimed.

"Yeah, let me take pictures first."

"Hey, Melinda," I said to the woman who ran the desk down at the sheriff's office. "I need a deputy to check out some vandalism at the old hardware store."

She took the information, and a few minutes after we hung up, Sheriff Cross herself showed up.

"Well, damn," she said as she got out of her SUV to survey the damage.

"Nobody reported this yet?" I asked her, and she shook her head.

"No, not many people come by the old store now it's closed. I'm guessing this is pretty fresh, though," she said. "Probably done last night."

"At least it was only done on the glass, so it'll be easier to remove."

"Yeah, that's... good," she said, as if she thought that was interesting.

I'd called Dad to let him know about the graffiti, and sent him the picture I'd taken. I also told him he probably needed to be here to talk to the sheriff himself, since he was the owner.

The rest of the day was clouded by the graffiti, although I figured it was probably done by some idiotic kid struggling with his own sexuality. While Dad and the sheriff went over the report, I showed Linc around the space.

"Well, had it not been for the unwelcome message out front, I'd say this is awesome. It's quite a bit more efficient than what we've got right now," he said.

"Yeah, and Dad's thinking about reopening the hardware store. His thoughts are that we can order in bulk and sell wholesale, meaning it'll be cheaper for us in the long run."

"Hey, that's a good idea. I'm guessing if our guys have to keep a record of what they're taking, it'll reduce waste too. Could save you thousands in the long run."

I smiled. "My thoughts exactly."

After the sheriff left, Dad came in and sat across from Linc and me. "Well, that was bound to happen. Crawford City's come a long way, but with Emanual and me comin' out, you moving back, and the gossip around you and Ash, I'm not at all surprised."

"You don't think it's just a dumb kid?" I asked, worried that it could be more.

"Nah, a kid wouldn't put the scripture on it. The sheriff and I agree it was probably someone older. The fact they only sprayed the glass also tells me they knew, even if caught, they'd only get a slap on the wrist since we can just scrape it off."

"Fuck that. If it was an adult, we can charge them with a hate crime."

Dad chuckled. "You've been in Nashville too long, son. Unless someone gets hurt, they won't press those kinds of charges out here. Well, boys, you might as well come on out here and help me. I've got razor blades and glass cleaner in the truck. We can scrape this off and clean it up like it was never there."

"What's gonna stop them from trying it again or worse?" Linc asked.

"Can't stop them, but I can turn the cameras back on, so we can at least catch them," Dad said.

"You've got cameras and they weren't on?" I asked.

Dad shrugged. "Didn't seem important with it being empty."

Linc helped for a few minutes and when it was clear we'd be done fairly quickly, he took off to take care of our other ongoing projects. Luckily, the spray paint came off easily since it was still fresh.

As Dad had predicted, no evidence remained that it'd ever been there when we were done cleaning. Now, if my concern over it could be so easily wiped away.

Jen and I had as much fun as we usually did when we visited. I didn't mention the spray-paint incident to her, mostly because, like her father, I'd like her to visit Crawford more often. As a black woman in a rural Southern town, she'd had her own fair share of racism and hatred tossed at her through the years. If she knew it was still happening, I doubted she'd be too keen on spending more time here.

Ash came over nearly every evening while Jen was visiting. I was shocked at how fast he fit into our little world. In the past, we would *Ash bash*, as we called it. Doing so was a bit strange now that he was sitting with us, but Jen used some of our more creative Ash bashes.

For some reason, they all sounded dirty now, causing all three of us to laugh.

I pouted when she finally had to leave. "Can't you move to Nashville? Buy one of those fancy houses on this side of the city so you can visit here more often?" I asked in a whiney voice.

She laughed. "You and my dad are conspiring, which, thanks for getting him to lighten up some. He told me last night you'd told him to stop with all the pressure."

"Yeah, I did, and I'm happy he took my advice."

"Me too," she said happily, then grabbed me into a hug, pulled back, and kissed me square on the lips, like she'd always done when getting ready to leave.

"I love you, Jen."

"I love you too, Toddy baby."

"You guys are... eew," Ash said behind us.

Jen threw her head back and laughed, then went over and began smooching on Ash. "Come on, Ashton, sweetheart, for old times' sake," she said when he pulled away.

"Hey there, sister, hands of my man."

"Come here, we can share him," she said, and Ash jumped back, and all but ran back into the house.

"Oh, that was fun," she said, when the door slammed behind him.

"You are so bad, not that he doesn't deserve it, but still..."

She pulled me back into a hug. "I'm glad you got back together. I miss you so much, and I'm also glad you got me to come home. I needed it," she said, flashing a glimpse of conflicted emotions she hadn't shown me until now.

Typical Jen. She was a closed book, and didn't share much when things bothered her. It was also infuriating as her friend to know she was hurting, and didn't just reach out.

"So, what have you neglected to tell me that's just comin' up now?"

She quickly masked her face again, and shrugged. "Just hard to see you cuddled up with Ash and all. I never thought I wanted to settle down, but... well, you two have made me start thinking domestically. Damn you, Todd!"

I laughed. "You'll get over it when you get back to Paris, or London... or wherever you are, and all the sexy men start flirting with you again."

She brightened up. "Hey, you're right."

With that, she kissed my cheek again, then jumped into the rental car her dad insisted on getting her while she was here. Waving at me and throwing kisses, she drove off. Damn, I really was gonna miss her.

THIRTY

ASH

So, TO SAY I was overwhelmed being in the middle of Todd and Jennifer was the understatement of the century. Knowing they were friends because of me, because they'd both hated me at one time, was even stranger.

Despite that, they both made me feel comfortable, not saying they didn't harass me, which honestly, I couldn't really blame them, but it wasn't hurtful.

At one point, Jennifer began talking about the *Ash bashes*. "I'm afraid to ask," I said, but I should've left well-enough alone.

Jennifer let out a wicked laugh, and said, "How many Ashes does it take to stop a hurricane?"

I shook my head and Todd smiled, matching the naughty grin on Jennifer's face. "None, they don't stick around long enough to do much of anything."

After the fourth one, something about "Ashes" and lye soap, I put my hands up in surrender. "Okay, okay, I give up. I was an asshole teenager."

Jennifer put her arm around Todd, and with matching grins, they both responded, "Yep."

By the time she left, I'd gotten as attached to her as I'd been before she and I had dated. Besides Todd, Jennifer had been one of my best friends. Smart, sassy and full of attitude. When Todd came into the house after she'd driven off, I saw the sadness in his expression.

"She really is amazing."

"Yeah, but not enough for you to leave me for her again."

I laughed. "She was my first and last girlfriend. I don't think you have much to worry about. Besides, I'm too small-town for the likes of Jennifer Cole, supermodel."

"I don't know. She has shit taste in men."

"Hey," I said and elbowed him in the side. He gave me a cocked eyebrow, and said, "Sorry, it's true. You were the first of many bad choices."

"It was probably true," I said, acknowledging his statement. "She did date a gay guy who could hardly stand to kiss her, much less do anything about all her yucky bases."

The sheriff pulled up in front of the house a few minutes later and got out of her SUV. Todd went out to meet her with me on his heels.

"Howdy, Sheriff," Todd said, and she smiled at him.

"Got some info on that graffiti," she said.

"What graffiti?" I asked, and Todd looked around at me.

"Dad's hardware store got tagged a couple nights ago."

"What did it say?" I asked.

"Some typical homophobic crap. It's fine."

"Well, maybe. Maybe not. Have you heard of a man by the name of Warren Jacobs?" the sheriff asked.

Todd nodded. "Warren *used* to work for me."

"I got a call yesterday from a preacher in McMinnville saying Warren stopped by his church and was ranting and raving about all the homosexuals in this town of sinners."

"I see. I'm kinda surprised a preacher called you about it."

"Well, that preacher is on probation for threatening to shoot up a clinic over in Bates County a few years back. They were one of the federally funded clinics, and he got it in his head they were doing abortions on every woman who walked in there. Anyway, he was arrested before he did something really stupid, and spent a few months in jail. The feds agreed not to prosecute him, even though he was threatening to attack a federal institution if he abided by his probation. When this Jacobs fella came in threatening to do all sorts of stuff, he got scared and talked to his probation officer, who forced him to call me."

"Well, still it's unusual for one of the wingnut preachers we got around here to call, but I'm glad. Warren has a few loose screws. I inherited him from my company's predecessor. He decided he didn't have to comply with my rules, or work where I told him to, so I fired him. Been awhile since I did, though."

"Has he given your team any grief?" she asked.

Todd shook his head. "Not as far as I know. I'll call my assistant, and Linc, my second in command, though, and find out."

"I'd appreciate that. Meanwhile, until I can meet with Jacobs and find out his angle, I'll tell you to keep a close eye out. He's probably full of hot air, but you don't ever know," she said.

Todd nodded. "I'm not too concerned about him, he's always been more bark than bite, but we can both guess he was the one behind the window spraying."

"Can't say without evidence, but he's a person of interest."

"Dang, Sheriff Cross," I said. "Look at you getting all *Blue Bloods*."

She just chuckled. "Well, if Marky Mark wants to come strut his sexy stuff around Crawford City, I ain't gonna say no."

"No doubt," I said, laughing at how quickly she turned the comment back to Mark Wahlberg's early hip-hop days as part of Marky Mark and the Funky Bunch. I was well-versed in the hottie's career since Dad had been a longtime fan of his, which had been weird growing up, since he didn't really follow pop culture. Guess it made total sense now. Mark Wahlberg did have a similar build to Amos. When I turned toward Todd, he was looking at me through narrowed eyes. "What?" I asked.

"Marky Mark can come do his *Boogie Nights* thing, and you better not even look. You know, now that I think about it, my dad loves that movie and I never understood why till this very moment," he said with a knowing smirk. "And you forget Jen just left, right? I can call her, and she'll be back here in less time than it'd take to make the call."

"I won't even pull her over for speeding either," Sheriff Cross said.

I just pouted. "I wouldn't touch, but you gotta admit, he's pretty hot."

Todd just leaned toward me, and said, "Well, you can peek, but that's it." Then, he gave me a nice kiss, right in front of the sheriff.

"Well, my work here is done," she said, and chuckled as she got in her car and left.

"I've missed those lips," I said when he whisked me into the house, and kissed me again for good measure.

"I'm glad, but I figured we better not do much kissing with Jen just getting used to us being a couple again."

"Oh, no doubt. I didn't want her to give me the butt-kicking she's been threatening since I broke up with her."

"You have no idea how close you came to that either."

"Don't remind me, but do kiss me again. Please?"

Thirty-One

Todd

A SH GOT CALLED BACK into work that afternoon, even though it was officially his day off. Apparently, Dr. Gib had to go pick up his niece from school.

I went to the dads' place and told them what the sheriff had said about Warren.

"That the idiot who was supposed to show up here after you fell off the roof?"

"That'd be him."

"Well, at least you know who the culprit is. I'll be honest, I know we got some folks in Crawford City that still don't like gay men, but they don't strike me as the type to cause any real damage. They are certainly not the type to go tagging the old hardware store," Dad reasoned.

"Sheriff Cross wasn't sure it was him or not, but I hope you're right, Dad. If I move all my equipment down here,

I can't afford there to be some idiot who'll get in there and create real damage."

"You're gonna be bringing jobs back to this area that's been lost since your dad retired and the hardware store closed down. These backwoods idiots might not like us being gay, but they won't have the nerve to do anything to harm your stuff," Doc said.

"I hope not, but I think I'll leave my stuff up in Nashville for a few more weeks till we know for sure. That place is tight as Fort Knox, and all the locks and security codes have been changed since Warren was fired."

"That makes me think, how did Warren know you were looking at moving into my building?" Dad asked.

"Good question. I'm not sure, but if I were to guess, one of the men who used to work with him probably told him we're selling the Nashville property and moving here. I've been letting the teams know, so if I lose any of them, I can replace them before the move is final."

"Good plan," Dad said. "But, before you move, you'll wanna try to flush out the snake in the grass, especially if this Warren fella is gonna be causing any more troubles."

I agreed with my father, and that afternoon, I called Linc and asked him who he thought might be giving Warren inside information. There was a list of about five people who'd probably be happy to rat us out. Of course, all of them were with the company under the previous owner, and none of them were happy about my ownership.

"Have any of them given their resignation yet?" I asked.

"Nah, I doubt they will. When we move, I'm just assuming they'll stop showing up."

"Sounds about right," I said. "Meanwhile, why don't you begin the process of replacing them? They might not have told Warren about where we're moving to, but if they're likely to leave us in the lurch, I'd rather be prepared, so it doesn't screw up a project's timelines."

"On it, boss," he said cheerfully, causing me to laugh.

"You love calling me boss, don't you?"

"Well, you've always been bossy," he said. Linc used to fuss at me for being a bossy bottom when we worked together before I took on ownership. Now, he left the bottom part off when he called me boss. However, I knew he didn't leave it out to be respectful, just less forward.

I touched base with my assistant, Jacklyn, but she said she hadn't heard from Warren or his crew since I'd let them go. I even checked with Ed, the attorney, but there was nothing going on with any of them. Maybe this was just a one-off, and now that Warren had gotten it out of his system, he'd move on and leave me in peace. I could hope, at least.

Thirty-Two

Ash

I HAD SATURDAY OFF, but I'd come in to make sure the nurse practitioner, Rachel, didn't need help, since Dr. Gib had scheduled to leave early to finalize the sale on the Cross Sisters' house. Todd was hanging out at my place, basically moving back in with me after Jennifer left, and I was excited to spend the afternoon with him.

Gib was sitting in his office when I arrived. "Hey," Gib said. "Does your boyfriend, Todd, do repair work? We'd like to get some renovations done before we move into the house officially."

"Yeah, he owns a construction company. He's just next door. Want me to ask if he can pop by to chat with you?"

"That'd be great. The Cross house is beautiful, but the nineteen-sixties lime-green kitchen might need to be replaced sooner rather than later."

I texted Todd, who agreed to talk to Gib about renovating the Cross house, but needed a few minutes to make himself presentable before coming over. The vision of him comfortably lounging around my house still in his pajamas made me smile.

By the time Todd arrived, the waiting room was empty, and Rachel waved me off, saying she could handle it.

The Cross house was just as I remembered it. Tall and stately on the outside, full of old Victorian furniture on the inside. "Do you know anyone who'd be interested in all this stuff? Gib asked Todd when we walked in.

"Well," he replied nodding. "I've been thinking about buying one of the local buildings that's endangered, and turning it into a historical museum and bed and breakfast," Todd said. "I'm going to donate most of the historical furniture from my home. Would you be interested in donating your furnishings as well?"

"Yes," Gib said, causing Todd to chuckle.

"Okay, I'll talk to Dad and Doc about where we can store all this while we're in the process of negotiating the purchase of the property."

Gib's husband ended up showing up right after that conversation, and expressed interest in the Mercantile deal with Todd. I didn't stick around for that conversation, going out onto the big open-front porch. Todd seemed to be taking on so much at one time, and I didn't want to get too involved and cause him to back out because I was being too pushy about things.

We left Gib at his new home and drove back to the clinic. As we pulled up, I saw a bunch of signs in the front yard. "What the hell?" I asked. As we got closer, I could read the signs, and my heart dropped into my stomach. *"God hates fags," "Leviticus 18:22,"* and several others.

I got out of the vehicle and was about to pull them up and start a burn pile when Todd stopped me. "No, I think this is an ex-employee of mine. Let me get pictures and give the sheriff a call, in case she wants to see for herself."

"If it's one of your old employees, why is he tagging my clinic? I don't want this stuff out here intimidating my patients," I said, and Todd nodded.

"At least give the sheriff a call first."

Luckily, Sheriff Cross was able to take Todd's pictures as evidence, and let us pull up the signs before taking them too. Rachel had been with patients, so she didn't see who'd put them out, and we didn't have security cameras. One of the neighbors said she'd seen some older woman, who appeared to be in her mid-seventies, putting the signs out. She'd never seen the woman before, and was sure she wasn't from Crawford City.

Sheriff Cross told Todd she believed his former employee had found support, and told us she would continue to investigate him. "Until we know for sure it's him, or people he's recruited for his hateful agenda, you can't do much about it, but if we could catch them red-handed, that'd certainly help."

"Unless he gets violent," I said.

"There's no indication he would. The only thing that's been done is tagging your property, but not in a way that couldn't be easily fixed, and putting signs out in your yard. Both are technically illegal, but neither carry much of a penalty."

Todd looked concerned. "I'm going to have to delay selling my property in Nashville, and maybe have to give up moving it here altogether, if we're gonna be at war with the wingnuts."

"I'm glad the doctor I hired didn't see this. If he thinks this is a prejudiced town, we could lose him. Sheriff, we need to figure out if this is outside or inside influences, because Crawford City has a lot to lose if this gets ugly."

She nodded. "Just don't anyone make any assumptions. Our little town has come a long way in the past few years. I know we still have a few who think like this, but most people are good folks and won't tolerate the hatred. Give me a chance to chase down my leads, and see what we can learn before y'all start getting chased away."

I couldn't blame her. I was the only doctor for miles around, and it was pure luck that I was able to attract Dr. Gib to my clinic. Todd's business would bring financial stability to Crawford City, and they didn't even know about his thoughts to fix up the mercantile building. That alone could increase the commercial businesses downtown by a third or more.

THIRTY-THREE

TODD

THE REST OF THE week went by without incident. Leslie did another x-ray of my foot after Ash demanded I come in, then Dr. Gib gave me a once over, saying I was good to go without the boot, as long as I promised not to jump off any more roofs.

"Everyone around here thinks they're funny," I said, but I'd already decided I liked Dr. Gib. As I sat grumbling about wasting my time in a freaking doctor's office, I realized how good the two doctors were together. They really did make a great team. When you threw in their highly capable nurse practitioner, Rachel, you couldn't have asked for a better group of people to keep Crawford City healthy.

I tried driving the day I got the boot off, and managed to get a nice cramp halfway between Ash's place and the dads'.

When I asked Ash about it, he shrugged. "You're gonna have to use it a while before it'll be flexible enough to drive with."

"You're cramping my style, Doctor Nash."

"Not me," he said smugly. "I didn't push you off the roof... although I've thought of doin' just that a couple times."

"Hey," I said, and began trying to tickle him, although he still wasn't ticklish. *Damn,* I thought, *Life isn't fair!*

Despite the hateful tagging and signs at the clinic, and even though I worried I was moving too fast, I decided to officially put in my bid for the mercantile building. I had old Tom draw up a rough sketch of my concept for the building, including an add-on to both sides to replace the old storefronts that'd long ago fallen in or burned. Although there were several vacant buildings downtown, this new edition would bring our downtown area back almost to the place it'd been in its heyday—long before I was born. I could also add several more rooms to the bed and breakfast, or as Tom called it, the boutique hotel.

I already had three people interested in moving into the shops, which would help when I went for a loan.

Of course, I had the mayor to get past. He, Doc, and Dad had gone to school together, and they were *not* friends. Mayor Thornburg lived up to his name and was a thorn in all our sides. Despite that, I believed the improvements this project would make to our little town would outweigh the mayor's objections, which were only based on his petty dislike of us.

⚘

Two weeks passed since we'd last been hit by the bigot squad, and we hadn't really heard much more. The sheriff had told me she was keeping her ear to the rails, so to speak, ensuring that if any talk was going on, she'd know. She kept assuring me that no one really supported them.

So, when Jake brought me an offer for the Nashville property, almost a third more than I thought I'd get, I went ahead and let the property go. I had one month to empty the entire place. One freaking month to move over sixty years of accumulated stuff.

Oh, well, no time like the present. Thank God I didn't have to wear that boot at least.

"Dad," I said, walking into his house after I got off the phone with Jake. "So, the property is under contract in Nashville, and the deal is good, real good, but I have to be out in a month. Do you have enough people in your magic contractor bag to help get all our stuff moved from there to here?"

He nodded. "I'm guessing there's a lot there."

"Imagine what you think, then add four times more."

"Dang! Well, we should probably go down and decide what can be sold or gotten rid of before we move it here."

"Agreed, I already thought I could get rid of a lot of it, but, Dad, I have a lot of great building equipment, some old, but most of it useful still. I also have a ton of building supplies left over from decades of work. I can't imagine parting with it. Heck, I can use most of it to renovate my house and the mercantile."

He thought on it for a bit, before he hollered to Doc, "Hey, Emanual, do you still have the number of the kid in Lebanon who started that moving business?"

"Yeah," he called back. "We were gonna use him to move all your stuff before we knew Todd was comin' back."

I cocked an eyebrow as Doc walked into the living room. "Oh, hey, Todd. Didn't know you were here."

I nodded. Clearly, he didn't, since I hadn't known they had plans for Dad's stuff had I not come back.

Dad turned to me. "So, that boy was involved in construction with his dad back in the day and knows all about moving equipment and such. I don't know what he'd charge, but I'd trust him, and he has good insurance too. If anything goes wrong, you'll be covered."

As Doc rummaged through papers to find the number, I set up a time for Dad and me to go to Nashville to go through my company's stuff before we had it hauled all the way out here.

After leaving there, I went back to the house, and just as I had the past couple of days, began taking inventory of things in the house to keep or move into storage, knowing I needed to so I could get my own renovations started. Ninety percent of the furniture was going into the mercantile building, but I still had to finish marking each piece, and pack all the odds and ends before hiring anyone to move it.

Dad had decided he wasn't going to reopen the hardware store right away, so luckily, I could put all the furniture from this home and the Cross sisters' house in there while I did the renovations. Linc and I had already gone to the hardware store and installed video surveillance, which provided additional coverage to the cameras Dad already had in place. Of course, we turned it all on this time. We also boarded up the windows knowing the furniture would be easily seen. It was old stuff, but it still had value, and I didn't want it stolen.

As I walked around the house tagging the various pieces of furniture, I kept thinking how incredible it was I was moving back to Crawford City, and that I wasn't upset about it. In fact, it felt like I was going back to how things were supposed to be, moving back home physically and metaphorically. That's what shocked me.

I also made it my mission to romance Ash. He and I had been apart for a lot longer than we'd been together. There were a lot of rough edges to smooth out if we were going to make it as a couple. I'd meet him with a picnic, or force him to get up extra early to go eat breakfast with me. All ways to get to know him better.

When he came home tired after a long day of seeing patients, I'd try to have something ready for him to eat. He seldom felt like going to the diner for supper, so I tried to cook, which I wasn't that great at, or if I ate with Dad and Doc, I'd bring something back for him. Either way, I'd keep him fed and happy.

I loved doting on him, making sure he felt relaxed and rested, and when he curled up next to me on the sofa,

I'd give him a nice shoulder rub. I loved that we kissed when he got home. I loved him... loved *us*.

So far, we hadn't done much of anything else to show affection. He still seemed leery of going too far too soon. We'd push things to a point, then back down. I wanted to do a lot more, I was *ready* to do a lot more. In fact, I fantasized about it almost daily, but I was afraid of hurting him, and fear had its own sort of power.

Thirty-Four

Ash

I WAS DONE PRETENDING to be virtuous. *Done*, I'd tell you. It took everything in me not to crawl up on Todd and take him all the way, especially with him being so sweet to me all the time.

Coming home to a man who loved me was worth all the gold in the world, though, so if taking it slow and easy was what I had to do, it was what I'd do.

We were both busy, though. That helped some. Most nights I came home and crashed on the sofa, exhausted from work. Gib was still waiting to get all the insurance companies on board before he could see a full load of patients, so Rachel and I were still doing most of the work.

Todd was working all the time too. Most nights, though, he made a special trip back to my house to be there when I got home. Lately, it was just to put supper together before he ended up going back to organize things in the new workshop, or manage his own home renovation.

Next week he was going to start his first job here in town with the Cross house renovation for Gib. Luckily, Amos was leading the charge on that, so Todd could spend more energy managing his company's move from Nashville to here.

On the weekends, when I wasn't on-call, I'd volunteer to help him. To be honest, I had no idea how he was going to manage all the stuff he was trying to organize.

We were done moving a load of wallboard from Nashville, when Amos called and asked him to stop by his home. I hadn't been back there since they'd moved all the furniture to the hardware store. Seeing the place empty for the first time in my life caused my stomach to do funny things.

"You okay?" Dad asked me when he saw my reaction.

"It's gut-wrenching to see the old girl empty after all these years."

He smiled. "Yeah, I thought the same thing, but if you hang out for a moment, it's almost like she's anticipating the changes. Almost like the old house is alive."

I waited a moment, and when I didn't feel the same, I figured the excitement was in him.

I heard Amos talking to Todd in the other room, and followed their voices. "If you remove the building entirely, you'll have the town down on you, and Mayor Thornburg being an ass. I'm gonna tell you right now, they won't approve the teardown, not completely."

"What do you propose?" Todd asked.

As I listened to Amos explain how they could gut the mercantile building, while leaving the basic structure, they could almost do the same without having to get approval from the city for new construction.

"So, Thornburg is givin' you grief about the permit?" I asked, concerned.

"Yes, since we got him and his jerk cronies overruled on the mercantile building sale, he's been kicking up a fuss about the house renovation," Todd said.

The city council meeting to discuss Todd's proposal to purchase the building from the city had been tense. The mayor had actively campaigned against it, pushing some lame idea of tearing the building down, and having a Walmart come in. When we pressed about Walmart's interest, he had to admit no one had even discussed it with them. It was clear to everyone this was the same vendetta he'd had against Amos and Dad, and therefore Todd and me, since they were kids.

"Instead of that, why don't you fight him at his own game? You know, this is an election year."

Todd looked at me funny. "What's your point?" he asked.

I looked at Amos and Dad, and said, "Well, it seems to me I know two men who are well-respected by almost everyone in this town who would both be great options for mayor, not to mention much better options than Thornburg."

Dad smiled and Amos cringed. "I'd rather go back to school to be an architect like Todd suggested than be a politician."

"Well," I said, chuckling, "I know someone who's had his eyes on that job for a while, though."

Dad blushed. Amos looked at him, and sighed, "You're wanting to run for mayor, are you?"

"Well, I've thought about it," Dad admitted.

"It would solve a lot of problems here, not to mention keeping you out of my hair all the time."

Dad smiled, and I figured this must've been an argument the two had been having.

"I'll talk it over with Amos," Dad said, and winked at me before grabbing Amos up into a big bear hug, and kissing him on the lips. "But, if my honey isn't on board, I'll have to decline. Nothing is more important to me than this incredible man."

Amos all but blushed in my dad's arms, and I had to struggle not to say *aah* as I watched my two fathers cuddling like newlyweds.

The mayor position in this little town was far from full-time, and the pay was a pittance, but with the recent growth, we needed a good one. Unfortunately, that wasn't Thornburg, who was petty and vindictive, not just with us, but with anyone who dared stand up to him. We all knew he wanted the position to push his overblown ego around town.

"So, you know—" I said, drawing attention away from the two dads, "—this town has some big decisions comin' up that will definitely need a strong mind and steady hand to lead it. If Thornburg has his way, we'll lose our small-town charm, and be like all the other towns around us, lost to progress with no respect to the townspeople, or its character."

Dad looked over at me and smiled, but didn't respond. I figured by how Amos was acting, they'd already decided Dad would be running, but maybe only if Thornburg and his city council cronies kept giving Todd a hard time.

To test the waters, Amos and Todd decided to submit the plans as they'd been drawn out by the architect, and see what happened.

"What's the prognosis on the approval for the mercantile?" I asked one night after getting back late from work.

Todd shrugged. "Dead in the water, at least at the moment."

"You gonna fight it?" I asked, stuffing my face with food he'd brought back from Dad's.

"I'm pretty sure I could win in court over it, especially since they've approved a variety of projects exactly like this one, but it'd be better for all of us if I could avoid a legal battle. What I really need is the town on our side if I'm gonna be successful with this long-term."

I couldn't help but agree. As much as progress was needed, and even wanted among the majority in Crawford, if any lawsuits were filed, they'd take that personally. Such were the ways of our little town.

Todd somehow managed to get everything moved from Nashville. Unfortunately, his proposal and building permits for his home had been denied, as we'd worried would happen. The mercantile sale had also been halted. With that, Dad officially announced his bid for mayor, causing quite the stink in town.

The town pretended to be aghast, but the truth was they were having more fun with this than they'd had with any local political race in over a century. Even though there were a few families against Dad winning a place on council, because of his relationship with Amos, most seemed to support him.

A couple of weeks into the campaign, Mayor Thornburg was overruled by the council, and the sale of the old mercantile building to Todd's company was completed. That was a big win for Dad. Of course, since the mayor basically controlled zoning and codes, no movement had been made on Todd's permits. To be honest, I didn't mind that too much, since the longer it took to get his home renovation done, the longer Todd stayed at my place.

Todd eventually had to give up, knowing he wouldn't get the work done in time to save his pipes from winter's grip. He winterized the old home and boarded it up to keep the windows safe from any potential vandalism. We were probably a bit more cautious these days after the bigot scare back in September, not to mention, the sheriff hadn't made any progress on finding out who had done it. The old house's windows had survived over a hundred and fifty years, and an idiot's temper tantrum wasn't worth losing them now.

Lisa flew back to help Dad campaign the week before the election, which was a good thing, since Thornburg had launched an all-out hate and mudslinging campaign against Dad, and all of us, for that matter.

"Doc Nash is a pervert, of epic proportions," Thornburg said early on to a local newspaper reporter. "Anyone who'd flaunt his deviant lifestyle should know better than to try to run for public office."

Frank, Lisa's husband, wanted to have an attorney contact Thornburg and threaten him with slander, but Dad just laughed, and said, "You gotta understand Tennessee politics. You don't go to court against an idiot, you let him step in his own poo, then point it out to everyone when he does."

I had no idea Dad was such an amazing politician, because he was right. Thornburg would make some sort of slanderous remark, and Dad would basically make an offhanded comment to counter it, often about how he was accusing him of stuff he'd done himself.

As a result of Dad's crafty tactics, the election was a landslide. Thornburg just wasn't popular, and Dad had been the town doctor for years, often giving his services away for free when people couldn't afford them. He was a beloved figure in our town, and it showed at the polls. Thornburg proved little competition.

Miraculously, even though Dad didn't take over as mayor until January, approval for both of Todd's projects went through the following week.

Todd immediately launched into the home renovation, since he said that was his biggest concern when it came to settling down in Crawford City. After seeing parts of it gutted, I decided I'd need to stay away until the old girl got her clothes back on. It just hurt too much to see all that history being ripped apart, even if it was my ideas that were being implemented.

Todd teased me, but was supportive as well. After seeing the crews start the demolition on the first day, he took me to the dads' house, and we snuggled on the sofa, while Dad served us both a shot of brandy.

"It's finally happening, boy," he said gleefully, lifting his glass in a toast.

Todd smiled and lifted his glass. "Thanks to you, Mayor Nash."

Dad cringed. "That's gonna take some getting used to."

Amos took his hand and kissed it. "I'm so excited for him, but I don't think he thought he'd win."

"There are a lot of changes comin'. I think most of the townsfolk were just relieved we had someone running who had a level head on his shoulders, someone they could all trust," Todd said.

"Have you spoken to Thornburg?" I asked Dad.

"No, the man refuses to acknowledge me, like I did something to him personally. I purposefully never said a negative thing about him, unless he was tossing mud at me. Even then, I only stated what the public already knew to be true. Trust me, I knew a lot more about the man than I shared."

"Dad," I said, and he shook his head.

"No, not from a medical perspective. He was never my patient. He always refused to see me as a doctor, which was fine with me. No, Jane and one of his ex-wives grew up together, and when they'd divorced, she came here telling Jane some of the things that man had done. It wasn't like he hit her or anything like that, but he wasn't a good husband, let's just put it that way."

"I think you could've said what you knew. He's had six wives, and the latest one just filed for divorce herself. It's not like we all didn't know already."

Dad sighed. "I wanna change the subject. Let's get back to celebrating the work on the Thompson house."

"Hear, hear," I said, and all four of us lifted our glasses to the sky.

Thirty-Five

Todd

IF I THOUGHT THINGS had been crazy moving the business from Nashville to here, it was nothing in comparison to what it was like once we'd arrived.

Not unlike with the construction company, Jake had agreed to finance the mercantile building project without my asking. In fact, he wanted part ownership, which I was considering.

If Jake took on another quarter ownership, that would still leave me as majority owner, and it'd free up a lot of my money and time to focus on other projects, like my home.

"You're finally letting me be a business partner with you? I never thought I'd see the day," Jake said as he walked through the old building, surveying the areas we'd already looked at before.

"Well, it makes sense, especially since you have more money than sense!"

"Hey, that's no way to speak to your partner-to-be."

"Well, if you think I'm gonna talk to you different now, you misjudged who you were getting into bed with."

He chuckled. "I know exactly who I'm getting into bed with, and it's not you." He looked sheepish for a moment, then admitted, "It's not been anyone lately. That sucks, you know?"

I laughed. "I thought you had a different man on your arm every night. What happened? Is the playboy finally getting too old to put out?"

"*No*. Damn, man, don't say such things, you're gonna curse me," he sighed, and plopped down on a dusty concrete pillar with no regard to his fancy slacks. "I'm tired of running around. I need to find a proper man and settle down, like you and the kinky stepbrother."

"Stop calling him that," I said, laughing in spite of myself. "What's brought all this on?"

He sighed. "I'm gonna be thirty, I never even thought about what that'd mean, but for some reason, it's sorta knocked me around a bit. I've been really successful in my career, know a lot of good people, have amazing friends, but I'm not complete. I feel uprooted. Does that make sense?" he asked.

I scooted over and sat on the pillar next to him. "Yeah, I didn't think I'd ever settle down, but mostly 'cause I didn't think I'd ever be with Ash again. Till we began to date again, I hadn't... I didn't feel... well, like you said, something was incomplete."

He smiled at me and nudged my shoulder. "So, when you two gonna tie the knot?"

"Probably when we get over this huge hump in the road."

Jake cocked an eyebrow at me. "What huge hump in the road?"

"Sex."

He looked at me funny. "It ain't good in the sack?"

"Don't know. Haven't been in the sack... at least, not since we were kids."

"What?" he asked, jumping up and looking at me in disbelief. "You and he haven't done it? You're freakin' livin' together!"

"I know, shut up. This is the most gossipy town on the planet. You don't need to announce my private information to the freakin' world."

"Sorry, but you can't drop that kind of information on a man and expect him to let it go without reacting to it. We're men, and gay men on top of that. Are you not into him?"

I laughed. Of course, my most randy friend would be all weird about my no-sex life. In retrospect, maybe he wasn't the one to discuss it with.

"Just 'cause we're gay, doesn't mean we're sluts."

"Since when?" Jake asked, almost like he was offended.

"Since not everyone is the same. Dude, calm down, or I'll go to Jen about all this."

He sighed and plopped back down next to me. "Okay, I'll try not to be dramatic, but tell me, if you want him like you seem to, why haven't you rounded the bases?"

"'Cause, I think he's afraid if we do he'll lose me."

"And you, are you afraid?"

I shrugged. "Yeah, maybe." And there it was—the truth.

Jake put his arm around me and pulled me close. "Listen, sex is sex. It doesn't have to mean anything, and I know you know that, but if you're in love with this man, sex could mean everything. Even a slut like me knows that. I recommend you take him out of town. Frankly, you're both too tied down here. Wine and dine the crap out of him, then y'all stay at a fancy hotel downtown, and get naked between the sheets. I'm gonna tell you right now, the longer you put it off, the less fun you're gonna have. You're two guys, for God's sake, just have some fun with it, and let the emotions land where they land."

I leaned into my friend and sighed. "I know you're right. I guess I just needed someone to say it. Okay." I turned to him smiling. "Help me figure out how to wine and dine him."

Now that the dating conversation was a go, Jake had forgotten all about the investment. That was fine, since Ed, the attorney, would handle all the details, and Jake would, as he always did, lean on me for the major decisions. Word of our little project had already begun to sweep through Jake's friends, and since a lot of them were famous country-music singers, I had no doubt his investment would ensure its success.

As the holiday season descended upon us, I was determined to get that fancy evening planned and take my man to Nashville, when the town got hit by the flu.

First, I got it, then Doc and Dad. Finally, it got Gib, then Rachel. Somehow Ash had managed to avoid catching it, which meant he was working overtime trying to get the town through the worst of it.

Lisa postponed her trip back to Tennessee, afraid the flu would harm her unborn babies, which meant Christmas this year was spent without the whole family together. We were all still managing the last of the symptoms when Christmas Day arrived, so we forwent the big meal, and settled for takeout from a grocery store in Lebanon.

We all agreed to put off our official Christmas celebration until mid-January, over the long Martin Luther King Jr. holiday weekend, which meant Frank would have time off and could join Lisa in visiting us. Of course, that was just a few weeks before Lisa's due date, meaning she would be heavily pregnant. Regardless, she said she'd rather be overly pregnant and spend time with her family, than not get to see us while managing two newborns.

On Christmas night, after we got home, I pulled Ash onto the sofa with me and confessed I was going to wine and dine him, so I could get him naked in a hotel bed. His surprised expression morphed into one of relief, and he sighed, "I thought maybe you didn't want to."

I crawled on top of him, pushing him further down into the sofa. "Dude, it's all I can do not to. Why the hell would you think I didn't want to?"

He looked shy all of a sudden, which was cute as hell. "I-I don't know."

I leaned down and began nibbling on his neck. "I want you so bad, I can feel it in my bones," I admitted.

"Mmm," he moaned. "I want you too."

"God, why have we waited so long?" I asked, but when I leaned back, I understood. Tears slipped out of Ash's eyes, and along his cheeks.

I crawled off him and sat on the edge of the sofa, concern wafting over me. "I'm fuckin' it all up again, aren't I?" Ash asked.

"No, baby. I just need to know what you want... what you need," I said, stroking his hair.

"I need you, and I don't wanna chase you away."

"Why do you think you'll chase me away?" I asked. We'd become as close to lovers as one could over the past few months without having sex, so I didn't understand his hesitance.

"I..." Tears streamed down his face now, and he sat up with his back against the armrest. "I can't do casual, Todd. I'm too invested in you. If you and I go all the way and you decide to leave, it'll be the end of me. I just know it."

I scooted over and pulled him into my arms. "I'm not going anywhere, Ash. I don't wanna be anywhere but with you." I pulled back just enough to make eye contact with him. "With or without sex, I just want you. Can't you see that by now?"

He shook his head. "No. All I can see is me pushing you away, and you leavin' me."

I could hear the *again,* even though he didn't say it.

"Okay, I'll tell you what. Let's make a plan... especially since I know how much you like those." That earned me a smile from him.

I went into the kitchen and turned his kettle on, fixing us both a mug of hot chocolate as I spoke.

"Let's set up some milestones. Those'll help us as we move this relationship further and it'll help me know how far to take things, while you're learning to trust that we're a long-term thing."

He came into the kitchen and wrapped his arms around me from behind, holding on tight.

"I love that idea, probably as much as I know you hate it."

I chuckled. "No, if it'll make you happy, I love it too."

I turned to him and let him snuggle into me. "God, I love you so much, Ash. I don't really even know how to tell you how much just having you with me feeds my soul. These past few months have been like balm on a gaping, festering wound. If you need time and milestones... then by God, you'll get them."

That night, we slept together for the first time, not in the bed as that would have been too much, and I wasn't at all sure I wouldn't have tried pushing things too far if we had shared his bed.

Instead, we pulled his sofa out into a bed, and cuddled together all night.

Falling asleep with Ash in my arms wasn't the only first of the night... I also had my first wet dream in over a decade. All the things I wanted to do with Ash in real life were being acted out in my subconscious, and damn, if it wasn't absolutely amazing. Not surprisingly, I woke up with a raging hard-on for the first time in I didn't know how long, and it hadn't been missed by my bedmate.

Thirty-Six

Ash

I WAS BEING RIDICULOUS. Hell, I knew it, but still, I didn't seem to have the power to stop it. Everything in me put the skids on when it came to being sexual with Todd. I wasn't lying when I told him if we went all the way and he left me that I'd be done for. For me, not taking things to the next level was self-preservation, even if it was as frustrating to me as it likely was to him.

Of course, if I allowed myself to admit it, the issue really was that I didn't trust Todd, not entirely. Even though we'd forgiven each other, even though we'd allowed ourselves to be intimate without sex, I still hadn't been able to give myself to him completely.

The week of New Year's was quiet at the clinic. Most of the town had either already had the flu, or didn't feel the need to see me about it. The frequent fliers were all still overcoming the holidays, so the usual rush wasn't there.

Todd's work had calmed too. Although they were still building, the cold, wet weather had held up most of the projects. Really, the only work going on was on the house and the mercantile building.

What it translated to was he and I spending copious amounts of time together, either hanging out at my place, or with our dads.

Dad was scheduled to take over mayoral duties the following Monday, so with Lisa and Frank on video chat, we had a big celebration on Saturday. Amos even baked a cake for the occasion, which floored Todd, since he was sure his father didn't have the skill.

We played virtual poker with Lisa and Frank until she lost all her money, and after having to go pee for the third time, she said, "I'm going to bed, and might not get up until these two monsters are born."

"Take it easy, sweetheart," Doc told her, and blew a kiss toward the screen in his very pregnant daughter's direction. She'd had a few complications with the pregnancy, because she was so freaking small, and my niece and nephew weren't in the least bit small from what I could tell from seeing her on the video feed.

When she and Frank hung up, I asked Dad, "So, do you think she's gonna deliver early?" Knowing he had a lot more experience delivering babies than I ever would.

"Possibly, she's riding pretty low for a month out." Premature birth wasn't uncommon with multiples, and I knew her obstetrician was keeping close tabs on her.

Despite that, I wished for the thousandth time she was closer, so Dad and I could keep a close eye on her ourselves.

Todd and I had been sleeping together every night on my pull-out sofa bed. I knew it was silly, but it seemed like a safe place to let things progress. We'd fooled around a bit, never going too far. The more we did, though, the more I wanted to just let go, and let whatever happened, happen.

We were both asleep Sunday night when Todd got a phone call. He ignored it since it was two in the morning, but when my phone began ringing, I looked and saw it was the sheriff.

"Hello?" I asked drowsily.

"Hi, this is Sheriff Cross. Is Todd with you?"

"Um, yeah, Sheriff. Why, what's up?"

"Can you put me on speaker? It's urgent."

I did as she asked, and Todd, who was fully awake by then, answered, "Hey, what's up, Sheriff?"

"Todd, I need you to come down to the mercantile building. It's on fire!"

"*What?*" he yelled, and jumped out of bed. "I'll be right there!"

We both dressed quickly, and I rode with him. We could see the flames as we sped toward town.

In the few minutes it took us to get there, the entire building was engulfed in flames, and it appeared as if it might catch the rest of downtown on fire.

It looked like every Crawford City firefighter was on the scene, and they weren't having much luck getting the fire under control. We piled out of the truck and were quickly met by the sheriff. "What happened?" Todd asked, his face registering his panic.

She shook her head. "We aren't sure, Todd, but it looks like it could've been arson."

"Fuck, why do you think that?"

She pointed toward a gas can that lay just a few feet from the entrance of the building.

"Damn, oh shit, has anyone gone to check on my other buildings?"

She nodded. "Yeah, there's a deputy at your home and the old hardware store. There's no evidence anyone's done anything there."

"Fuck," he said again. "I'm not sure why..." He stopped talking then and looked at me, then at the sheriff. "Have you spoken to Thornburg?"

She shook her head. "No, he wasn't home, and his soon-to-be ex-wife said he hadn't been there in over a week."

"You know he's probably who did this," Todd said over the noise.

She nodded sadly. "We'll have to investigate, of course, but he's a person of interest."

Just then, Lebanon's fire crew showed up, and it appeared like it was just in time as a tree behind the old drugstore was beginning to smolder. If it went, it could catch the main buildings on fire as well.

With their help and a couple of other neighboring fire departments, the fire was finally contained, but nothing was left of the mercantile. I could see the impact of the loss on Todd, though he didn't actually say much. It was like someone had kicked the life out of him.

He dealt with the fire's aftermath the following week. The insurance company was refusing to pay, because until an investigation proved otherwise, it could've been an arson attack led by one of the investors. Although no one had seen hide nor hair of Thornburg, or Todd's former employee, we were all confident one or both were behind all this.

Todd went back to sleeping in his own bed after that night. As concerned as I was about him, I didn't really say anything about it, knowing what kind of pressure he was under.

As the week progressed, he became more and more distant. "Todd," I told him right before Lisa and Frank were scheduled to arrive. "You need to talk to me, don't push me away."

He shook his head. "I'm sorry, Ash, I'm not able to handle all this right now. I think I need some space. Just for a little while as I navigate all that's happened. If people are trying to drive me out of town, they could ruin me. I mean, like, *I can't come back from this* ruin me."

"So, let me help," I said.

He looked at me for a long moment, and said, "Baby, you know how much I love you, but you don't trust me, not really. You keep me at arm's length. Right now, I don't have the energy to keep the boundaries in place and manage my own emotions. I'm not leavin', I promise, but I do need to be somewhere that I can just be... okay?"

I didn't see, and no, it wasn't okay.

I shook my head. "No, this is exactly what I thought would happen. You're leavin' me again, so just go. Run away, Todd. That's what you do."

I locked myself in my room while he gathered up what remained of his stuff and left. I knew I was making it easier for him, but damn, if he was leaving, I'd rather him be gone and be done with it. I'd rather be hurt than destroyed.

I kept saying to myself, "*At least you didn't go all the way,*" but I was lying to myself. Even if I'd held back physically, I'd gone all the way with my heart.

Thirty-Seven

Todd

WITH MY HOUSE ALL torn apart, I couldn't go there, so I packed my belongings and with my tail appropriately tucked between my legs, I went to the only place I could: The dads'.

They didn't ask for an explanation, and I didn't offer one. Instead, I let Dad lead me up to the third floor, a room Ash and I used to play in that was seldom used. I guessed they knew I needed my privacy, as much as they needed theirs.

I stared at the ceiling for what felt like hours, before Dad knocked on my door and told me they had supper done.

"I'm not really hungry, Dad, but thanks."

He looked at me for a moment, then said, "I'm not gonna pry, but because you're my son, and I happen to know you tend to make the same kinds of mistakes I do,

I'm just gonna say, don't let things go too far before you work it out."

I looked at my dad through squinted eyes, and he shook his head and left, saying, "Stubborn," under his breath as he closed the door.

I dove into work after that, focusing on trying to save my business, and trying not to think about my wreck of a love life. Ed got the fire marshal's report, and sent it to the insurance company, which of course, they didn't want to accept. He warned me we'd possibly end up in court over it, and I resigned myself to that possible, if not inevitable, outcome.

I spent my days and most of my nights working on the house, determined to get enough done that I could at least move in while the new construction was completed. Hell, even if I could just move into the upstairs, although that wasn't really much of an option since the entire back of the house had been removed, and the only thing keeping the weather out was plastic.

Regardless, with the mercantile project dead in the water, and Dad and Linc working the other projects, I wasn't really needed for much more than to work here and work hard.

Lisa and Frank showed up on Friday, and that night I was faced with Ash for the first time since our fight. I resolved to keep my distance and be civil, if not detached. It appeared Ash had decided the same, and although there was a distinct chill in the air that night, it wasn't horrible.

Lisa kept looking between us, but luckily, her being at the end of her pregnancy seemed to keep her occupied enough to save us from too much scrutiny.

I went to bed early, determined to avoid too much discomfort, and I looked out of the third-floor bedroom in time to see Ash leaving shortly after.

I was about to climb into bed when I got a knock at the door.

"Come in," I said, expecting to see Dad or Doc. Instead, in walked a very perturbed, very pregnant Lisa.

"So, what the hell?" she asked.

"Lisa, why did you walk up those steep stairs in your condition?"

Frank walked in behind her and waved before leaving just as quickly, shutting the door behind him.

"You and my brother are being stupid again, and I wanna know why."

I looked at her, and was about to tell her it wasn't any of her business, but the expression on her face was enough to make me reconsider.

"Lisa, it's nothing you can do anything about. We're just not meshing."

"Explain, and don't make me pull this from you. My god, it was bad enough I had to climb up here to do this. Do you have any idea what it's like to haul two squirming babies around with you all the time?"

I chuckled, but didn't dare respond to that question.

"I needed a little space, that's all. It's not Ash this time, it's all me." Judging by the frustrated look on her face,

I knew my half-assed explanation did little to convince her.

"And you couldn't get space when you were with the man you love, and who loves you?"

"No, not when he keeps me at arm's length." My irritation got the better of me. I hadn't meant to admit that, not to Lisa, and certainly not when she was visiting and uber pregnant.

"What do you mean, at arm's length?"

"Nothing that I should be discussing with his sister."

"Fuck that. I'm just as much your sister as his, so spill."

I chuckled again. I wasn't sure whether to be touched or annoyed at her words, maybe both were fitting. "This how you handle your clients?"

"No, I'm nice to them, but I'm not related to them, and I don't do therapy when I feel like I've got a dump truck inside my uterus. This is special family treatment. Spill!"

I plopped down on my bed, and pointed toward a chair next to it, not that the chair was comfortable, but I was guessing it'd be better for her to have a back to lean against.

"I really shouldn't be talking to you about this. I mean, you're right, you're my sister as much as his, but you are still his sister. I..."

"Okay, got it. My god, you can strangle an issue better than my long-winded clients can. I don't have time to listen to all the bullshit, nor do I have the patience. Spit it out, Todd."

"We haven't had sex!" I felt my cheeks heat at the revelation. "Fuck, he cringes when I even try."

Lisa let out a long sigh. "Well, I'm not really surprised." She stared at me for a long while before she finally said, "I'm not gonna make excuses for him. He's one of the worst about getting his emotions all wrapped up and messed up, and, well, if you'd open your eyes, you'd see he's always been that way, all his life, and when it comes to you, he's like ten times worse than usual."

I didn't really know how to respond. My own emotions were screwed up and wrapped up in a bundled mess.

"I may lose my business, or at the very least, a major chunk of it. I'm in over my head, and what I need more than anything is someone to hold me, to love me without all the past..." I shook my head, and looking Lisa in the eye, repeated, "Without all the past. I can't compete with what happened to us, Lisa, I lose every time."

Lisa struggled up out of the chair, cussing as she did, then sat on the bed next to me. When she was able to put her arm around me, she said, "I love you, Todd. Honey, what you're goin' through is shit. Stupid shit."

She rubbed my shoulder, as she said to herself, "My brothers are both stubborn, stupid, and couldn't pull their heads out of their asses if their lives depended on it."

She pulled me around, so I was looking at her. "So, here's what I'm gonna do. I'm gonna take my enormous self downstairs, get in Dad's monster whirlpool tub, and soak. Then, tomorrow, you, Ash and I are gonna go to the donut place. We're gonna do all this in public, so I don't bump your heads together, or say something hormonal that I'll regret once I'm done carrying Frank's spawn around inside me, and the two of you are going to talk this out."

She got up and waddled to the door, and I was just about to call for Frank to walk her down, when she opened the door and I saw Frank's redhead appear. I smiled as the attentive husband walked in front of her, ensuring she got down the steep stairs back to the second level.

"Lisa," I said, before she descended. "I love you."

She smiled at me. "Don't think you can butter your way out of tomorrow, and if you think you'll be able to slip past me, well, just consider how much hell they'll be to pay when all this—" She cradled her pregnant belly. "—comes after you."

I chuckled. "I'm not gonna give you the slip. Just wanted you to know how happy I am that you're my sister."

She looked at me for a moment, fondness nearly hidden behind a smirk. "Whatever. I love you too, you idiotic, romance-inept dufus."

She began her descent, and I watched until she and Frank reached the final step, before I closed the bedroom door.

I might have agreed to breakfast, but I still didn't want to see Ash. In fact, it would've been much easier to continue pretending he didn't exist, as shitty and unfair as that was to even think, but I'd already given my word, so I steeled myself for a forced meeting I knew I couldn't avoid,, not with Lisa pulling the strings.

THIRTY-EIGHT

ASH

LISA PHONED ME MOMENTS after I got home, and told me I would be having breakfast with her and Todd tomorrow morning at the donut shop.

When I was about to argue, she hung up on me. Clearly, I wasn't going to win that argument, no matter how much I wanted to argue. The woman had always been difficult, and it seemed pregnancy had turned her into a dragon. So, after a restless night, once again with little to no sleep, I got up, took a shower, and waited for my overbearing sister and *unboyfriend* to show up, and take me to an uncomfortable breakfast.

Lisa texted me when they arrived, and I left the house only to see Todd was driving, and Lisa was sitting in the middle seat of his truck. I scooted in next to her, and none of us spoke until we arrived at the donut shop.

When I got out, I helped Lisa across the seat and out of the truck. She mumbled something I didn't quite hear, but I could tell she was irritated that we were arguing, and that she'd felt compelled to intervene, a circumstance that if she hadn't been incredibly pregnant, I'd have told her to butt out of.

When we got inside the ancient donut shop, Lisa plopped down on one of the rickety old wooden chairs, and hollered at Jamie, the owner Jim's son, to bring her a Long John with Bavarian cream. "I need coffee too!" she demanded, and I had to smother a smile as Jamie quickly complied, without comment or complaint.

Jamie was just a year or so younger than Lisa, if I remembered correctly. He and his wife already had two children, and I could only imagine he knew not to contradict a pregnant woman this close to delivering.

As soon as she had her donut and coffee, she wasted no time launching into her lecture. "I'm ready to pull the hair out of both of your stubborn heads. Which one of you wants to start this confession?" She paused to take a bite of her donut, and moaned. "If I wasn't so angry at you two, I would really be enjoying this donut."

When neither of us spoke, she swallowed, and said, "Okay, then we'll start with you." She pointed at Todd. "Say what you need to say to get this worked out once and for all."

"There's nothing to say," he said flatly, looking Lisa in the eyes and avoiding mine.

She slammed her hand down on the table, causing both of us and poor Jamie to jump. "There *is* something to say, if after all this time, you get back together just to end up back in the same damned place, so spit it out!"

"He doesn't want me." If I hadn't known him so well, I might've missed the hint of hurt in his voice, and only then did what he'd actually said register.

"What?" I nearly shouted. Thank God the donut shop was nearly empty, or the tongues would already be wagging across town at our public display.

"You don't. I've been patiently waiting, and you push me away. You like the thought of me, but you don't want the real me. Of course, now you've got your fancy medical degree, it's not like I'm that surprised." Both Lisa and I stared at him. *Where the hell was all this coming from?* "I'm sorry this isn't working. I have a ton of work to…"

When he stood to go, Lisa pointed at him. "You'll do no such thing. You sit your ass right down in that seat, and finish what's been started." Then, her pointed finger turned to me. "Ash, are you pushing Todd away 'cause you think he's below you?"

"That's a bunch of shit," I said, frustrated and angry he'd even think that. "I've been in love with him since we were kids, and besides, he's one of the most successful businessmen I know. Why would I be ashamed of him?"

My answer seemed to satisfy her, because she turned back to Todd, but he still wouldn't meet my gaze. "Todd, why do you think he's ashamed of you?"

"Why else would he be pushing me away? I mean, he says it's 'cause he doesn't trust me, but I know it's more than that… it has to be." He blushed a bit, then let out a heavy breath. "We couldn't keep our hands off each other... before."

With everyone's eyes on me now, I could only stare at my uneaten donut, knowing what I was about to admit. "Todd, I'm screwed up. This hasn't really got anything to do with you. I'm just a mess."

"Why don't you be specific. What are you a mess about?" Lisa asked.

"It's like I already said, I'm afraid you'll leave me again, and I can't handle givin' you my heart just to have you break it."

I glanced up only to see Lisa give me a pained look, before sighing. "You two are such an emotional wreck. Not just you, Ash. Both of you. Listen, Ash, if you want Todd, you're gonna have to get over it. Nobody is going to sit around and wait for someone who keeps them locked out. It's just not how we humans do relationships. Besides, this is sounding more and more like you're still punishing him for how things ended when you were both teenagers."

She turned to Todd. "Todd, I'm guessing you blew up, instead of talking about your feelings. I know you're a guy, and a stubborn Southern man at that, but if you wanna be in a relationship, you gotta talk about things before they blow up." Taking a deep breath, she then addressed us both. "Here's what we're gonna do. I'm gonna finish eating this incredibly delicious donut, because your niece and nephew are hungry, and when they're hungry, I'm *hangry*. When I'm done, you're gonna take me back to Dad's, then you're gonna go on a nice long country drive, and you're gonna *talk*, and you're gonna work all this out. I don't wanna hear a damned complaint either," she said, before pointing at both of us in a stern motherly way that left no room for discussion.

Lisa took her time finishing her donut, moaning like it was a delicacy flown in from Paris, then finished her coffee and got up to leave. Neither Todd nor I had spoken as she finished her food. We hadn't even looked at one another. I knew Lisa was right. I had pushed him away and refused to let him in, and Todd had blown up, which I knew he would, because I was pushing him into it.

Frank met us as we pulled up to Dad's house. Before she got out, Lisa said, "I mean it. You are not to come back until you've worked this out. I'll not be raising these two kids around two bitter old men who can't get their act together and love one another like... well, like Fate has dictated. These two deserve to know love is stronger than your heads are thick!"

I hopped out of the truck, and she crawled over the seat and into Frank's waiting arms, and didn't even look back as he helped her into the house. As soon as I was strapped back in, Todd took off and headed down the road toward Lebanon.

Unable to stand the silence any longer, I took the plunge, and spoke first, "Todd, Lisa was right. I haven't been fair."

He didn't speak for several moments, before he sighed, and said, "I should've talked about it, but we all know that's not my greatest strength." When he got to Bargerton Road, he pulled off and parked in a wide graveled area where a large propane tank used to sit.

"I can't play games with you, Ash. I get that you're leery, I get that you don't trust me, but I've forgiven you, I've opened myself up to you. I've loved you in spite of all the things that happened in our past. I never stopped loving you."

He leaned his head back against the headrest, and stared out at the traffic that passed us by. Instinctively, I knew not to respond, not yet. I needed to let him work through his thoughts, then let him have his say before I had mine.

"I'm so afraid I'm gonna fuck up this business. I've always felt like I'm too slow, too backwoods to accomplish much, and when we were kids, you kept pushing me to go to college. I knew college wasn't for me. It's not just that I hate school, but even when I was young, I would look forward to the summers when I could just work and get my hands dirty. You pushing me to get a degree made me feel dumb, plain and simple. I felt dumb and inadequate. Now, even though the business is working, happening... I'm confronted with the fact that you're a freakin' doctor with a freakin' medical degree. You've done exactly what you planned to do, and I'm so proud of you, but I can't help but feel like you're looking down on me, and when you weren't interested in being intimate, well, that felt like I'm not... like I'm not enough!" He rubbed his hand over his face, and sighed, before continuing, "If Lisa hadn't interfered, I would've probably let this end here and now. I'm not sure if I'll pull through this mess with the mercantile building, and on top of that, your new doctor is investing in the damn thing. It was just too much, Ash. I can't be in a relationship with someone who sees me as less than them. It doesn't matter that I love you with all my heart. I still have my pride."

I had to force myself to keep my hands in my lap. I could feel the pain rolling off him, and all I wanted to do in that moment was throw my arms around him, but it wasn't time yet. Todd needed space when he was like this. He always worked through it, but only if I didn't interrupt.

He glanced at me, but when I said nothing, he continued, "I'll figure out a way to pay Doctor Gib back, even if the insurance company refuses to pay. I don't want you to worry about all that. When I take on a partnership, I'm someone others can rely on. When the house is done, I'm probably gonna have to sell it, but I don't really need a house that big anyway. So, I know I don't have your fancy degrees, but I've got integrity."

"Bullshit!" I blurted out when I could no longer contain myself. "You think I've been pushing you away 'cause I didn't think you measured up? I thought, even after all these years of hating me, you'd know me better than that, and, dude, your partners are as responsible as you are for the fire. They took the same risks you did with the building, so you don't owe them any more than you owe yourself. Stop trying to be a damned martyr." I sighed in frustration, and stared hard out the window.

After giving myself a moment to calm down a little, I turned to him. "Listen, I didn't allow us to be intimate, 'cause I was being an ass, though not intentionally. I don't even think I realized that was until Lisa said I was punishing you. The truth is, I knew you'd eventually blow, and when you did, I could justify why I didn't give myself to you completely. Now that I can see that, it feels slimy as hell. I'm sorry, Todd. *Really* sorry. You deserved better than that. As far as your business, you have to see how much I admire what you've accomplished."

Todd shook his head. "No, I don't see it, Ash. You've not said anything like that. In fact, you've basically kept me confined to a little part of your world. You rarely talk about your life, what it was like up till now. I know more about what Lisa's been up to for the past decade than I do about you."

"Lisa doesn't stop talking. That's not fair to compare me to her," I said, only half-joking, but hoping I'd get a smile out of him.

Todd chuckled. "That's probably true, but you have to understand, from my perspective, it really looks as if you're keeping me at arm's length. I've told you about my business, Linc, even Warren the jackass who was probably involved in burning the mercantile. I've told you everything about my life. Besides knowing you went to the University of Tennessee for undergrad, and Quillen for med school, I have no idea what those years were like for you, who your friends are, who you dated. You're a closed book to me. I mean, I can ask Doc or Lisa or even my dad for information, but you haven't shared much."

I nodded. "Yeah." It was hard to admit, but I knew I needed to. "Todd, I didn't wanna give much, 'cause I figured it was just a matter of time before you were gone again. Really, deep down, I still don't believe you're gonna stick around."

"Where am I goin', Ash? I'm moving here. My business is here. My family is here. Everything's here. *You're here.* So, where do you think I'm goin'?"

I shrugged. "I didn't say that what I feel is logical. It's just that you've not been one to stick around. You left the day after our high-school graduation, and haven't looked back. I've been here this whole time and you never came back."

"I guess we still don't know each other very well," Todd said, sounding exhausted. "You need to spend more time with Jen and Linc. I'm solid as a rock and as settled as one too. At least, I was before all this happened. Before I bought the construction company, I'd lived in the same apartment since high school, one I used to share with Jen. When she moved out, I had enough money to live in it alone. Then, after buying the company, I moved into a tiny house I renovated on the construction lot. If the dads hadn't talked me into moving back, I'd have stayed in that house, probably till I died."

Our conversation had me on the verge of tears, which surely would've halted our heart-to-heart, so I was re-lieved to hear him let out a small chuckle. "You see, Ash, I'm not one for big waves and changes. I like a settled and simple life. I'm happier when things are that way. I did leave right after high school, but that was because I didn't wanna watch you fall in love with someone else, and be forced to see it day in and day out. Really, when it comes down to it, I don't think I ever wanted to leave Crawford City. It's home. The fact that Nashville seems to be expanding all the way out here, and the people comin' in have big money for big homes, well, that's a boon I'd never seen comin', but that's how it is. Even if the company folds, I can get a job with any number of contractors out of Nashville and still live here."

"So, what you're saying is," I said, still staring out the front windshield, "I'm pushing you away, 'cause you might leave, but you ain't leavin'?"

A deep chuckle came from him. "Well, yeah. I'm not gonna leave now. If we fuck this up, we'll just be stuck here staring at one another from now on."

I was just about to tell him I was ready to go all the way to make the relationship work, when both of our phones began dinging from incoming texts.

"Oh shit!" I practically yelled, upon reading the first message.

"Yeah, okay. This'll have to wait, unless you wanna deliver your niece and nephew in your clinic!" Todd said.

"Nope, that's a part of Lisa I'd rather never see!"

"Agreed," Todd said, and shuddered as he threw the truck into drive, and skidded through the gravel, then onto the highway back to town.

As we reached Dad's house, I jumped out and rushed to where Frank, Dad and Amos were loading Lisa into the front seat of the truck.

"How far apart are the contractions?" I asked.

Lisa called out, "Not far enough. I love you and Dad, but I don't want either of you delivering my babies. Get this truck moving to Lebanon."

Frank rode with Dad and Lisa, while Amos rode with us. I phoned Sheriff Cross and told her we were rushing Lisa to Vanderbilt Wilson County Hospital in Lebanon as fair warning, so no deputies would pull us over on the way.

She chuckled. "Trust me, my deputies don't wanna deliver any premature babies, but y'all don't be crazy on the drive," she said. I could tell she was excited about the news.

Less than thirty minutes later, we pulled up in front of the ER. I'd called ahead, telling them we had a visitor from Oregon who'd decided to go into labor. Of course, when Dr. Frost heard it was my sister, she laughed. "That don't surprise me in the least. Your sister probably planned it, so she could give birth to her kids while she was home."

I'd forgotten that she and Lisa had been in the marching band together growing up.

"You're probably right. I'm glad you're there, Doctor Frost. That'll make her feel a whole lot better about givin' birth here."

As I rushed to the side of the truck, Lisa was having another contraction. I sent Todd in to get a wheelchair and let them know we'd arrived.

"The contractions are close," Dad said. "These two are comin' and they ain't gonna wait."

Lisa was panting when Todd returned with the wheelchair. "Nice and easy, sis. Frances Massengill, your old band friend, is the doctor on duty, and she's gonna deliver the babies. She's called Doctor Frost now."

"Fran? Cool," Lisa said between pants, as Frank pushed the wheelchair through the emergency doors. Dr. Frost must've called down, because Lisa was wheeled up to labor and delivery shortly after our arrival. Dad stayed with Frank, and helped him fill out all the paperwork to admit her, while I went with Lisa.

"Where's Frank?" Lisa asked, panicking when we finally got to the delivery room. "He's with Dad filling out paperwork. Dad won't let them keep him down there for long. He still has a lot of weight here. You've got a few minutes, so don't fret."

"*Don't fret?* Just like a stupid man to tell a woman in labor not to fret."

Just then, Dr. Frost walked in and squealed, rather unlike a doctor, when she saw Lisa. "Oh my god, look at you, girl! I heard you were pregnant."

Lisa smiled, and as Dr. Frost bent down to give her a hug, said, "I'm so glad it's you. I had an image of some old man with cold hands and a condescending drawl as the doctor helping deliver my babies."

"No, he just retired," Dr. Frost said, and I had to keep from laughing. Dr. Freemont had a reputation as a total ass, who still practiced medicine like it was the nineteen eighties. No one really liked the man, but until Dr. Frost took over labor and delivery, he'd been the one to run the place. Rumor was the two clashed like wild animals.

Luckily, she won. Not really surprising, though, since she'd graduated from Vanderbilt University School of Medicine, and the university had taken over the hospital.

"Okay, brother, we've got this," Dr. Frost said to me. "When Lisa's husband gets here, send him to the nurses' station to get scrubbed up. We're just gonna check and see how far along Lisa is, and then we'll give you all an update."

I went to the waiting room, but I didn't have to wait long before Dad brought a very anxious Frank up with Todd and Amos.

Frank was immediately escorted down the hall by a nurse, and was probably being put through the husband treatment. Our job was done, at least until the little ones were born, and our duties to spoil them rotten began, so now we waited.

Rather than take my own seat, I sat on the extended chair next to Todd and curled into him. I didn't even think about it, my body just moved there instinctively. When he put his arm around me, both of the dads cocked an eyebrow.

"So, you worked it out?" Dad asked.

I looked at Todd, then tried to slide out of his embrace, only to be pulled back in. "Not quite. We were in the middle of that when we got your texts."

I settled back against him. "I still have some more groveling to do."

Todd chuckled and gave me a little squeeze. "I think we probably both do."

Both the dads smiled then, and Dad slipped his arm around Amos. We all four sat happily, our family's new additions occupying our thoughts.

THIRTY-NINE

TODD

WHEN THE EXCITEMENT OVERTOOK Ash's consciousness enough for him to naturally snuggle into me, I realized he had been telling the truth. If he was embarrassed by me, he'd have never reverted back to snuggling so easily.

There was a lot to work out, for sure, but it was worth it. Ash was worth it.

It took a while, but eventually Frank came out, a look of wonder on his face, saying the birth had gone well. Both babies were being cleaned up, then we could meet them.

He quickly took his phone out to call his parents, and was telling them everything went well as he walked back toward Lisa's room.

We were all smiles then, none of us really comprehending that our little Lisa had just given birth to two babies. None of us would ever be the same again, and happily so.

The rest of the day was one of small, happy moments. Lisa and Frank named their son Martin, after Frank's grandfather, and because he and his sister had been born on Martin Luther King Jr. Day, and their daughter Margaret Jane, after Ash and Lisa's mom.

That night, I dropped Ash off at his house. He kissed me and invited me in, and I told him I was happy we were working things out, but I wanted to finish the conversation we'd started before anything more happened between us.

The truth was, I wanted Ash so badly my entire body hurt from it. I'd managed to push my libido down while we were learning to be around each other again, but now I just wanted him—needed him, really. I knew I wouldn't be able to be alone with him and not take what I'd needed for so many months, but we needed to fully clear the air first.

The babies were able to come home with Lisa two days after they were born. They were a month early, but both were totally healthy. Returning to Oregon was delayed since the babies weren't allowed on a plane for at least a month, and since the doctors preferred it be three months since they were born prematurely, Lisa and Frank decided to remain in Crawford until the spring. It also meant, though, that poor Frank would be flying back and forth from Oregon to manage work and spend time with his new family.

A week after the babies had come home, Sheriff Cross came by and told me they'd apprehended Warren after he'd been pulled over for a DUI. He'd admitted to helping set the fire, but he swore it was all Thornburg's idea. Apparently, our former mayor was upset with his election loss. The scariest part was Warren said Thornburg had also planned to have someone take out my home and the storage area in the old hardware building.

Thankfully, those threats never materialized, or I would've indeed been ruined, not to mention someone could've been hurt.

"Sheriff, was Thornburg or Warren responsible for the spray paint and yard signs too?" I asked.

She nodded sadly, "Warren was pretty toasted, and confessed to it all, but, no, I don't think Thornburg was behind the spray paint, and the yard signs were put up by a church group from Kansas of all places."

"So, nothing local then?" I asked.

She shook her head. "I told you, Todd, this town is different. Thornburg, well, he was having issues that your dad and you got mixed up in... but even that wasn't about who you are, more about him... well, enough of that," she said, to stop that conversation before it went too far. "Just know that most of the locals love you, and are happy you're home." With that, she patted my arm, then left.

My attorney, Ed, called a week after Warren's confession, and said he'd been contacted by the insurance company. Since the confession proved I wasn't involved in setting the fire, they were finally going to pay out.

Their refusing to pay when there was no evidence that I'd been involved in the arson still stuck in my craw, but at least I'd be getting the funds.

Refocusing on the mercantile project, I sat down with old Tom to discuss the architectural plans. Luckily, we'd already measured the size of the building and captured a lot of its nuances, so I asked Tom to redraw the blueprints, making it much larger. That way, it would fit the entire space including the two vacant lots on either side of the old building. Thornburg might've destroyed the old historic structure, but we could still put something there that represented the historical element that'd been lost.

As for Ash and me, our relationship had taken the back burner once again. We were spending less and less time together, mostly because our schedules were so busy, but also because the opportunity to clear things up had been interrupted, and we'd let it be.

The day we finished the new construction on the third floor of my home was a big day for me, because it meant two things. One, we were well on our way to completing this massive project, and two, I could move back into my house, instead of having to live with Dad and Doc.

I'd already had the crews close off the exits downstairs, and I'd installed a makeshift heater for the new third-floor master suite. I was looking forward to using the whirlpool in the en suite, and because the master suite was huge, I had some of the workers bring up the old range, microwave and refrigerator, so I could create a makeshift kitchen up there too.

I'd just finished helping to lay the floor in the new office and carriage house, and was about to head upstairs for my first night in the master suite, when Ash showed up.

"Hey, what's up? Lisa and the little ones okay?" I asked, concerned.

"I assume they are fine. I came to see you."

"O-okay," I stammered. "Come on up. I was just about to climb into the shower. You can see the finished master suite while you're here."

A blush came over Ash, and knowing what his thoughts must've been, I quickly walked away, sporting my own obvious embarrassment.

When we walked into the third-floor master, Ash gasped. "Oh, God, Todd, this is *beautiful*. I can't believe... it turned out better than I imagined."

"Wait until you see the en suite and master closets."

Ash's eyes widened as he followed me into the extra-large bathroom with a monster whirlpool tub, large enough for two people, and a beautifully tiled shower with dual showerheads. The double vanity that sat along the center wall to avoid the slanting ceilings above was marbled, with large mirrors over each sink.

The master closet was through a door that separated the vanity and the whirlpool tub, and could've been a room in itself. We'd installed shelves and clothes hangers that would've made any clothing fanatic happy.

When we came back out into the bedroom, Ash sighed. "This room is bigger than my house."

"Do you like it? Is it what you imagined?" I asked, both hopeful, and a little nervous.

He nodded. "It's so much more than what I imagined," he said, and turned toward me, stepping into my arms. I instinctually wrapped them around him.

"I miss you. Can we be boyfriends again now?" he asked.

"Are you sure that's what you want?" I asked.

He looked up into my eyes, and nodded. "Can I show you?"

"I guess," I said, not understanding what he meant by showing me, not until he freed himself from my embrace, and began to unbutton his shirt.

"Whoa, Ash, I don't want you to do something you're not ready for."

"Fuck ready for, I'm more than ready. I shouldn't have denied you what you needed, 'cause I was only denying myself," he said, as his shirt slid down his arms and onto the floor. "I've wanted you for so long, and I'm finally taking what I want. Now, *strip!*"

I laughed, caught off guard by his sudden assertiveness, but turned on by it too. "Calm down. I'm covered in dirt and grime. I need a shower, and..."

Ash launched himself at me, his mouth latching onto mine, and began tugging my shirt up over my shoulders. "Not waiting any longer," he said with determination, after he pulled back.

His hands roamed all over my bare chest before wandering lower, exploring me. When he kissed my neck, I could tell he was trying to pretend like he didn't just get a mouthful of sawdust, and I couldn't help but laugh.

"Come on, I was about to try out my new shower. You can test the dual showerheads with me."

I woke up around three in the morning. It was quiet except for Ash's soft breathing next to me. It was familiar, even after all this time. I lay there with him curled into me, remembering the stolen times in our youth when we'd spend the night with each other, and make passionate love, then fall asleep just like we were now.

We were boys then, and although making love with Ash was just as amazing as I remembered, there was another element to it now. It was something I hadn't expected, something more.

Ash had always been a cuddler. Apparently, that hadn't changed, as I had to roll him off me, so I could get up to pee.

He fussed as I pulled away, making me smile. I loved having his warm body pressed up next to mine. That was something I'd never stopped craving.

As soon as I was done, I crawled back into bed, and pulled his body close to mine. He immediately turned over, so I could spoon him. "You okay?" he asked groggily.

"More than, you okay?

"Mmm-hmm," he moaned, and I curled my arms around his body, and nuzzled into his neck.

I inhaled the intoxicating scent of him. I'd stocked the bathroom with the designer soaps and fancy shampoo he used, and their smell on his skin and in his hair mixed perfectly with his own masculine scent.

I was, of course, overthinking what we'd done, but probably nothing like he was. The fact that he was able to sleep, though, was something at least.

I wasn't able to fall back to sleep, and ended up getting up early, and turning on the new coffee pot I'd bought for up here. Ash woke up a few minutes after the coffee started, and rolled onto the side of the bed, his hair sticking straight up after going to bed with it still wet.

He'd always been adorable, especially when he first woke up. He got up and kissed me, then said, "I'm gonna grab a shower, then you can tell me why you're fretting so much."

"I'm not fretting," I lied.

"I'm a champion fretter, in case you've forgotten. Do you have creamer, or am I gonna have to drink that black?"

I smiled. "For some reason, I bought creamer, and even have some sugar packets."

He turned to look at me with a smirk, before going into the bathroom. "Were you expecting someone?"

"You never know."

Ash hmphed and disappeared into the bathroom.

I thought about joining him, but I was too uptight. Making love to Ash was clearly making me the crazy one. I was like a string on a guitar tuned too tight, and ready to break at any moment.

When Ash came out, I'd finished my second cup of coffee, and was sitting staring out the large window that looked out over downtown, or at least the little strip of woodland that separated this and the dads' property from downtown.

Ash poured himself a cup, put almost as much cream in it as coffee, and sat on the bed across from me.

"Okay, so let's talk about it."

I chuckled despite the stress I was feeling. "There isn't much to talk about, really. I wasn't prepared to do this without some more... well, more discussion."

Ash gave me a knowing grin. "We were never gonna discuss it. I realized that while sitting across from you last night at the dads' place. Yesterday, all I could think about was you, and the way it used to feel when you'd touch me, then instead of repressing the memory and emotions... okay, the desire, I decided to come here and make good on it."

His smile disappeared as he took a sip of coffee before cringing. "Where did you get this stuff? It tastes worse than Amos's coffee."

I laughed. "It *is* my dad's coffee. I found it in one of the old boxes of stuff we were supposed to be throwing out. It was a new container, so I decided since it was just me..."

"Dude, it doesn't matter if it's just you, you deserve better than this!"

I got up and set my coffee cup on the makeshift night-stand, then took his and did the same. He was about to squawk about it, until I put my hands on his chest, and gently pushed him backward onto the bed, then crawled on top of him and began kissing him slowly.

"I've missed this," I murmured into his ear when we came up for air.

"Me too. So, don't miss it anymore, *let's get it on*..."

He began serenading me with the classic Marvin Gaye song we'd both memorized long ago as my lips were busy elsewhere. My dad used to have a record of it, and as kids, we'd listen, laugh, and sing along to the lyrics... before we understood what it all meant.

Before we broke up, it had become our theme song.

We were just heating up, when the sound of hammers and saws beneath us drowned out Ash's crooning.

"Probably shouldn't 'get it on' with all my crew under us," I said on a sigh.

"We can be quiet."

I burst out laughing. "Wanna bet?"

"Hey," he said as I continued laughing, and rolled off him.

"Come back here tonight."

"We've got supper at the dads' tonight."

"Come over after."

"And let Lisa see she was right?"

"Lisa knows she was right," I said, grinning. "Besides, she's occupied with two very demanding little people at the moment."

"They are amazing, though, aren't they?" he asked, practically beaming.

"More than! Ever thought of having your own?" I didn't know where the question had come from, but now that I'd asked, I was really interested in his answer.

"Eventually. You know I've always wanted kids."

"Me too." I crawled back on top of him, and said, "Think we can make some?"

He laughed out loud and shoved me off. "We'll try again tonight. Meanwhile, I gotta get to work, or Doctor Gib might fire me."

I kissed him and got up. "I've gotta get downstairs. I swear if I don't keep my eyes on the kid Dad and Linc hired, he'll put wallboard over my doors and freakin' windows."

I smiled, remembering that was the same thing Dad used to say about Ash and me if he didn't keep an eye on us. It was both funny and disconcerting hearing his old sayings come out of my own mouth.

ASH

I HAD DECIDED THE hell with it, no more waiting, and God, I was glad I did. Making love with Todd was just like I remembered, sweet, loving, and hot as hell.

I danced into the clinic, quietly singing, "Let's get it on," and got an inquisitive look from my staff at the front desk as I walked by. "What?" I asked, and laughed when I saw Leslie's knowing smile.

No way was I gonna admit what she thought she knew.

The day spun by as I happily worked through seeing my patients. Thankfully, I was mostly dealing with minor issues, since the flu had finally worked its way through the population, so that evening, I was able to leave early, instead of having to work overtime to get all my documentation done.

When I got to the dads' it was strangely quiet. Frank's family had visited and already gone home, but it was rare to show up without one of the little ones crying about something. I came in quietly, guessing my niece and nephew were both asleep, and not wanting to wake them.

Lisa was sitting in Dad's old recliner, a baby in each arm. All three of them were passed out cold.

I smiled at the sight. It was amazing to see my sister as a mother, and a mom of two on top of that. Slowly, I pulled my phone out and snapped a picture. If this was as good as I thought it'd be, it'd need to be framed.

I slipped into the kitchen, assuming at least one of the dads would be in there cooking, since the smell of something wonderful met me at the door.

I walked in just in time to see Dad kiss Amos sweetly, then pull away smiling like he was the earth and the moon. I cleared my throat before anything more personal happened, and then slipped onto the stool on this side of the island.

Dad continued holding onto Amos as I sat down, then winked at him before letting go.

Whispering, he said, "So, you seem happy. What's going on?"

"Oh, you know... just got everything I've ever wanted."

"Hmm, that so?" he asked, and winked at Amos again.

"What?" I asked when the two looked over with matching grins.

"Honey, you know we can see the driveway at Todd's place," Dad said.

"Our bedroom faces that way, remember?" Amos added, chuckling.

"You saw that I spent the night," I said, feeling a blush creep up my neck.

They both nodded, their grins never leaving their faces. "It's about time. I thought the two of you were gonna never work things out," Dad replied as Amos continued to nod.

"Well, apparently we have, and God, it's so awesome. Not that I'm gonna discuss the particulars with you."

I was about to change the subject, when I heard the telltale signs of a baby waking up. I quickly turned and headed toward the living room just as Lisa woke up. Martin was stretching and yawning, so I quickly lifted him out of Lisa's arms, and began swaying with him, the way you would naturally when holding a newborn in your arms.

Lisa looked up, smiling. "I must've fallen asleep. I don't get much more than three hours at a time, especially when Frank isn't here."

"We both told you we'd take baby duty, honey," Dad said as he walked in behind me.

"I know, Dad, but it's just so much on you and Amos. I don't wanna interfere with your relationship."

"That's crap and you know it," Amos said quietly behind Dad. "We wanna love on our grandbabies. Why don't we sleep in the nursery tonight, and you can sleep in the guest bedroom? We'll wake you when they need to be fed."

Lisa sighed, sounding exhausted. She'd been resisting their help, wanting to do all the work herself, saying it'd help her bond with the babies, but we could all see she was in serious need of a good night's sleep.

"Okay, but if there's any..."

Dad put his hand up. "Dear one, I raised you both and helped with Todd. I also have a very well-used medical degree. I'm sure I'm up to the job."

"I know, Dad," she said, sighing again, and this time wiping away tears. "I just wanna do it right."

Dad went over and kissed her head. "And you *are* doing it right. You're an amazing mother, and we all know it, but learning to accept help is part of the whole *doin' it right* thing."

She nodded. "This postpartum emotional stuff is crap too. I thought my hormones were out of whack with the pregnancy, but I cry at the drop of a hat since they've been born." Both Dad and I looked at one another and turned to her before she shook her head. "No, there is no depression. It's just me bein' emotional. I'll tell you if it gets to be too much."

"With your mother's history, it wouldn't hurt to let Ash prescribe you an anti-depressant," Dad said.

"No, I'm breastfeeding, and I'm not having any diffi-culty with bonding. In fact, it's the opposite. I wanna be with them all the time, it's almost like I'm obsessed," she said, chuckling.

"Well, sis, this isn't something to mess with. You have some of the symptoms, and you know as well as we do, if you don't treat it, it can get out of hand."

"I know. I'll call Doctor Frost and see what she thinks. No offense to the two of you, but she deals with this every day. If she thinks I need an anti-depressant, we can deal with it then."

Both Dad and I nodded. I was going to suggest she call Dr. Frost anyway. It was one thing for your dad and brother to push something, and another for a bona fide obstetrician to have an opinion.

When little Martin started to make faces, I sighed. "I'm guessing this is a sign that I get to change my first diaper, huh?"

Lisa chuckled. "That would be a yep! It'll be good training."

I must've looked pained, because Lisa immediately asked, "What was that look for?"

I shrugged. "Todd asked me this morning if I wanted to have kids."

"This morning, huh?" she asked, and I knew I'd probably given up too much information, but I needed Lisa's advice, and it couldn't hurt to get Dad and Amos's too.

"Yeah, so we're crossing bridges that have been burned to cinders until now, and after... well, you know? After... he asked if I wanted kids."

"Isn't that a positive thing?" Dad asked.

"Well, yeah, but you know me, I get too carried away. I don't wanna chase him away like I did..."

"Geez, Ash," Lisa said, then started rocking when Margaret Jane began fussing. "You've got to give yourself a break. You were a kid, and you were a kid in love. It's okay to have dreams and hopes, even at the beginning of something. You know how to keep those thoughts in check."

"Todd has always wanted kids too," Amos chimed in. "When he was little, he used to talk about when he would become a dad."

"I'm just being too weird about things. Me being overbearing."

"I think Lisa was right, you *were* a kid, but you know Todd isn't a kid any longer. I think he can handle someone who knows what he wants. Trust him, Ash. Let your heart just *feel*, and stop trying to do it right," Dad said.

Just then, Martin let out a wail, alerting me that he'd finished with whatever he'd been up to in his diaper. I grabbed a fresh one out of the bag next to Lisa, and walked into the study, where I'd seen they'd put a changing table.

When I came back out, Lisa immediately had to take care of Margaret Jane.

Even though the conversation drifted away from my concerns, I continued to think about what they'd said. Maybe they were right, and I could just be myself. I could just let Todd know how I felt and what I wanted, and not worry about him running away. That gave me hope, even though it also scared the crap out of me.

FORTY-ONE

TODD

T HE NEW KID CUT through the cord of the power tool he was using first thing that morning. The electrician was two hours late, because, "I got drunk with my brother-in-law last night, and didn't pay attention to the time, so I overslept this morning. Sorry, man!"

By the time afternoon hit, I was fit to be tied. I was also exhausted, running on little to no sleep.

When Linc came by after picking up supplies, he took one look at me and forced me to go with him to, "Check something out at the headquarters."

Of course, when we got out of sight of the house, he pulled over and forced me to spill. "What's up, man? You look like you're about to blow a gasket!"

"I didn't sleep last night."

"Really, why?"

"Ash," I said with a sigh, though I couldn't help but smile saying his name. When I looked at Linc, his eyebrow was cocked, causing me to laugh.

"Yeah, we're back... well, we're back together, all the way. But, that's not why I didn't sleep."

"Okay, well, why don't you tell me what's up. Ash is hot as the day is long, and you've *had* the hots for him all your freakin' life, so what's up?"

I gave him the hairy eyeball at the 'Ash is hot' comment, but quickly shook it off, knowing it was a ridiculous thing to be jealous over. "He's just too important. I mean, I'm worried that we're moving too fast."

"For him, or for you?"

I thought for a moment, not really sure. "Well, for both of us, I guess."

"So, I'm guessing he made a move then?" I nodded, but didn't reply. "Listen, if you hadn't grown up with him, would you be worried about all that, or would you just be enjoying his body, like a normal man who's getting some after like what, twenty years?"

I gave him the stink eye again, and replied, "You know, I wouldn't be worried about it, we'd just be having fun."

"So, have fun, stop overthinking."

"You don't get it, dude, I *love* this man. Like, thinking about weddings and babies and shit, in love. I even asked him this morning if he wanted kids."

Linc laughed. "Then, you probably just need to be straight up with him. He clearly feels the same, seeing as he didn't run for the hills, and if he made the moves on you last night, then you need to get over yourself, and let this be what it was probably always meant to be." I shook my head, but didn't say anything. "Listen," Linc said. "I've got to get this stuff to the build site, so we can finish the damn thing and I can turn the keys over to the evil mistress of the manor, then I'll come back and pick you up, and we'll go have a drink at the local bar, and you can tell me all your woes."

"Nah, can't tonight. We're having supper at the dads', then I've got a date with Ash for a repeat performance," I said, unable to hide my grin at that last part.

Linc just laughed. "You're already married, dude. Just tell him how you feel. He's probably fretting over the same thing. Then, you can make sweet love, and get all gushy and pudgy around the middle, like the old married man you were born to be!"

I playfully punched my friend on the arm. He was a dork, but he was an amazing friend.

When he dropped me back off at the house, I wandered through the building site, and seeing it was a total mess, decided to send the crew home, since it was just getting worse the longer they were here.

"Listen up," I yelled over the noise. "Y'all cut out of here early and get your fuckin' heads screwed back on before you show up here tomorrow, and I'm gonna tell you, if any of you come in here tomorrow with the unprofessional attitudes I've seen today, I'll fire the lot of you! Now, make sure your workspaces are spotless before you go, then get the hell out of my hair! Oh, and tomorrow morning, I want you all here fifteen minutes early!" I gave my electrician a look, and when he blushed and looked down, I figured I'd got my message across.

As they were cleaning up to leave, I climbed the stairs and crawled into the shower, before lying down for a nap. The sheets still smelled like Ash, which calmed me. Linc was right, I needed to get my feelings for the guy out in the open, and stop worrying about what that meant. I loved him, I wanted him, and I wanted to stop dancing around those facts.

I fell asleep thinking about what it'd be like to wake up every morning as we had today, with him curled up against me. The thought was better than any I could've even dreamed of.

Forty-Two

Ash

A MOS TEXTED TODD TO let him know supper was ready, but when Todd didn't respond, he asked me to run and check on him.

I jogged over, not really thinking it necessary to drive the short distance to his home. It was strange that the crews were gone. They usually worked until after six, especially with Todd wanting to get this done, so he could free up the crew for another build he had coming up in a couple of months.

Todd's truck was still outside, so I went in yelling for him. When he didn't answer, I dashed up the stairs calling him. When I reached the third floor, I saw why there'd been no answer. Todd was curled up in the cutest little ball on his bed, the pillow pulled up against him like he was spooning it.

I couldn't help but smile. He was the most handsome man I knew, and when asleep, he had the most innocent-looking face. Over the years, that face had matured, but it still held that same sweetness.

I went over and kissed his eyelids, then his nose, like I'd done long ago when I wanted to wake him. When he finally opened his eyes, he reached over and pulled me onto him. "I was just dreaming of you."

His cock rested hard against my stomach, and I chuckled and reached down to rub it. "It's a good thing with this being like it is. Otherwise, I might be jealous."

"Hmm," he moaned sleepily. "It's always you I dream about."

The statement reached inside me and tugged at my heart. "Same for me."

Todd buried his face in my neck, before he began sucking on it. "You've got to stop all that, 'cause we have a family all waiting on us to come down and eat."

"M-mm," he moaned unhappily.

"I know, but the sooner we eat, the sooner we can come back here and deal with all this," I said, still rubbing against his hardness.

When he didn't get up, I pulled away, or tried to. "We need to talk," Todd said, holding me tight against him.

"Yeah, and we will, but right now—" Todd cut me off with a delicious kiss that melted my insides and my resistance. I all but forgot why I was here. A few seconds later, I heard Lisa's voice calling from downstairs.

"Hey, guys, where are you?"

I laughed, when Todd whispered, "Oh, shit, it's Lisa."

"We're up here," I yelled out, and reluctantly climbed off Todd.

He jumped up and dashed into the bathroom. "You could've given me a minute to get dressed before telling her where we are," he said, before closing the door behind him.

Lisa came in a moment later, and exclaimed when she saw the room. Her eyebrow went up when she saw the unmade bed, and me standing next to it.

"Did I interrupt something?" she said, a feral smile crossing her face.

I chuckled. "Yeah, but it's probably best, since Dad and Amos would kill us if we missed supper."

Todd came out a moment later, dressed in sweatpants and a t-shirt. "Hey, Lisa, I'm surprised to see you without two little ones attached to you."

She chuckled. "Yeah, I've been overly protective, so I let Amos and Dad take baby duty, while I came to see your progress. Looks like things downstairs are comin' along."

He smiled. "They are, wanna see the master suite?"

"Of course!" She proceeded to look around the expansive room, and when she walked into the en suite, she sighed with delight. "This is magnificent, Todd. Oh, and all this storage," she said, when she walked into the master closet.

"I wish you were closer and could do an attic reno on a house Frank and I are looking at in Salem. He's gonna have to be closer to the state offices with his new position, and there's a big farmhouse we're looking at.

It's cool, but old and stuffy. I would so *love* this," she said, making a sweeping gesture toward the whole room.

Master-suite tour done, we walked back down the new staircase and onto the second floor. Todd showed her around, and discussed how he was gonna just clean this level up. "There's plenty of room for your niece and nephew to stay, I see," she said, smiling.

"Like Dad or Amos will let them stay here when ya'll are in town," Todd said, chuckling, before we all went back down to the main floor.

"Unfortunately, it still requires a lot of imagination to see what the first level will look like, but basically, my offices for the business will be the new construction over there, and the back level will be the family room. The old kitchen and dining room are being combined to offer a large meeting room, which can be used for the office or for formal family events, and the kitchen and dining room will now be on this side of the house."

"It's going to be so amazing," Lisa said wistfully. "I'm just so happy to see this old place getting a nice facelift. It's not like it was bad before, but it just feels like you're breathing new life into it, while making it your own."

Todd looked at me, and his expression held a lot of meaning. Not saying anything, he turned back to Lisa and smiled.

We walked back to the dads' place, and after Dad sent us to wash our hands, not unlike when we were kids after coming in from playing outside, we sat down for another amazing meal.

"You two seem to have picked up the quality of food prep," Lisa said. "I don't remember either of you being this good at cooking before."

Dad smiled. "Well, we took a cooking class together last spring, before Todd came and fell off Amos's roof. Between eating crap food, or eating out every evening, we had both gained several pounds, so in an effort to be healthier, we decided we just needed to figure out how to cook better food ourselves."

"Who'd have guessed we loved cooking together this much?" Amos added. "It's like we were made for couple's cooking."

Dad glanced at Amos and smiled. The looks between the two had grown even more fond since Lisa had been staying with them. It's almost like having the babies and their family under their roof had somehow enhanced their relationship. It was like looking at pure happiness and it did nothing but warm my heart and make me yearn for the same thing with Todd.

I quickly put that thought aside, though, convincing myself I just needed to give it time. I was learning that letting things happen as they would, instead of putting too much pressure on our relationship to be what I wanted it to be, would be a key to our success as a couple.

Todd and I walked hand in hand all the way back to his house. When we got up to the bedroom, he pulled me over to sit on the bed. I was ready to strip, but he held my hand, saying, "I wanna get this out in the open, do you mind if we just talk a minute?"

"Sure, what's up?" I asked, feeling my heart rate pick up.

Todd sighed and stood before he began pacing the floor.

As I watched him, fear began to take hold of my heart. Was he about to dump me, because I'd pushed things too fast? *Fuck, I'd done it again.*

"Ash, I can't just go at this like we don't have a history. Like it isn't you and me in the middle of all this."

Hearing he wasn't comfortable going forward, I stood to go, barely holding back tears. He'd wanted me to be intimate with him, and when I had, he'd freaked. Why wasn't I surprised? I'd been stupid believing that he'd really changed, stupid for thinking this time would be different for us.

I started walking toward the door, when he grabbed my arm, and asked where I was going.

"Todd, I can't do the cold-hot thing. If you're uncomfortable with what we did last night, then—"

I didn't get the words out before he crushed his mouth to mine. His kisses had a way of melting my brain, so when he pulled back, I could only stare at him. I was truly dumbstruck.

"You are my life, Ash. There's no cold and hot between us, it's always just been hot." He chuckled then, which eased my worries a fraction, before he continued, "I don't want you to go home, ever again. I want you here with me. I know it's too soon, I know we just made love for the first time in like forever, but I don't wanna be without you any longer. I want all those things you used to talk about when we were young. The house, the garden, the kids, the dog with the amputated leg..."

I looked at him, confused for a moment, before I remembered telling him we needed to keep a dog that no one else wanted. I'd seen some show about a three-legged dog who was about to be put down by the shelter, but had been rescued by a family who'd ended up being saved by the dog when their house had caught fire.

"I can't believe you remember the dog," I said, chuckling as Todd wrapped his strong arms tightly around me.

"Baby, what you don't seem to understand is I remember all of it, every dream you ever had. I remember the color of the bedspread you picked out from that old interior design magazine you swiped from your dad's waiting room. I remember the names you wanted to call our three kids, as well as the name of the three-legged dog."

Tears were beginning to well up in my eyes again, but not from sadness, but because Todd was confessing feelings I'd thought were long dead, the same feelings that had never died in me.

I didn't have words. I just stared at this amazing man who had always had such power over me. "I love you too," I finally got out as the tears spilled over.

"Then, let's get married."

My eyes grew to the size of saucers. "What? Todd Amos Thompson, did you just propose to me?"

He fell to his knees in front of me then, staring up at me before taking my hands in his, and kissing them. "You are the only man I'll ever want, Ash. It's stupid to keep dancing around that fact. I want you with me, here in our home. Hell, it's always been yours and mine. I realized this evening as I lay in the bed we shared together last night, I'm renovating this fuckin' house for *you*, not me. I moved back to Crawford City for you! It's *all* for you." He looked overwhelmed, then and began backpedaling. "I know it's too soon. I know I'm jumping the gun, but..."

I fell on my knees in front of him, pulling him into my arms and crushing my mouth to his. We ended up rolling around on the floor, kissing each other's brains out, before he landed on top of me. He lifted up, grinding his cock into mine, and asked, "So...?"

"So, what? You knew my answer before you even asked. Of course, I'll marry you. I'm yours, Todd, only yours, forever and always!"

FORTY-THREE

TODD

"**D**AD? ARE YOU SURE?" Lisa asked.

"Yes," Doc chuckled, and kissed his daughter on the forehead, before looking back lovingly at Dad. "They've had a cancellation at the state park, the couple broke up last minute, so Fall Creek Falls is available over Valentine's Day weekend."

"Like in two weeks?" I asked, surprised at how fast things were going.

Dad looked over at me, like he was concerned I'd blow up or something. I supposed that was fair, seeing as it had been my past go-to reaction. "Son, it's not that fast for us, we've loved each other for... decades..." he said, smiling as he looked back at Doc. "It just makes sense for us to get married now, while Lisa is stuck here, and has the babies here too. Our whole family is together, and... well, and we are ready to make this official."

My heart melted at the way Dad and Doc looked at each other. I imagined it was the way Ash and I looked at each other these days too... not that I wasn't above givin' them shit about it, though.

"God, you two have it bad. Well, you better make sure to clear it with Mr. Wedding Planner," I said, just as Ash came into the living room.

He gave me a withering look, then smiled. "They have, and I've been on the phone already. The florist in Mayville has already agreed to do the flowers. I guess she was doin' the wedding that got cancelled, and had already ordered a ton of red roses and white chrysanthemums. Are those colors okay, Dad, Amos?" he asked.

"Personally," Doc said, "I couldn't care less about flowers, so long as I get to marry this man." He then tugged Dad into an embrace, and thoroughly kissed him right in front of us without a care.

I all but hid then as Lisa and Ash went to work planning the last-minute wedding. God help me if this was any indication of what our wedding was going to be like. *Our wedding.* Just the thought had me grinning like a lovesick fool.

I chuckled as I got roped into going to the state park to help with event setup, because it really didn't matter how over the top Ash got with planning our big day. Like Doc had said about Dad, the only thing that mattered to me was marrying the man I'd loved for so long, but had been too much of an idiot to admit it.

I stood back in shock as Lisa, Ash, and the Mayville florist transformed the lodge's ballroom from an ugly conference room to a beautiful wedding chapel.

It was fortunate that they'd been able to book the ballroom, because I think every person from the county showed up for that wedding.

I couldn't help but wipe tears as Ash, Lisa, and I stood on either side of our dads and watched as they professed their undying love.

"Best Valentine's Day *ever!*" I said as Ash cuddled up against me that night.

He kissed me and sighed. "We really are just like them, waiting so long to fix us..."

"Yeah, but at least we figured it out before we turned fifty."

Ash lifted up and looked at me. "I can't even imagine not having you. I love you so much, Todd, you know that right?"

I smiled and pulled him to me, kissing his amazing lips. "I know and I love you just as much... maybe even more."

"No way..." he said, and when he tickled me, it turned into a wrestling match that ended with us making love.

Ashton Nash was finally mine, and I was his. An impossible dream we hadn't even dared to dream since we'd been kids was coming true for the both of us.

Forty-Four

Ash

O UR WEDDING *HAD* TO be held in our new home. I mean, it wasn't like I hadn't dreamed of this my entire life, so planning really had been a snap.

The house renovations took longer to complete than Todd had expected, mostly because the building was like an old Southern woman, and as Todd put it, "Demanded that we do things her way instead of the way we thought they should be done."

My heart continued to swell as my fiancé did what he could to make the wedding everything I'd ever said I wanted. We'd finished the house in mid-September, but he told me he wanted to wait until the wedding to officially move in.

"You've waited for this so long, Ash. I want it to be perfect and this old lady is as much a part of your dreams as our wedding." So, we were having our wedding on

October first. The first Saturday in that month. Even that date felt right.

I cried that night in his arms, amazed that I'd not only gotten the wedding and the house I'd always wanted, but especially because I'd gotten my dream guy.

"You know I'd marry you in front of a justice of the peace, and move into a shack and still be happy, right?" I told him later that night as we snuggled.

He kissed me before he laughed. "Maybe—" he said, "—but you'd have given me shit about it for the rest of my life."

I laughed silently. He knew me too well, seeing as I really did want the house and the perfect wedding too.

Even before we moved in, I loved walking around the incredible property, and did so every day, looking at all the beautiful workmanship Todd and his crew put in, and how they'd managed to take an old house, preserve all her historical beauty, and still make her a magnificent modern home.

Like perfect icing on the cake, Amos and Todd's landscaping crew met with me right after the dads' wedding.

"You should be the one to run point on the garden's design," Todd told me, before sitting back and letting me take charge. The landscaping crew chuckled when I just took his handsome face in my hands, and gave him a huge kiss. God, I was so in love with that man.

Luckily, the crew had understood me when I told them I didn't want the formal Southern plantation-style garden. I didn't really go for all that intense formality and

Victorian sensibilities that were often associated with racism and hatred toward anyone not straight or white.

As a result, the gardens that separated the dads' place from ours were designed more along the lines of English cottage gardens, with lots of blended lines that drew your eye naturally to the beautiful forests that surrounded both properties.

We built several walkways among wildflower fields between the two homes, which included areas to sit and just enjoy the insects and birds attracted to the flowering plants. The land between our properties had been an open field that dipped into a drainage area. Now it was beautiful, and when all the wildflowers were in full height and bloom, it was much like an old maze. I could envision the kids running through there and playing hide-and-seek during the summers. The only issue was Lisa was convinced copperheads and rattlesnakes were gonna lurk around every turn, waiting to strike her babies. It wasn't like there weren't always copperheads to worry about, but we'd learned as kids how to watch out for them, and her kids would as well.

We always played ball on Todd's side of the property, so we left that as a grassy field, but built up the grass there, so it wouldn't turn into the mudhole it sometimes did back then. Even if we never had children of our own, I dreamed of the town's kids coming out to use that field again one day.

With all of the landscaping improvements, we decided to have an outdoor wedding in the fall, not long after the house was completed. Neither of us wanted to wait any longer than that.

It was a simple family affair. We hadn't told that many people about it, because neither of us wanted an enormous wedding. Lisa, Frank, and the twins flew back from Oregon for the occasion. Jennifer and Todd's friends Jake and Linc were there, too, along with some select friends from town.

Despite its scaled-down nature, or because of it, our wedding felt sweet and intimate. Amos knew someone, who decorated the new gardens with twinkle lights that dotted the walkways, and led to a small event tent.

The ceremony took place in the open, and both the dads escorted us up the formal aisle to where a minister from the local Methodist church stood.

Surrounded by wildflowers and our family and dearest friends, I'd never felt more loved in my entire life. It may not have been the fanciful wedding I'd dreamed about as a kid, but as I stood next to Todd in front of our loved ones, and we tearfully pledged to love each other for the rest of our lives, I realized this was an even better dream because it had come true.

FORTY-FIVE

TODD

I WATCHED ASH AS he took in our surroundings, and was pleased and relieved when I saw the same level of happiness that I felt, mirrored in his smiling face.

"I've loved you forever," I began, when the minister asked me to recite the vows we'd written. "Like our souls were destined to be together, you complete me, and make me whole. You are and always have been my love, my family. I vow to be yours until the end of all time, and maybe even longer than that."

Ash chuckled and wiped at the tears that fell from his eyes. "Todd, you are my soul. There is no one I've ever loved as intensely as I love you, and even though it took us a long time to accept it, we are soulmates."

The group chuckled around us, making Ash smile. "I promise to be your beloved husband, to give everything

I am to make you happy, and to make your life as rich as you make mine."

Then, it was the minister's turn to speak. "Do you, Todd, take Ashton to be your lawfully wedded husband?"

"Of course, I do!" I exclaimed.

The minister smiled and turned to Ash. "Do you, Ashton, take Todd to be your lawfully wedded husband?"

"With all my heart, I do."

"Then, by the power vested in me, by the state of Tennessee, I now pronounce you husbands. You may kiss your spouse!"

At the minister's words, I cupped Ash's tearstained face in my hands, and kissed him deeply. I could hear distant claps and whoops from our family and friends all around us, but in this moment, no one outside the two of us existed. I'd meant every word I pledged to him, we were destined to be together, and I was going to spend the rest of our lives proving that to him.

The evening was a lovely blur as we danced under the twinkle lights, drank Champagne, and ate a surprisingly delicious wedding cake the dads had made.

Neither of us could get away for a proper honeymoon, but our newly renovated home was like being in paradise anyway. That night, as we lay in the bed where we'd fully rekindled our relationship, all of the intense emotions we'd felt for each other for more than half our lives washed over us as we made love for the first time as husbands.

FORTY-SIX

TWO YEARS LATER: ASH

MY PERSONAL AND PROFESSIONAL life was better than it'd ever been. After formally moving in with Todd following our wedding, we set about renovating my little house downtown to be part of the clinic. Expanding the clinic had long been my hope after we added another doctor to the team, and with Todd's expertise, we were finally in a position to do so.

We converted the living room and kitchen into a waiting area, so we could renovate the rest of the clinic at the same time When the project was complete, our facility was large enough that Dr. Frost even started coming once a week to help treat the community's pregnant women who couldn't travel to Lebanon on a regular basis.

The clinic was better than I'd ever dreamed it would be. I'd fully intended to do the work to turn our clinic into a public one, so when we were approached by a federally funded practice to join them, I was overjoyed. It helped that the entire team agreed that joining them was what was best for the people of Crawford City. The transfer of the clinic out of my name and into the larger program would mean I'd actually get vacation time and weekends off, something that hadn't happened since I'd finished my internship years before.

The timing was fortunate, since the twins turning three and Lisa was all but demanding we fly to Salem to see them and the family's new house. Taking time for vacation hadn't been an issue. I easily talked Gib and Rachel into handling my side of the practice. Of course, considering this was the first time I'd been out of the office for more than a couple days since I'd come to work here, helped me convince them.

Todd's business was growing in leaps and bounds, and I knew it was difficult for him to get away with all the new building happening in the area, but he hadn't complained a bit about taking time off. But, of course, that was mostly because the twins had completely stolen our hearts, and we wanted to see them.

Luckily for Dad, it was easy for him to get away, since, as mayor, January was when the town needed him the least. He'd taken to the job like a duck to water. Most of his meetings took place in his home, and when he needed a larger space, they'd use the meeting room in Todd's and my place.

Every year, more and more people moved to our little town, and as a result, careful planning had begun to ensure Crawford City grew steadily, while maintaining its rural Southern charm.

With happiness and hope in mind, we all loaded onto the plane on our way to see Lisa, Frank and the kids.

Once we landed in Salem, Lisa greeted us, and took us back to the house. Frank had stayed home with the kids, who were currently trying to wreck their playroom.

The property included thirty acres surrounding the house, and I was surprised at the beautiful view. Not unlike our part of Tennessee, the hills rolled and although we had a lot more forest, I could see how Lisa and Frank had made a comfortable home here.

Frank's sister, Donna, and her wife, Louisa, were playing with the kids in the playroom when we arrived. I'd met them once before when they'd flown out to see the babies while Lisa was stuck in Crawford.

The two women had moved into a smaller home on the property, and helped Lisa take care of the rambunctious toddlers.

We were shown to our rooms, and when we came back down, Lisa asked us to sit down in their oversized living room that'd been added on to the back of the original structure. Dad and Amos were taking care of the kids, which wouldn't have been suspicious, except Lisa, Frank, Donna, and Louisa were all sitting like they were waiting for Todd and me.

"What's up?" I asked as we sat on the sofa.

Lisa sighed, and Donna blushed. I realized then this was going to be an interesting conversation. Todd took my hand, like he tended to do when we sat next to each other, and snuggled close to me.

"So, we wanted to talk to you about something... maybe a bit strange, but important," Donna said.

I nodded and Todd looked at me inquisitively.

Lisa looked at her sister-in-law, who took a deep breath, before taking her wife's hand. When her wife nodded, Donna continued, "So, I have endometriosis, and Louisa and I have decided that it might help me if I give birth. For some women, my mother included, their pain was reduced because of the process. The problem is, neither one of us want children."

Lisa chimed in then. "Frank and I have agreed to adopt their baby. In fact, I've already had my own eggs harvested, but..." She looked down at her stomach and sighed again. "We ended up making our own, again."

"What? You're pregnant!" I couldn't contain my excitement at the news that Todd and I would be made uncles again. Todd chuckled beside me as Lisa nodded and grinned.

"Anyway, my eggs are already frozen, and since you two mentioned that you eventually wanted kids, it seemed like a great way for you to have one. What do you think?"

I took a deep breath, before looking at Todd, whose eyes had gotten significantly larger. "Um, so you'd use your eggs and I'm guessing Todd's sperm, and the fetuses would be implanted in Donna?"

All three women nodded eagerly. I shook my head, still grappling with the magnitude of what they were proposing. "It's all a bit too 'in the family,' isn't it?"

"Well, yeah—" Lisa said with a huff, "—but it's not like anyone is related by blood in this equation. The baby would be completely healthy. Besides, gay guys do this stuff all the time. I have several friends who have harvested egg donations from their sisters."

I looked over at Todd, who seemed to have forgotten how to breathe. "Honey, breathe before you pass out," I said, and he let out a long breath. "So—" I said, squeezing Todd's hand, "—we need some time to think about this. We haven't even discussed the whole kids thing that much." Lisa nodded. "Now, let's talk about you being pregnant, which is huge news, totally overshadowed by this conversation!"

Todd had relaxed considerably, after having been totally caught off guard with the baby conversation, but he acted strangely the rest of the night. He was studying Donna closely, but occasionally would look over at me. I could tell he was still processing their proposal.

Finally, I broke away from the group, telling Lisa I needed to borrow her car, so I could take Todd for a drive before he exploded. Of course, she laughed, and I could tell she wanted to rib Todd a little, but seeing his expression, even she knew better than to push it... well, at least not yet.

The moment we shut the car doors, Todd grabbed my hand, and said, "What do you think? Do you wanna do this? What is endometriosis? Would it put the baby in jeopardy?"

I squeezed his hand before starting the car, and pulling onto the road toward downtown, convinced my husband needed space and at least three beers to process all of this. I decided to drive and answer his questions as we drove along.

I explained that endometriosis could result in lesions forming in the reproductive organs, and that pregnancy has been traditionally used to help minimize the pain. It wasn't necessarily something that would hurt the baby, although it might cause premature birth, or force the mom to need a C-section.

I realized I was lapsing into doctor-speak when Todd's eyes glazed over, so I switched the conversation to his other questions.

"I don't know, the idea of you and Lisa having a baby together, and it being carried by her sister-in-law is weird. I'm not sure how I feel about it. How do you feel?" I asked.

He took a deep breath, before answering. "Like, it's the absolutely perfect solution to having a baby, and, oh God, it would be as close to having your baby, one with your genes and mine, as we can possibly get, and that the baby would be beautiful and smart, and good with his hands, like my side of the family, but smart like yours. He or she might become a doctor, or maybe take over the business from me..."

I laughed. "Breathe, honey. I don't want you hyperventilating, and here I thought you were freakin' out 'cause you didn't like the idea."

"No, I'm freaking out, 'cause it's perfect!" I glanced over to see sparkling eyes staring at me. I'd rarely seen him so lit up with excitement. So much for needing those three beers.

"Well, not perfect. We have to look at the laws in Oregon and Tennessee," I said, trying to be practical, but I'd be damned if his excitement wasn't infectious.

"Yeah, I already did on my phone, and according to Google, it's legal in both states. We'll just have to get an attorney," Todd said excitedly.

"I can't believe you're so okay with this. I really thought you'd be freakin' out."

"Oh, I am freakin' out, but in a good way. I'm happy adopting, Ash, more than happy, if that's what you want. To be honest, it's what I thought we'd eventually do, but at the same time, I secretly always wanted a baby that was genetically related to us, I just didn't think it'd be possible. I know that sounds ridiculous. I shouldn't care, but..."

I took his hand in mine and kissed his knuckles. "Baby, it's not ridiculous, it's sweet, but let's think about all the ramifications of this, like the fact we both work incredibly long hours. Your business is just now taking off, and mine is, well, typical doctor's hours. Do we have the time to dedicate to raising a family right now?"

Todd shrugged. "I mean, you work less now than you used to, and since you're selling the practice, you'll be making more money, and you won't have to be there all the time."

Todd squeezed my hand. "I've talked to Doc and Dad about this several times over the years, and they'd love to have a little one. They're built-in babysitters, and after seeing them with Martin and Margaret Jane, we both know they'd be like two mother hens anyway. Besides, we can hire someone if we need to, it's not like we don't have the income to support that now."

Todd looked at me with pleading eyes, and I couldn't help but laugh. I already wanted to say yes. I'd always wanted children. I, like Todd, had assumed we'd eventually adopt, but this did seem like the perfect opportunity.

I tried to think about any other objections there might be, and I was sure there were millions, but looking at the happy expression on my husband's face, I couldn't think of any more at the moment.

"So, you're saying you're a yes?" I asked.

I glanced over to see him nodding eagerly, and I shook my head. "I guess I'm a yes too. God help us both!"

Todd yelled, and had we not been driving down the road, he'd have probably picked me up and swung me around, as had become his favorite thing to do when he was excited about something.

Instead of the bar, we went to a local box store, found a ridiculously expensive bottle of Champagne, the kind actually from Champagne, France, as well as some sparkling grape juice for Lisa, and drove back to their farm.

When we entered, the little ones were down for their afternoon nap, so we slipped into the living room, where all the adults, including Donna and Louisa, were sitting.

"Lisa, can you help me in the kitchen?" I asked, and she stood and followed me out.

When she saw the Champagne, she squealed, clamped her hand over her mouth to keep her squeals from waking the little ones, and then jumped into my arms. "So, you're both a yes?" she squeaked.

"Seems like it. Todd is actually over the moon with the idea."

"And you?" Lisa asked with a little worry in her expression.

"It's a bit weird for me, you and Todd making babies." When I scrunched up my face, she hit my arm just like the little sister I remembered. "I'm not making babies with anyone but Frank, and it's as close to you and him having a baby together as you can get at the moment, thank you very much." She said it with a note of sass, but I could tell she sincerely wanted this for Todd and me.

I nodded. "I'll come around, but the part about us having a little one and that your sister-in-law is the surrogate, it actually sounds nice. So, no matter what, they're surrounded by family."

"Exactly," Lisa said, and hugged me again.

That afternoon, we passed the Champagne around, talked about how mind-blowing this decision was, and how it would change our lives forever. Todd ended up forcing everyone to take a group picture to commemorate the night we all decided to make a baby together.

Dad and Doc sat in wing-back chairs, wearing matching smiles as big as I'd ever seen, and holding their two wriggling grandbabies on their laps, while Donna and Louisa sat in front of them on the floor. Lisa, Frank, and Frank's parents, who'd arrived that afternoon, stood behind Dad's chair, and Todd and me behind Amos's. That ended up being one of the most cherished pictures of our family, and Todd had it blown up and placed in a prominent space in the nursery he built for our little ones.

Forty-Seven

Todd

"Three?" I asked again, sure I hadn't heard right.

When the doctor nodded affirmatively, my stomach felt like it might fall out of my body and roll around on the floor. I looked at poor Donna, who looked as if she was about to pass out. I instinctively reached and took her hand in mine.

"Are you going to be okay with this?" I asked.

She nodded. "I think so. It's just a lot to digest."

"Uh-huh. It is."

Ash hadn't been able to get away from work for this latest trip to Oregon, and Louisa was stuck in traffic on her way here, so it was just Donna and me at the appointment.

I sat down next to her as the doctor explained that selective abortion was an option, but would most likely put the other babies at risk. "We don't currently know if the babies are identical or fraternal. Until we know that, we won't know whether they share a placenta or not, but our best guess is that they aren't identical."

"I won't have an abortion," Donna said. "I'm sorry, Todd. I just won't."

"It's okay," I quickly consoled her. "We're happy with whatever decision you make."

The doctor and Donna discussed the impact having triplets could have on her endometriosis. I sort of zoned out then, and wished for the hundredth time that Ash was here, so he could explain all the medical nuances to me. I secretly swore this would be the last time my husband weaseled out of coming with me to support Donna and Louisa through this.

When the doctor left us alone, Donna called Louisa, and I called Ash. Luckily, they both answered at the same time, so all four of us could talk to one another. Both Louisa and Ash were quiet after getting the news. I looked at Donna and we both nodded in agreement to sit quietly as they processed the information, which I'd only begun to wrap my mind around myself.

"I've already decided to fly out on Friday," Ash said. "I'll see if I can get off a day earlier."

Donna shook her head. "There's no need to come earlier, Ash. I already know I'm going to carry all three, but do come on Friday. We need to discuss the pregnancy, as well as the transition to you and Todd. I'm guessing now that you're gonna have three little ones, you're gonna need all the help you can get."

Ash cleared his throat. "Yeah, I thought Lisa's two were a lot."

Donna chuckled. "We'll talk over the weekend. Maybe Louisa and I can help."

It ended up that Donna and Louisa wanted to be god-parents for the babies. They'd already discussed it and even though they didn't want children of their own, they still wanted to be an active part of our babies' lives.

Since they weren't technically related to us, officially making them godparents sort of made them family too, even though we'd always consider them family regardless. It ended up being a wonderful decision, and with it our babies gained a pair of adoring aunts, and by extension, extra sets of grandparents. Our family tree got a bit confusing if you thought about it too much, with Donna being the surrogate, her and Louisa being godparents, but more like aunts, Lisa being the biological mother, but family-wise an aunt, and Ash being the biological uncle, but their father in every way that mattered. However, it worked for us, and only solidified our growing group as a tightknit family.

Donna gave birth at thirty-three weeks, which the obstetrician had planned for. Lisa already had three little ones in her care by that time, so Dad and Amos joined Ash and me to help with caring for our triplets when Ellen, Lynn, and Jessica were born.

Donna and Frank's childhood home was enormous, so it was decided that everyone, with the exception of Lisa and Frank, would stay there. Initially, the hospital thought they'd have to keep the babies for six weeks or longer, but all three were so healthy, they ended up coming home at four weeks old.

We fully intended to hire a nurse to help us out, knowing we wouldn't be flying the little ones home to Tennessee for at least a couple of months, but Donna and Frank's mom had been a labor and delivery nurse, and Donna and Louisa were also more than happy to help. So, for the first three months of our newborns' lives, they were utterly and completely surrounded by their loving family.

I only had to fly back to Tennessee twice to deal with work issues. With the official sale of the clinic, Ash was able to officially take paternity leave, meaning he had six months off before he had to be back at work.

Mayor Doc, as nearly all of Crawford City now called him, held most of his meetings virtually, so he and Dad were able to remain in Oregon with us too.

With three infants, one six-month-old, and two toddlers to contend with, our time in Oregon was intense, to say the least. However, I don't think any of the adults in our complicated little brood had ever been as happy as we were. Exhausted for sure, but happy.

FORTY-EIGHT

EPILOGUE: ASH

I HIRED A NANNY to help out for the first few weeks after we all returned home to Crawford City. Three babies were a hell of a lot of work, and Todd and I were outnumbered from day one, even with our dads' help, so it worked out perfectly.

Dad and Amos spent three nights a week at the house taking baby duties, which allowed Ash and I to catch up on sleep, and spend much-needed time together as a couple. It took all five of us to pull it off. I internally blessed the hearts of the families, including Lisa and Frank, who'd had multiple births without all the help Todd and I had.

Probably because we were so busy chasing babies, the days and months passed quickly, and before we knew it, our kids were a year old.

The entire family descended on Crawford to celebrate the milestone. Lisa, Frank, and their three kids, along with Donna, Louisa, and Frank and Donna's mother Clair, all flew in from Oregon.

Lisa's little ones were tucked into their beds in the nursery at Dad and Amos's house, while Donna, Louisa, and Clair each held one of ours.

Dad had passed out drinks, and we all sat around enjoying the first moment of quiet since they'd all arrived.

"So," Louisa said. "We should probably tell you now, when there isn't one of the nieces and nephews screaming for attention."

Donna smiled and blushed, and I noticed Clair's expression darken a bit, before she checked it.

"I've finished my doctorate as a nurse practitioner, and I've been hired at the hospital in Lebanon, working with Doctor Frost. Ash, I think she's hoping I'll end up working between there and your clinic here in Crawford City, so she can focus more on deliveries, and doesn't have to be here every week to see patients."

I stared at her and Donna, a couple who'd ended up becoming great friends of ours, let alone considered family.

"So, you're moving to Tennessee?" I asked.

Both Donna and Louisa nodded. "We love it here. As you know, Donna is hoping she can get into the PR side of country music, and when she met your friend Jake, they seemed to get along great. We also love the idea of being closer to our godchildren. Besides, after spending the day with these three, I can see you need all the help you can get."

The entire room chuckled at that.

I turned to Clair, and she nodded at me. I could see she wasn't happy with their impending move, but she'd somehow made peace with the decision.

"Would you two consider livin' here in Crawford City?" Todd asked.

They both nodded. "We've actually found a home less than a mile from here, but we didn't want to put an offer on it, until you two knew about our plans. We don't want to... um..." Louisa hesitated, and Donna quickly jumped in.

"We don't want you two to think we're overstepping."

Both Todd and I laughed. "If you're willing to take on kid duties, you can't overstep. Like you said, we need all the help we can get."

"So, you don't mind if we move close? We have visions of the kids stopping by to hang out with us from time to time. Maybe even taking evening duties, so you two can get a break."

Todd stood up and came to kneel in front of the two women. "I've grown to love you both since you've become a part of our family. I don't care if you move next door. If you're willing to move to this part of the world, we want you as close as you feel comfortable being."

A tear rolled down Donna's cheek, and she leaned over gently, so as to not wake the baby, and kissed Todd on the cheek. "We do feel like family, and these three are so important to us." She looked over at Lisa and

Frank, and smiled. She whispered, but loud enough for everyone to hear, "Now, you two can help us figure out how to get the rest of the family to move here as well."

Frank just shook his head, but Lisa smiled. That gave me some hope that maybe my baby sister was in on this conspiracy. Although, I couldn't imagine the attorney general for the state of Oregon moving to a podunk little town in the middle of Tennessee.

The house they wanted to buy was one we all knew very well. It'd belonged to Mrs. Scott, an old lady who'd hired Todd and me to mow her yard during the summers. She used to invite us in when we were done, and spoil us with homemade lemonade and cookies. We'd both loved the woman with our entire hearts.

She had died over a decade ago, and her home was given to a distant relative who had done little with it. For the most part, the basics had been cared for, but it was musty and dirty, and clearly not lived in for years.

With Frank and the nanny staying behind to watch over the six little ones who'd all been put to bed, the rest of us walked the short distance to Mrs. Scott's old house. Todd and I shared our good memories of the place as we went, and Donna and Louisa lit up like candles as we told them how the home had meant so much to us when we were young.

Todd and Amos quickly went through inspecting the house, and confirmed it needed all new electrical, the plumbing showed signs of needing to be replaced, the roof was shot, and they guessed it all needed new windows and insulation.

"So, how much?" Donna asked.

When Todd told them, they smiled. "We're able to buy this place cheap, so you can actually do it for what you're quoting, we'll still have savings left to spend on stuff to spoil our godbabies," Donna said.

Todd laughed. "Well, if you two can help, we can probably get the costs even lower than that."

Donna cringed. "Um, I'm no good with that at all, but Louisa loves all that construction stuff."

"So, what do you think? Willing to get into this for some sweet equity?" he asked Louisa. Her face lit up as she eagerly nodded.

As we walked back toward ours and the dads' houses and the chaos that now occupied them, it felt like the world was right. Our kids needed Donna and Louisa as much as they did us. Two little girls and one boy were a lot to deal with all on our own. It really would take a village to raise them up right, and with their adoring godparents moving to the area and their loving grand-daddies just down the road, it seemed like our three little ones were going to have exactly that.

Choosing to forgo his inheritance instead of losing his identity leaves him adrift, can the sexy wine grower be his foundation or will he be lost forever?

Continue the Coming Home Series with Discovering Home.

Available at your favorite bookseller.

Join Blake's email list to get advance notice of new books and receive his occasional newsletter:

www.blakeallwood.com

MM Romance
By Blake Allwood

Transitions Series
Aiden Inspired
Suzie Empowered (MF Romance)
Bobby Transformed

Chance Series
Love By Chance
Another Chance <u>With</u> Love
Taking A Chance <u>For</u> Love

Romantic Series
Romantic Renovations (1)
Romantic Rescue (2)
Romantic Recon (3)

Melody Series
Melody of the Heart
Melody of the Snow

Road to Rocktoberfest Anthology
Changing His Tune - 2022

Coming Home Series (2023)
A Long Way Home
Family Home
Discovering Home
Finding Home
Bound For Home
…and many more

Novellas
Tenacious
Moon's Place

Romantic Fantasy
By Adam J. Ridley

Big Bend Series
Love's Legacy (1)
Love's Heirloom (2)
Love's Bequest (3)

The Witch Brothers Series
Emerald Earth (1)
Diamond Air (2)
Ruby Fire (3)
Sapphire Water (4)

Blake Allwood was born in west Tennessee, then moved to Kansas City MO after earning a degree in Early Childhood Education from Graceland College in Lamoni, Iowa. He met his husband Shaun in 1995 and they officially married in 2015, once gay marriage was legalized; although they still consider Valentines Day 1995 as their true "anniversary date". Twenty-two years later (2017), after fostering 12 children together, he and his husband sold their home, purchased an RV and began traveling the country with their two dogs.

Typically, Blake can be found relaxing in the RV or by the fire with his laptop and their Jack Russell Terrier, Buddy, curled up between his legs demanding attention. Denver, their Siberian Husky mix is often asleep at his feet or playing tug of war with Blake's husband.

Most of Blake's stories are inspired by the places they have visited in their ongoing travels. His first book, *Aiden Inspired*, was released in 2019 and he has now written over 20 books. In 2023 he is releasing the *Coming Home* series which is comprised of ten-plus sweet contemporary romance novels that are based on a fictional town in his home state of Tennessee.

Blake also writes under the pen name of Adam J. Ridley for his urban fantasy fans looking for stories revolving around gay characters. His first series is The Witch Brothers Saga, starting with ***Emerald Earth***.

BIBLIOPRIDE.COM

BOOKS BY LGBTQ+ AUTHORS